THE
DYING
TIME

ANTHONY CARRAGHER

The Book Guild Ltd

First published in Great Britain in 2024 by
The Book Guild Ltd
Unit E2 Airfield Business Park,
Harrison Road, Market Harborough,
Leicestershire. LE16 7UL
Tel: 0116 2792299
www.bookguild.co.uk
Email: info@bookguild.co.uk
X: @bookguild

Typeset in 11pt Minion Pro

Printed on FSC accredited paper
Printed and bound in Great Britain by 4edge Limited

ISBN 978 1916668 294

British Library Cataloguing in Publication Data.
A catalogue record for this book is available from the British Library.

For Siobhán, eternal love and thanks.
Mila and Gavin, love always.

'Those stars are the fleshed forebears
of these dark hills, bowed like labourers,
And of my blood.'
– Ted Hughes, "Fire-Eater"

'It takes the whole of a life to learn how to die'
– Seneca

I

Nothing in that calm foretold of the storm to come or the havoc it would wreak. I can picture it still. On the promenade, an eager spaniel tugged a phone-gazing youth along by its lead. Two young women jogged past the bandstand, heading towards the cliffs. An old man on a wooden bench negotiated his flapping newspaper as seagulls bobbed on the chill breeze. In the houses overlooking the shore, the inhabitants of Blackcliff woke to another sleepy Sunday morning.

I stood alone on the sand. The town, the beach, the smell of the air, it was all foreign to me, yet somehow eerily familiar, as if I'd stood before in that very spot and witnessed that very scene. The jagged rocks to the west. The strand arced in a large horseshoe around the bay. The pier to the east. That creeping sensation came again. The feeling that I might implode. Gravity, fastening upon my bones. The imperceptible shift of the sand beneath my bare feet. The earth pulling me to its core.

I shielded tired eyes from the glare of the winter sun and watched as the pair played by the water's edge. A mother and her young daughter stepped in and out of the wash as the waves lapped outwards on the low tide. I moved closer. Close enough to hear their voices over the screech of the birds. Their laughter a dance on the wispy air. In my hands, a batch of letters. Papers stained by words that could never be unread. Closer still. Touching distance. They had not yet noticed this stranger in their midst. I called her name, 'Kate?' The mother turned, a quizzical shadow crossing her face as our eyes met. In that moment, our worlds intersected and locked tight. There would be no going back.

6:05a.m. (Friday, one month later)

Kate O'Connor began to turn from the window when she saw them. One, two, ten wispy flakes drifting on the wind, circling, falling to settle on the ground. Suddenly, there were hundreds, thousands, a sea of white dancing in the inky blue. The storm had arrived early. She could hear the thunder of the waves as they battered the rugged cliffs beneath the lighthouse. She wasn't sure how long she'd been standing there just gazing into the dark, thoughts adrift like the newly arrived snow, never fixing on anything certain. These silent purgatory hours before dawn were the bleakest when neither the dead nor the living offered a voice of solace. An all-too-familiar tide of dread began to rise within her. Kate breathed deep and slow. In, hold. Out, hold. In, hold. Out, hold. Thinking only of each breath, nothing else. Kate pulled her shawl tight about her shoulders.

Across the bay, the waking orange lights of Blackcliff began to appear. Kate glanced behind her to where her daughter lay asleep. The clock on the bedside locker glowed 6:10a.m. She should try for more sleep. The floorboards groaned as she tiptoed gingerly back to the bed. Amy didn't stir; she was a solid sleeper. Kate slid carefully under the blankets. Her feet felt like ice, but she avoided the temptation to hold them against her daughter's warm legs. When her body temperature had risen, she snuggled as best she could into the angled form of the spreadeagled child. Her mother once told her that you never know which occasion would be the last. Suddenly, a night arrives when your child no longer wants to share your bed. They no longer desire you to nuzzle into them, to smell their hair, to envelop their half-grown gangly forms. If you knew the last time was to be the last, then you'd hold on and never let go.

Amy was an only child, and to Kate's eternal regret, that she would remain. At thirty-eight, she still had time on her side, but not her husband, Peter. He was holding steadfast. He had a busy career; one child was enough. More and more, it was just Kate and Amy sharing the bed, Peter almost always away on business. Qualifier: *important* business. Peter was a politician, another of the Kavanagh clan to be elected to public office, in the European Parliament no less. Peter's business was important, but so too was his family. Many times, she had reminded him that you didn't get to see your daughter grow up twice. It was a one-time gig with no encores. While Kate was determined to savour every morsel of Amy's childhood, Peter didn't seem to get it. He said that he understood and always promised change, but any fool will tell you that change comes hard, particularly for those who like things as they are.

Kate's eyes grew heavy, and she began to drift. She and her father were out to sea on her uncle's boat, white sails billowing on the warm summer wind as they navigated the waves from Doolin to Inisheer. Kate leaned over the starboard side and let her hand cut through the sparkling wake. Her father stood at the wheel, his back to her, the island looming ahead. She leaned out further, stretching her hand farther into the deep. Her father looked back from the helm. 'Kate,' he called. 'Kate,' he called again sternly, 'be careful.' She lost sight of him in the sun's blinding glare. A buzzing came. She couldn't place it. *Buzz, buzz*, it continued. Kate's eyes opened. Her mobile glowed on the nightstand. Amy didn't budge. Kate stretched her arm and lifted the phone. She manoeuvred the screen to her face, careful to tilt the light away from her daughter. An uneasy sensation crawled beneath her skin at the recognition of the number. She held her breath and opened the text.

Remember, none of this is your fault.

Kate pictured again the stranger on the beach. The cold, empty eyes. The steely matter-of-factness. Hardly a month had passed since he'd gate-crashed her life. She angrily pressed delete and stifled the urge to fling the phone across the room. Kate rested her head back on the pillow. There was no chance of sleep now. Amy moaned slightly and turned in her slumber to face her, eyes still closed. Kate's little princess adrift in her innocent dreams, unaware that the castle walls around her had begun to fissure and crack.

7:55a.m.

The chair rocked slowly back and forth like a hypnotist's pendulum. It creaked beneath Król's weight, and he wondered when it had last been sat on and by whom. One of the arms had dislodged from the main wooden body, and the seat was tattered and torn – a collector's piece in need of loving care. The cushioning had been cold and damp at first, but his energy had infused warmth and new life. Its owner was probably dust now, yet here in this old shed, their throne still survived. It, too, would eventually disintegrate to nothingness, but for now, on it rocked.

The shed was a neat affair. Stone walls bordered a concrete floor. Along the far wall, paint cans were stacked in an orderly fashion alongside an old ride-on lawnmower. Rows of shelving held garden supplies and tools. On the highest shelf, an old tabby cat perched nonchalantly, surveying its kingdom. The rusting corrugated roof rattled in the wind. These dark hours lasted forever, time creeping slower without witnesses, the deep stillness conjuring the ghosts that had led him here. Through the grubby window, he watched as the sun began its slow rise above the horizon. He closed his weary eyes and imagined how pleasant it would be to fall into a deep and never-ending sleep.

Król awoke with a jolt. He checked the time. He'd drifted for five minutes. The dream had seemed so real. Life, dreams, dreams, life - at times, he found it hard to tell them apart. He'd been hiding in a backyard concealed behind a tree. In the dark, he watched through the rear window as a mother and child hung decorations on their Christmas tree: his wife, his child. The child glanced in his direction. Had she seen him? He wasn't sure. The lights came on, and the tree was aglow. He started to cry. He should be with them. Suddenly, his wife was before him, screaming his name, flailing her fists upon his chest. But when he stared into her soulless eyes, it wasn't her. It wasn't her at all. He could feel the intense heat rising. Everything was ablaze. The inferno spread rapidly, swallowing all before it. The tree, the house, and the yard were all engulfed in horrible licking flames. He roared after his wife and child, but they were lost in the toxic smoky haze. His eyes began to burn, and his skin melted. All was gone. That's how he always woke. To sleep was to suffer.

Król rubbed callused hands up and down his face. He lifted his phone and checked for messages. Still no reply, Kate wasn't biting. He had meant it; none of it was her fault. Król took the watch from the inside pocket of his weatherproof coat. He twisted the crown. Another collector's item, this one still cared for tenderly. His father's once, now his. He pushed the crown inwards, and the gold cover sprang outwards to reveal the glass face. Ten past eight. He counted the hours. Eighteen, that was it. After all this time, just eighteen hours.

Outside, the snow fell heavier. Caught in the swirling wind trap of the courtyard, it flitted and flurried in manic tumbling loops. An ageing stocky retriever trudged through the fresh covering, its warm breath rising like fog. It seemed both intrigued and frustrated by the weather. Frozen earth meant cold trails. The dog ambled slowly and lazily, its snout sniffing the white ground. Suddenly, its ears pricked, and its head rose. It must have caught sight of his movement at the window. Thankfully, it didn't bark or fuss. Indeed, it exhibited a peaceful air that suggested it hadn't barked in a long time. The dog shuffled unworriedly towards the shed. Król had been expecting to see Rocky out for his morning jaunt. They had formed a bond of sorts, and with each of his visits, the retriever understood their alliance better – treats for silence. Król had left one side of the double-doored entrance to the shed slightly ajar, and in the opening, he'd laid the necessary delights. The dog spotted the easy pickings and made its way over. 'Good boy, good boy,' Król whispered. The dog cocked his ears, looking up briefly to acknowledge his presence before proceeding to gnaw earnestly. Król reached into his holdall for another snack and then proffered his cupped hand towards the dog. Rocky lumbered closer. As the dog chewed on the additional kindness, Król rubbed its head softly, murmuring, 'Good boy, good boy.' Rocky's legs slowly buckled, and he collapsed quietly to the ground.

Over on the top shelf, the tabby squatted down on set paws, its feral eyes furtively scanning for danger. Król smiled; he liked cats. He admired how they were always ready for the end of the world. Poised for flight. Prepared to fight. Everywhere lurked danger, and everything was about survival. People could learn a lot from cats. He stretched over, and with his fingertips, he slowly closed the dog's eyes. 'There, there,' he whispered. 'Good boy, Rocky.' Dogs, too.

Król peered out the window and across the yard to the

rear of the old single-storey farmhouse from where the dog had ventured. Nothing stirred.

Two cars were parked to the back of the farmhouse since the night before. Blue and yellow letters spelling *Garda* were just discernible beneath the covering of snow along the side of the closest vehicle. The first time he'd seen the police car at the house, he'd been alarmed. Had he been spotted? Yet nobody came to search for him or warn him not to trespass. Instead, the car continued to come and go, and Król realised it wasn't about him. Grace Quigley had a new man in her life. That he would be a policeman was a wrinkle, yet it didn't change his plans. Nothing could.

The rumble of an approaching car engine and the muffled crackle of tyres on gravel broke the snowfall's cloaking quiet. Beyond the house, a pot-holed driveway overhung by tall wind-gnarled trees stretched for half a kilometre. A vehicle was weaving its way erratically down the long approach. It skidded around the back of the farmhouse and slid precariously to a halt next to the parked squad car. A young man wearing a dark, short-sleeved T-shirt over faded blue jeans climbed out and stumbled towards the house, leaving behind an open driver's door and a humming engine.

'Grace!' the man shouted as he thumped his fist on the red door. His ungainly movement caused him to lose balance and slip in the snow. 'Grace! Get out here!' the man yelled again as he clambered clumsily back to his feet. The back door opened, and Grace's new beau, Dan Brady, stood tall, blocking the entrance. Król wondered how many times events such as these had played out through the ages: same scene, different characters. Back and forth, back and forth.

Like the hands of a watch retracing its ticks over and over. He closed his eyes. These matters would unfold as they willed. They were not his concern; his time would come.

8:05a.m.

Dan Brady leaned against the frame of the open farmhouse door. Before him stood a flush-faced Tommy Molloy. The stench of sour alcohol and leaden exhaust fumes fouled the crisp air. Over Tommy's shoulder, beyond the walled yard, rolling white fields stretched to the horizon. A wistful notion of Dan and Grace pulling on their boots and going for a hike drifted from Dan's mind as quickly as it arrived. He stifled a yawn and finished buttoning his sky-blue uniform shirt.

'What's all the shouting about, Tommy?' he asked calmly, but to no reply. Instead, Tommy attempted to brush past him into the kitchen. Dan deposited a stern hand on Tommy's chest, easing him backwards. 'That's far enough, big man,' he said. Tommy slurred some barb, but Dan couldn't make out the words. Better off. With a sigh, he wiped some of Tommy's spittle from his cheek. At six-three, Dan towered nearly half a foot over the new arrival and was in considerably better physical shape. It would be foolish of Tommy to try something, but then again, there was no accounting for the actions of a drunk.

'I see you've hired the pigs for protection,' spat Tommy, aiming his words past Dan in the direction of Grace Quigley, who sat pensively at the kitchen table. Dan looked at Grace, and his heart sank. She cut a forlorn figure. Her shoulders slumped in the puffer jacket she'd hastily pulled on over her nightie and slippers. Tears pooled in her eyes. *She deserved better*, thought Dan. Was this as far as evolution had come? Men like Tommy, fuelled by hate and vitriol, forever transferring their inadequacy onto others, never to blame, never to improve.

'Dan lives here now, Tommy. You shouldn't call, not without my permission,' said Grace. From the stunned look on Tommy's face, it was clear that this revelation was breaking news. That wasn't a surprise. Grace and Dan hadn't exactly advertised the fact about town. In truth, even Dan was still processing his recent move, the stamping of their relationship.

'I'll come whenever I fucking want, okay!' growled Tommy. 'Have you been drinking, Tommy?' asked Dan. It was a rhetorical question. From Dan's experience, if Tommy was awake, he was under the influence. Not just drink – weed, pills, whatever was in supply. Grace had briefed Dan all about her ex-boyfriend and the father of her child, Niamh. Her life-sentence. Tommy seemed incapable of goodness, and the fatigue of countless parenting battles had worn Grace down. Dan and Grace had agreed that, if nothing else, they would behave with dignity. He admired that about Grace. She did the right thing. Despite the hardship, the bullying, and the trouble, she persevered with a decency few he knew possessed. One good adult, wasn't that the adage? Well, little Niamh would be okay.

'You been fucking, Officer?' asked Tommy, his face tattooed with hostility. Dan didn't need any further inducement. He grabbed Tommy's upper arm and began to frogmarch him back out to the yard.

'Daddy, what's going on?' came the voice of a child. Niamh had emerged sleepily from her bedroom and was ambling into the kitchen. Grace stood and walked to her daughter, lifting her into her arms. 'It's okay, baby. Daddy came by to see if we needed anything, with it snowing and all. He didn't want to wake you.' Dan released his hold of Tommy's arm.

'Hey, sweetie, come here for a big hug from your daddy,' said Tommy. The young girl ran to her father and jumped into his arms. Tommy twirled her around in an arc, stumbling a little as he did, and finally, set her down safely.

'Look! Look at the snow, Daddy!' squealed Niamh gleefully as she pointed excitedly out the open back door. 'Can we build a snowman?'

'Not now, sweetheart, okay, I gotta go. You have fun, and then tell me all about it when I see you.' Tommy ruffled the little girl's hair and pushed her gently back towards her mother. Head down, Niamh offered no complaint. Dan could see that the little girl was used to disappointment. 'We'll build one after school,' said Grace to help soften the blow. Suddenly, the look in Tommy's eyes changed from dull to angry, and he began to move threateningly towards Grace. Dan quickly reached out and stopped him in his tracks, voicing a simple but firm, 'Time to go.'

Dan shepherded Tommy back out to the yard, careful all the while not to alert Niamh that her father was being evicted. 'Leave your vehicle here, and I'll drop you into town on my way to the station,' said Dan quietly so the little girl couldn't hear. Tommy looked at him incredulously. 'Are you fucking serious? I need to...' Dan interjected, cutting him off mid-sentence. 'Not in front of Niamh. C'mon, be smart,' he whispered. Dan opened the door to the police car and eased a now-silent Tommy into the backseat. Dan cleared the loose snow from the roof and windows and then crossed the yard to Tommy's souped-up BMW. He leaned in and switched off the engine, closed the driver's door, zapped the lock and put the keys in his pocket.

Tommy stared out from the patrol car, bemused and silent. Grace stood watching from the doorway, hands in her coat pockets, pockets wrapped around Niamh, who snuggled between her legs. Dan walked to Grace and gave her a kiss goodbye. Niamh looked up, and Dan patted her head softly. 'I'm giving your daddy a lift to town as his car is low on petrol. He'll be okay with me,' he said. Niamh nodded an okay, but her eyes betrayed worry and sadness.

Dan returned to the police car, sat in and started the engine. He cranked the heating up to full blast. Like a retreating shadow, the frosty fogginess cleared from the windscreen. 'I'll have your car towed to the station, Tommy. You can collect it there later. No need for you to come back here,' he said. Tommy grunted some unappreciative acknowledgement and rested his head backwards, closing his eyes. From the doorstep, Grace called aloud, 'Rocky! Here, boy, Rocky. Here, Rocky!' Dan looked in his mirrors, but there was no sign of the dog. When he was sure that the retriever wasn't going to end up under his wheels, he drove out of the courtyard and up towards the main road.

Across the yard, hidden from view, Król watched on. He listened as Grace hollered in vain after the dog. The sun's glare blinded the windowpane, and Król spotted the faint trace of a fingerprint on the glass. He set his right index fingertip on top of it. His was larger, maybe twice the size. How long ago had it been placed, and by whom? A fingerprint can last for forty years, he'd been once told, but he couldn't remember why or where. After the police car had left, he watched as Grace and the child went back inside the farmhouse. Król lifted a pair of binoculars from his bag and scanned the farm's hinterland. Nothing stirred but the eager snow.

8:15a.m.

Most of the time, Amy's face glowed like a warm summer evening. Eyes gleaming and hinting at mischief. Rosy freckled cheeks. Mouth open wide in a toothy smile, some crooked, some missing, yet somehow all perfect in their imperfection. All this beneath a wild tumble of russet curls. And when she laughed, sheer joy rippled through the house. This morning, there was neither radiance nor giggles. Today's Amy was quiet and brooding, head down, frowning pensively, eyes locked on her cereal. She toyed with the milk-sodden flakes in the bowl, moving them back and forth but not to her mouth. Kate knew the troubled look. Eight-year-olds didn't hide their emotions well. That was the preserve of their parents. Maybe it was the planned sleepover at Niamh's, her first time to spend a night away from home. 'Is everything okay, baby?' she asked. No answer came, just more swirling of soggy cereal. 'Amy? What's up? You look a bit sad. Don't worry, you can tell Mammy, no matter what it is.'

Amy raised her head. She seemed to be on the verge of tears, and Kate felt a bolt of fear run through her.

'Do you still love Daddy?' asked the child.

The question smacked Kate full in the face. Shit. She smiled as she reeled from the accusatory blow, never looking away from the inquisitive eyes scanning for any betraying reflex. 'Of course I love Daddy, baby,' she replied as quickly as she could, but not quickly enough. From the sad realisation creeping across Amy's face, it seemed that even eight-year-olds could detect a hesitation's reveal.

Once, Kate's counsellor had asked her to say the first three words that came to her mind when she thought of her husband, Peter. Love had not been one of them. Nor happiness.

Regret.

Disappointment.

Disillusionment.

They were but three of many that had sprung readily to her tongue. Anger. Frustration. Selfishness. Loneliness. Sadness. There were so many, and even if they were all bound together in one large encyclopaedic tome for the unhappy, they still couldn't start to describe how truly lost and disenchanted she felt.

'Why would you ask me that, baby?' Kate asked nervously.

'I don't want you and Daddy to split up. Sean, in class, his daddy left his mammy, and now his mammy is cross all the time. The kids in school tease him, say that his home is broken, that he has no daddy. He says his mammy shouts a lot and that she told his daddy to fuck off.'

'Now, Amy, don't use those words.'

'I didn't say it. Sean did,' said Amy, with an impudent scowl.

'I think you just joined him in that, so not again, okay?'

Amy nodded her head, her face displaying a mix of acquiescence and frustration.

Kate knew Sean's parents well. It was hard to keep secrets in a town the size of Blackcliff. Their split had loomed ominously, and when it eventually came, it was fractious and angry. They'd both had flings. Mike first and then Helen in spite. Now Mike had moved into his girlfriend's flat over the butcher's on Main Street. Helen bitched about him constantly at the school gate, and to be fair, it sounded like she had good cause. However, these days, Kate steered clear. It wasn't for her to judge who was right or wrong in the affairs of others. She'd enough on her own plate.

'The children shouldn't pick on Sean like that. It's not fair. I hope you don't do that.'

'No. I like Sean. I stick up for him; it's not his fault,' said Amy.

A surge of pride flushed through Kate. After a thousand soiled nappies and innumerable sleepless nights, after all the worrying, protecting and caring, the countless bedtime stories, forehead kisses, never-want-to-let-go hugs, now, here before her, sat this independent marvel. A being created of her own flesh, blood, sweat, tears and toil. Her miracle. Her Amy displaying compassion and understanding that seemed lost on many five times her age. Worry too. Worries she shouldn't have. Kate could have cried, but somehow, she held back the tears. This was a moment for calm.

'That was very kind of you, Amy. Sean needs good friends now.'

Kate crossed to the table and sat down. She stared directly into her daughter's eyes.

'Why do you think Daddy and Mammy might split up, baby?'

The words nearly caught in her throat, but somehow, she'd extracted them before they choked her. Amy fidgeted some more, the spoon now buried deep in the mushy cereal, but finally, she answered. 'I dunno. Daddy's away all the time, and when he's home, you two fight a lot. You're not happy when he's here. He always seems to be cross, like Sean's mammy.'

Kate looked at her little girl. So innocent, so beautiful, so full of everything good with the world. She could feel her stomach churning. So this, this was the happy home that they had built? As much as Kate liked to believe she was the innocent party, the bottom line was that, as parents, they were collectively failing their daughter. She, too, was complicit. What the proportions of guilt were, the ratios of culpability, that Kate couldn't tell for sure. There was plenty of blame to go around. She began to respond when she was startled by a loud screech. Their heads turned in stunned unison.

'Look, Mammy, look!' cried Amy, pointing out to the back garden.

Kate rose from the table and hurriedly crossed the room to the glass patio doors. Perched outside on the garden table was the most stunning creature she had ever seen. The yellow eyes of a snowy owl stared straight back at her, piercing hers in their unblinking resoluteness. Black barring speckled the pristine white plumage. A female, larger than the males. Had it sailed south on the crest of the coming storm?

'Amy, slowly, ssshhh, come closer, get a better view.'

Amy tiptoed to the door and took her mother's hand, her eyes never leaving the owl. On cue, the bird screeched a loud *kerrawk*, spanned its wings wide and rose into the frosty air. It hovered for a while above the backfield and then descended at speed in an elegant swoop towards the white earth. The instinctive movement occurred in a split second, a primal evolutionary reaction to the minute twitch of a hair on the nose of its prey. No time for thought. Just hardwired to hunt, to stay alive. At the surface, the bird's outstretched talons clasped onto its victim, and together they rose into the sky. Amy gasped aloud. 'What was that, Mammy? What was it?' she cried.

'I'm not sure, baby. Maybe a mouse or a small rabbit. It was too far away to see.'

'Will it kill it? Will it kill it?' asked the child excitedly.

Kate hated to lie to her daughter. She rarely did, and once was already enough this morning. 'Yes, baby. I think it will.'

8:15a.m. (9:15a.m. Brussels)

Peter Kavanagh silently groaned as he scanned the mountain of documents still to be finalised before he departed Brussels that evening on his flight to Shannon. He could do without the trip home, but Kate had ordered a war council. 'Time to clear the air,' she had said. Peter glanced up from his computer, suddenly aware of a presence haunting his open office door. Despite his broad frame, Commissioner Wagner had the uncanny ability to steal up when he least expected it. Peter wondered how long he'd been standing there watching him. It was his own fault for leaving the door ajar in an attempt to alleviate the dry radiator heat that had amped into overdrive ever since the cold snap had frozen the city.

The commissioner's ego preceded him along the corridors of the EU Parliament building. When Peter first arrived, he had hardly settled behind his new desk when he received his first warning not to cross Herr Wagner. It was hard to believe that five years had since passed. Oddly, he and the big German had struck up an unlikely partnership. They shared a liking for some of the finer things in life. Late nights carousing in Brussels' smoky dens had seen them forge a pact of mutual convenience. Peter could keep a secret, and Wagner could open doors. In managed doses, Wagner was bearable, and till now, Peter had kept his exposure to acceptable limits.

'Have you a moment, Peter?' enquired Wagner.

'Yes, always. Come in.'

Wagner entered, closing the door behind him. He made himself as comfortable as he could in the swivel leather seat positioned in front of Peter's desk. Peter hoped the chair survived the ordeal – it took forever to get anything new requisitioned. He closed his laptop and placed a napkin over his half-eaten breakfast. 'What's up, Commissioner?'

'You never joined us last night. Can I assume you had a better offer?' Wagner asked with feigned disappointment.

Peter smiled. 'You might say that.'

Wagner laughed and dug a pack of cigarettes from his pocket. He offered one, but Peter waved his hand to gesture no. Peter allowed himself one in the evenings with a glass of wine, but otherwise, he'd managed to give them up. This was a non-smoking building; however, it appeared that these rules only applied to lesser mortals than the commissioner. Soon, billows of sweet-smelling tobacco filled the small office.

'We had a few vintage brandies without you – to keep us warm,' said Wagner, pointing past Peter to the snow that was falling outside the fifth-floor window.

'Anything else on hand to keep you warm, Commissioner?' Peter asked. He knew all too well, if true to form, Wagner and his cronies probably ended their night's revelry in one of the town's less reputable establishments. The commissioner chortled aloud but didn't respond. Instead, pleasantries over, a serious look shadowed his face. 'How's Tanya getting on?' he asked. Tanya was Wagner's daughter. Mid-twenties, full of confidence, not all of it well placed. Two years previously, Wagner had asked Peter to offer her a job as an assistant. Peter could hardly have said no, and he didn't. Tanya was fresh from college and had just moved to Brussels from the family home in Munich. Working in the Parliament, Wagner could keep a watchful eye on her, or that was his plan anyhow. Tanya was a feisty girl, keeping watch of her had proven difficult.

'She seems fine. I've been travelling a lot with all this migrant stuff, so I haven't seen her much. Is everything okay?'

The commissioner shifted a little in his ill-equipped, undersized chair. *Ease up on the steak and wine, Herr Wagner*, thought Peter.

'She seems off. Worried even. Something is troubling her.'

Peter felt his pulse quicken, and his palms began to moisten. 'Did she say what?'

'She won't tell me, but I know something is on her mind,' said Wagner. 'A father's intuition, you might say. Her mother says she is going to visit and sort it out, and that's all I need.'

Peter breathed a little easier; maybe Tanya could be trusted after all. 'I'll talk to her discreetly, see if I can learn anything,' he offered.

The commissioner's eyes narrowed ever so slightly as he looked straight into Peter's. 'You and Tanya. You know not to cross the line?'

'That's crazy! Come on, you know me better than that,' said Peter, laughing aloud. Wagner just stared unblinking, watching for any tell of a lie. 'No way. No way!' declared Peter, shaking his head adamantly, matching Wagner's stare eye to eye.

'Okay,' said Wagner. 'But don't ever forget this, Peter. She's not just any employee or just another girl. She's my girl.'

Peter could feel his heart trying to burst through his chest, yet somehow, outwardly, he maintained a calm demeanour. 'Why this, now?' he asked.

The commissioner rose to leave, and having opened the door, he stood once again in the frame, filling both its length and width. 'I passed her on the steps last week. She was talking to an older man. More, he was talking to her, telling her something. He looked the rough type. Tanya seemed stressed and agitated. I went to her to see if I was needed, but she was at pains to push me away, to tell me everything was okay. I left – I don't like to treat her like a baby, you know – but as I was walking away, I heard a name being mentioned angrily.'

Peter waited nervously in the pause and then asked, 'What name?'

'Your name. Peter Kavanagh.'

II

I went to see Amy at her school. It was just before Christmas. She and Niamh were playing in the yard at break time. I waved to her, and they came straight over. She remembered me from the beach when I gave the letters to her mother. 'Mammy's friend' was how she described me to Niamh. I guessed they were seven, maybe eight years old, their little bodies already changing, taking shape. Children that age are innocent. They believe every word you say. They see the good in all. They can't imagine why someone might cause them harm. Of course, they display reticence at first, but that quickly dissipates if you know how to talk to them and see things from their perspective. I asked what Santa might be bringing, and the two reeled off a range of hoped-for toys, which they naturally assumed I knew about, for what else could be more important? Kids will tell you anything. They really will. I could barely look into Amy's earnest eyes as she informed me that Niamh was her best friend forever and that every Wednesday afternoon, they had a play date on Niamh's farm. The longer I spoke to the two girls, the more unsettled and queasy I felt. Amy asked my name. 'Król,' I said, 'it means king.' 'That's cool,' she replied, smiling. That horrible fear rose within me. Tears welled, and I wiped them away. In Amy, I saw her again. Her delicate face, her glowing smile, her wavy locks of hair. I could smell her. I longed to reach through the bars and touch her, lift her into my arms, hold her tight and never let her go.

8:20a.m.

Dan's gums ached. He was grinding his teeth again. His dentist had remarked upon it. Near invisible hairline cracks in the enamel, frayed caps worn by attrition. 'Do you suffer from anxiety?' the dentist had asked. Dan replied that he was a policeman and left it at that. What he hadn't added was that, yes, absolutely, he was stressed more often than not. No matter how hard he tried to make a difference in his work, little seemed to change for the better. For a small town, Blackcliff possessed more than its fair share of what his father had dubbed *useless life-suckers*. Slime who leached the marrow out of anyone or anything they came into contact with. A sad realisation had come, he could never say exactly when, that his efforts were, on the whole, pointless. He'd grown up with the notion that people were inherently good, but these days, he wasn't so sure. Good to themselves, and if watched, maybe occasionally others too. He drove on towards town. Beyond the car's wipers, a new wondrous landscape had appeared. The scruffy

23

verges, scrags and troughs now resembled an idyllic winter postcard under their new blanket of snow.

Dan glanced behind him. Tommy Molloy's head bobbed up and down in a sleepy stupor as the vehicle navigated the country road. The fermenting reek of alcohol and sweat was making Dan queasy. He lowered the driver's window a little and breathed deep the cold air. A flurry of invading snowflakes landed wet on his hair and cheeks. Tommy stirred awake. He yawned loudly and wiped away the drool that had seeped from the corner of his mouth. 'Jesus, shut that, will you? It's fucking freezing,' he growled.

'It'll do you good, clear your head,' said Dan as he closed the window an inch to placate his passenger. 'That must have been some night you had. What did you get up to?'

'None of your business,' said Tommy yawning. 'I know what *you* were up to, though, between the legs of my missus.'

Dan's teeth clenched, his disgust simmering again. From nought to one hundred, it didn't take Tommy long. Dan was well used to dealing with mouthy local warriors trying to wind him up. With Tommy, though, it was more than that; *it was personal.* He was Niamh's father. If Dan and Grace were to last, then Tommy would be a constant presence in his life. That was not a pleasant thought. 'She hasn't been your *missus* for a long time, Tommy. Was she ever really, for that matter? Getting her pregnant and her being your beloved are two entirely different things.'

'Yeah, you believe what you want, Mr Garda, but it was me that let *her* go. She cried when I left.' Somehow, Dan couldn't picture Grace, or anyone for that matter, crying after Tommy, but the world was a peculiar place. That he knew well. Dan checked the rear-view mirror. Tommy's face was a smirking annoyance that begged to be smacked. There were times when Dan regretted being a Garda, bemoaned his duty to do the right thing. He drove on, passing the GAA pitches and then the industrial park on the edge of town.

'Did you ever hit Grace?' Dan asked, the muscles in his arm tensing as he gripped the wheel, his eyes resolute on the road ahead.

'What? No way, I never laid a hand on her. Why, did she say I did?' snarled Tommy in reply.

Dan was silent. He'd seen plenty of domestic abuse perpetrated against defenceless women by so-called hard men. Grace had never called out Tommy explicitly, but Dan had his suspicions. He suspected that she was holding her tongue for Niamh's sake. They reached the old single-storey police station, which occupied a prominent corner site at the top of Main Street. It always reminded Dan of the old Western movies he'd watched as a child with his dad. As the bandits rode into town, they would invariably have to pass the sheriff's office first, where a stare-off would ensue. The outlaws always looked so menacing and heartless, but in the end, you knew that somehow the sheriff and his small band of motley strays would win out despite the odds. Nothing seemed so clearcut these days.

'What's done is done, Tommy, the past is the past. But mark my words, if Grace ever feels threatened by you again, then just know, I'll never let it rest, okay?' said Dan, with an anger in his voice that he wished wasn't there. Tommy remained silent as Dan steered into one of the station's parking bays. Dan turned and locked eyes with his passenger. 'Did you hear me, Tommy?' he asked sternly.

'Yes, sir,' replied Tommy in a derisory tone as he glanced away furtively. Dan still hadn't decided whether to charge Tommy for driving under the influence. To be honest, he'd enough on his plate with the storm coming in. He didn't need the hassle.

'But listen, I'm really confused. Something doesn't make any sense,' coughed up Tommy suddenly. 'When I stayed over at Grace's just before Christmas, she never mentioned feeling threatened. She didn't even mention your name. That's odd, isn't it?' Dan could sense the malign smirk without the need to look. 'Who knows, maybe my dates are wrong. I get bombed a lot.'

Dan knew Tommy was lying, but the ugly thought still annoyed him. He wondered again how Grace had ever been involved with this excuse for a man, this vulgar asshole who fathered her child. Had he, a police officer, been selected as the safe and reliable choice? The dependable one you turned to when you'd had your fill of the bad boys. Dan flushed the negative thoughts from his mind and switched off the engine. 'Do you know what, Tommy? I have an idea. A few hours in the cells to sober up might do you some good.'

8:35a.m.

Niamh ran excitedly from the farmhouse into the back yard. Grace followed, calling after her to be careful. The laughing child scooped snow from the ground and, rolling it into a ball, flung the missile at her mum. Grace fired a return volley. Król watched on from the shed. After a short while Grace called her daughter, 'Okay, Niamh, come on, we've got to go, or we'll be late for school'. She zapped the alarm on her Micra, and the two of them climbed in. The engine coughed into life, and exhaust fumes plumed into the crisp air. Grace clambered back out and repeated the same process of wiping snow from the windows and mirrors that Dan Brady had performed only a short while before. Job completed, Grace stood tall and gazed around the yard. She called again for Rocky. Inside the shed, Król bent down and patted the unconscious retriever's head. He'd grown fond of the dog these last few weeks and wished it no harm. After a moment or two, Grace gave up and sat back in the car. Soon, the Micra eased its way around the side of the house and proceeded slowly up the long driveway.

Król leaned forward, steadied the chair with his feet and pulled his large holdall towards him. He stretched the opening wide and drew a photograph from an inside pouch. With his index finger, he traced each of the faces. He hardly recognised himself. His wife Jude stood smiling happily by his side, between them, their daughter Theia sitting proudly on her new bike. Król tucked the photograph into the inside pocket of his coat. He checked the new smartphone he'd acquired for cash the week before. The battery read ninety per cent. He typed in his regular mobile phone number and dialled. He felt the vibrating in his inside pocket, and he ended the call and placed the new phone back into the bag. Król took stock of the remaining contents. Three rolled-up sleeping bags, some plastic ties, builder's tape, and a pair of mini binoculars.

Beneath these, at the base of the bag, lay a large manilla folder stuffed full of papers and bound by two sturdy elastics that formed a cross. From a zipped side pocket, he drew a Luger pistol. He checked the magazine. Eight live rounds. He raised the barrel and squared the tabby cat in his sights. The cat stared back, unamused. Król lowered the gun and eased back into the chair.

8:50a.m.

Kate pumped the brakes. On, off, on, off, just as her father had taught her, never foot down in snow, hail or ice. Getting to school alive made better sense than getting there early, so they slowly descended the winding road which ran from the elevated clifftops of the island headland in the west to the bay and the town of Blackcliff in the east. The snow was sticking, and most of the road surface was already covered. Negotiating one precarious bend after the next, eventually, they reached the base of Cliff Road and veered left to cross the wooden bridge that spanned the narrow causeway to the mainland. In town, the roads were gritted and easier to negotiate. They passed the cemetery and church on their left. Ahead, just past the community centre, was the primary school. Kate loosened her tight grip on the wheel as they slowed to a stop at the gates.

In the back of the car sat a gloomy Amy. Kate had been explaining to her that all married couples fought. It was natural. She and Peter were no different to the parents of the other kids in school. 'The important thing is to make up and try to do and be better the next time,' she had continued. Amy, though, had remained quiet throughout the journey. When Kate looked in the rear-view mirror at her precious cargo, the sight of her child's dejected little face brought tears to her eyes. She decided to drop the subject, not force it any further. 'Grab your overnight bag too, baby,' she said as she turned the engine off. As Amy leaned over to gather her things, Kate quickly dabbed her wet cheek with a tissue. Kids never liked to see their parents cry. If they weren't in control, then who was?

Outside on the pavement, Kate slid up the navy-blue zipper on Amy's pink puffer jacket. Red leggings and yellow wellies finished the colourful outfit. Next to her daughter, Kate felt drab and grey. She reached into her coat pocket and retrieved one of the many hair slides she regularly carried for just such occasions. Kate gently pinned back a wayward lock of her daughter's hair with the yellow and orange flowered clip. 'Have a wonderful time at Niamh's later, and don't forget to call Mammy on Grace's phone anytime you need to. Now, what is it that you know for certain and that you want to tell Mammy?'

Amy hesitated for a moment, but finally, she relented. 'I want to tell you that I know you love me,' she said, giggling as she spoke. Kate felt her heart lift.

'You sure?'

'I'm certain,' said Amy.

'And how much does Mammy love you?'

'More than everything in the whole world,' said Amy, her hands stretched out wide in elaboration.

'And for how long?'

'For always.'

Kate held her daughter tightly and kissed her head. She took the pink woollen hat protruding out of a side pocket of the child's coat and nestled it snuggly down over her head. 'I love you soooo much, baby. Don't you ever forget.' Before Kate had even finished the words, Amy let out a whoop for joy and ran excitedly to where she had spotted Niamh in the schoolyard.

'Best friend forever,' she had described Niamh as she packed that morning. *Forever is a long, long time*, Kate had thought. Suddenly, Amy stopped in her tracks and came running back towards her. 'What is it, love?' Kate asked as her child approached. Amy beckoned her to lean her head down, and Kate obliged.

'I love you too, Mammy,' said Amy, planting a big kiss on Kate's lips, and then she was gone again. Tears welled once more in Kate's eyes.

'How cute was that?' came a voice from over Kate's shoulder. 'I was just coming over to say hello. I couldn't help but hear,' said Grace Quigley.

'I know, that makes it all worthwhile,' said Kate as she stood again from her hunkered position to greet the smiling Grace. 'How are you, Grace? Are you and Niamh still okay for the sleepover if school finishes early? If it's any trouble, I'll gladly—'

'No, Kate, it's grand, no problem. More fun for the girls. They can build snowmen,' said Grace.

'I'm surprised the school is even open. They say the weather is going to get worse.'

'I think we might be closing at midday. We're just waiting on word from the principal. He's phoning schools in the other towns to see what their plans are,' replied Grace.

The two women looked over to where their children were busy throwing snowballs at each other, both now seemingly oblivious to the fact that their parents even existed. Grace glanced at Kate as if she wanted to say something, and then her gaze shifted awkwardly.

'How's Dan these days?' asked Kate.

'Yeah, he's good. Tommy's a pain, though, hanging around, making things difficult. I hope he doesn't scare him off.'

'I don't think Dan scares easy,' said Kate reassuringly.

'I hope not.'

Kate exhaled, and her breath drifted in a steamy cloud above her. She thought of Amy's sullen face in the car on the drive down from the lighthouse. She thought of her husband in Brussels. She thought of a summer's evening years ago, lying on the heather overlooking the Atlantic, Dan Brady by her side.

'Dan will do what's right, don't you worry,' she said.

She could see the effect of her words on Grace. A weight lifting. A sparkle starting to glint in her eyes.

'I'll ring you later when I'm settled with the girls. Have a lovely night off, and enjoy yourself. You deserve it,' said Grace.

'Thanks,' replied Kate and made her way back across the gritted tarmac to her car. For a while, she just sat there watching her little girl playing in the snow with her pals. The previous night, she would have sworn that Amy hadn't a care in the world. Now she knew that wasn't true. Everybody hurt, even the children. The bell sounded, and the kids scuttled side by side into the grey single-storey school, which, but for the coloured pictures stuck to the inside of its windows, could have passed for a prison. Kate hoped Amy would look back before she entered, but she didn't.

10:05a.m.

The Clare County Hotel was located about five miles north of Blackcliff along the coast road that led to Galway. The call had come into the station early that morning. A guest had left the hotel without paying. Dan would have sent the rookie Edwards, but he was busy at the scene of a road accident. The hotel had insisted that a Garda report was needed. Dan hoped it wasn't going to prove a waste of his valuable time; unpaid hotel bills were not a police matter.

A young girl greeted him nervously at an old-fashioned wooden reception desk. Dan asked for the manager, and after a few minutes, a lady, probably in her early forties, arrived and introduced herself. She asked Dan to follow her up to the first floor. Dan noticed the threadbare carpets and chipping paint as he climbed the stairs. The hotel had seen better days. In his childhood, it was a destination resort with sports facilities and private access through a wood down to a shingly beach. Now, it served as a budget hotel and was often used by the immigration services as an interim accommodation solution for asylum seekers.

They arrived at room 107, and the manager turned the key in the door and invited Dan to enter. The room was basic enough. A faded brown curtain was pulled to the side of a small window that looked out to the hotel car park. A dressed double bed filled the centre of the room. In the corner, a small and not very smart-looking TV sat atop a cheap desk. Beside the bed stood a heavy wooden wardrobe. Next to it, a door opened to a tiny bathroom. *Not unlike a million other hotel rooms*, thought Dan, *except this room was jaded; it didn't want any more visitors.*

'So, what exactly is the problem?' Dan asked the manager.

'I spoke to Garda Edwards at the station this morning. Did he speak with you?' she replied.

'Yes, yes, of course,' lied Dan, 'but if I can hear the story straight from you.'

'Okay, this guest has been staying with us for nearly four weeks now. He checked in on December 7th, paying three weeks cash in advance. That was the first unusual thing. Not many people pay cash these days.'

'It is legal tender,' commented Dan dryly, but the manager didn't seem to hear him.

'He stayed through Christmas, and then a few days after New Year's, he renewed for another week,' she continued. 'He said he would clear the final bill upon his departure, which was due to be yesterday. But the last time anybody saw him was two nights ago, and we've seen nothing of him since. He was always adamant that we never entered his room when he wasn't there, so we gave him a little grace. He'd been a good customer. But, when housekeeping checked this morning, it looked like he'd packed and left. His car is also gone, a blue Corolla. The bed hasn't been slept in for a few days as it seems to be tucked in just as the housekeeper made it on Wednesday evening.'

Dan listened to all that the manager had to say and found nothing too odd, really. 'So, it looks like he's bolted alright. You'll need to phone him, email him, follow up by legal means,' said Dan, sure now that he had indeed wasted his time.

'He left some personal things behind,' continued the manager, undeterred, 'that's why I called. We put them in here.' She opened the doors of the wardrobe, lifted out a storage box and placed it on the bed. 'The box is ours,' she said.

Dan scanned the contents. He felt his interest levels spiking. He picked up the passports – four of them. One by one, he checked the identity pages. Two were for the same person, Nicholas Król, one British and one Polish: a dark-haired man, mid-thirties, strong face, prominent cheekbones. The next was a woman named Judyta Wojcik, long blonde hair, a few years younger. The last was a young girl, Theia Król, seven years old. These passports were Polish. Dan wondered who departed their hotel room without paying but left their passports behind and then didn't return to retrieve them. Now, that was odd. 'Is this him?' he asked, showing the manager the passport picture of Król.

'Yes,' she replied.

'And the woman and child, did you see them, were they here at any time?' asked Dan.

'No, he was always alone. Well, actually...' the manager hesitated mid-sentence.

'Yes?' teased Dan.

'Sally, our cleaner, thought she saw a woman leave his room one afternoon. There was no other room that this woman could have come from. Sally didn't recognise her, and nobody else saw her.'

'Did you show Sally the passport picture?' asked Dan.

'Yes, she didn't believe it was the same woman, but she wasn't sure.'

'When was this?' asked Dan.

'Before Christmas,' replied the manager.

Dan placed the passports back into the box and rummaged around the rest of the contents. He dug into his jacket pocket for a pair of nylon plastic gloves, snapping them on carefully without breaking the sheaths. He took a half-used syringe from the box and put the needle to his nose. There was a familiar scent, but he had no idea from what. He stared at the remaining fluid in the vial but didn't recognise it from sight. Two additional used syringes lay in the cardboard box, but he left them where they were. Dan lifted a printed photograph of a young woman in her early twenties. The woman stood next to a very broad man. Behind them was the glass façade of what seemed to be an office building. A nearby street sign said Place de Luxembourg. The manager had moved to the corner of the room by the window, and now she came back to him holding a small aluminium bin.

'This too,' she said and handed it to him.

Dan took the bin from her and peered inside. Charred paper and ashes filled the container. He sifted through them carefully until an image caught his attention. He lifted the blackened paper, and a few brittle pieces of ash fell to the carpet. The partial face of a man looked back at him. Just the nose, eyes, chin, and the rest of the head had been burned away. Dan felt his jaw tighten, his teeth grinding again. He had a vague notion that he recognised the face, but he couldn't figure out who it was. In truth, it could be anyone. He placed the charred picture into the cardboard box.

The chest of drawers and wardrobe were empty, and the floor was clear. Dan entered the bathroom. A red toothbrush stood to attention in a ceramic holder. He drew an evidence bag from his jacket, placed the toothbrush into it, and shoved it into his pocket.

'That's all his stuff,' said the hotel manager, shrugging her shoulders, 'I just thought it was strange, him leaving these things, then taking off without paying.'

'You were right to call us. Don't worry, we'll check him out,' said Dan as he made his way back into the bedroom. Out of the corner of his eye, he spotted an object resting on the top of the wardrobe. It had been pushed too far back to be seen from inside the bedroom. Dan crossed the room again to the old wooden closet. He couldn't reach so he stood up on the bed and poked about the top of the unit. He dropped back down from the bed, smiling, a thick black book in his right hand. He held it up for the manager to see. It was a Bible, King James version.

'Hotel issue?' Dan asked, even though he felt sure few hotels kept Bibles anymore and certainly not the fire and brimstone of the Testaments.

'Not ours,' replied the manager.

The hardback cover had a number of circular punctures roughly the diameter of a fingertip. Dan pushed his baby finger through one to a depth of nearly an inch. He opened the tome and leafed through the pages. The holes tore at the paper as the pages parted. About three-quarters of the way through, the punctures ended. 'Anybody hear gunshots around here lately?' asked Dan as he closed the book.

'What? No, nobody said anything like that,' replied the now alarmed-looking manager. Dan placed the Bible into the box.

'I'll take these down to the station,' said Dan. 'Keep us informed if your guest returns, and we'll follow it up from our end. Ring in the details of that car of his and anything else you can remember that might be of interest. Also, tell Sally that we may wish to talk to her. Ask her if there is anything else she can remember about that woman, please.'

Dan made his way into the corridor, and the manager followed. Together, they proceeded down the stairs and out through the lobby to the front entrance. An old man and woman were entering the hotel, and they stared curiously at Dan in his uniform. 'Good morning,' said Dan to the inquisitive couple and then thanked the hotel manager for her time. He said goodbye and plodded back through the snow to his patrol car. He opened the passenger door and placed the box on the seat. He scanned the surrounding countryside. A path ran from the hotel entrance around the side to a lawned green area, which was now snow covered. Behind the green was the dense wood that led down to the shoreline. Dan wondered how far the sound of gunfire would travel through the thick trees. He sat into the car and dug the Bible from the box. He flicked through the damaged pages carefully until an underlined section caught his eye.

24:17-21 If a man takes the life of any human being, he shall surely be put to death.

Dan put the Bible back into the box and started the car. He had no idea what to make of the peculiar assortment of items he'd collected and was always loathe to jump to quick conclusions. All the same, a nagging worry had seeded.

10:10a.m.

Król crept around the perimeter of the courtyard that separated the shed from the farmhouse. He crouched low behind an old tractor that was slumped in permanent rest on a bed of weeds. Earlier, he watched as the policeman and the early morning visitor departed together and then later, as Grace and Niamh had left for school. Grace was a teacher there, so neither would be back until the afternoon. All the same, he was careful to take cover where he could as he traversed the cobbled ground. His circuitous route would leave as few visible footprints as possible.

Reaching the farmhouse, he sidled up next to the gable end window. The sash window was split into two halves, each consisting of six single-glazed panes interspersed between metal muntins. He poked the fragile glass with the tip of his index finger. It would only require a solid tap. He lifted a thin metal bar from the pile of scrap that was heaped along the wall, and with one light crack, the bottom-left pane shattered inwards. Król pulled out any remaining shards and discarded them into the snow at his feet. Reaching in, he released the catch lock. The curtains billowed inwards as he lifted the bottom half of the window upwards.

Standing on an upturned bucket, he clambered in and hauled his bag in after him. He closed the window and scanned the room. Cardboard boxes were packed high along the far wall. A doll's pram was parked in the corner.

A pink bicycle rested precariously against a vanity table, the hose of a vacuum cleaner tangled in the spokes of one wheel. Suddenly, he could see her, hear her. His daughter, learning to cycle, no stabilisers, screaming hysterically as she freewheeled down a laneway, he, heart pounding, running behind. 'Again, again, again,' she joyfully shrieked. These fleeting recollections came less and less, and he struggled desperately to pin them down, to capture them in his mind before they frittered away, never to return. Deep sadness filled him. He was so far from anything he loved. He didn't want to end it this way, but what else could he do? There was no way back.

III

I was always a watcher. In the shadows, you learn to hide. That way, nobody troubles you. At university, I'd roam unnoticed, observing the students, the professors, and the visitors. I knew everything and everyone on that campus, yet so few knew me, or if they did, they rarely showed it. In Poland, I'd look down on the passers-by from the rooftop balcony. All I'd see were heads, no one different from the next. Ants busying about the city.

Here in Blackcliff, I am invisible again. After our first meeting on the beach, I followed Kate most days from afar. An hour here and there. I'd pick up the trail at the school gate after she'd dropped Amy off. I learned her habits. Once a week, she'd visit her parents' grave. I would crouch out of sight behind the trees and shrubbery along the far wall of the cemetery. I remember thinking what a lovely place to rest one's bones with the cliffs in the distance and the sea below.

But Blackcliff is not my town. These dead are not my dead. My mother and father are buried across the sea. It's a strange feeling when both of your parents have passed. They tether us in all of this vastness. When those roots have withered, the branches where once we sat, they hollow and break. We are left to stand alone.

Kate would say words to her parents that I couldn't hear, and then she'd bless herself and leave. One day, after she'd gone, I weaved my way between the rows nearest the abbey ruins. There, by the stone wall, the headstones are worn bare by time. The oldest I found was dated 1786 – only thirty-one orbits around the sun for Michael Riley. I think the name spelt Riley. It was almost indecipherable. The ground was hard and flat, with no sign that a once-mortal creature reposed beneath. With every passing year, the last traces of Riley will slowly but inexorably fade.

I stayed amongst those tombs until darkness descended. My teeth chattered in the ferocious cold, and a hunger ached in my stomach. Across the bay, the lighthouse sent its warning beacon out over the seas until slowly the light dissipated, and its wispy trace seeped into the unending black. As I looked at that canopy of stars, I thought of my father's words as he tried to explain to a small child the outlandish scale of everything. As he tried to demonstrate to me that the entire history of the universe was mapped out above us, every single moment in time and space frozen in a photograph, nothing erased. 'There are more stars in the sky than all the grains of sand on all the beaches in all the world,' he said, shaking his head as he did, as if even to him, with all his knowledge and years, this very idea was preposterous. Is he out there now with my mother? And when I follow them, what then? Like Riley, I, too, will

be lost to the winds of time. Yet, here, Kate, Peter, and Amy,
they will never forget me.

10:15a.m.

Kate pulled the lapels of her coat closed with her gloved
hands and leaned into the squall. The wind whistled hard
from the sea below, sending large white flakes flailing on
its icy gusts. She pushed open the iron gate to the cemetery
and made her way along the age-old path. The cemetery
had been here longer than most people could plot their
family trees. It was something she'd been planning to do,
but like a lot of things, she hadn't quite got to it yet. Her
grandfather and her great-grandfather were buried here,
but before that, she had no idea. She crossed between the
rows and stopped at her parents' graveside.

Tears filled her eyes. They still came, no matter how
many years had passed. She missed both of them so
badly. She'd loved them in different ways. She'd bickered
endlessly with her mother because she could. Because her
mother would allow her to. She'd allowed her voice to be
heard, empowered her to question, and encouraged her
to improve upon the blood that had gone before her. Her
mother had forged an iron will within Kate, for she had
known that only strength would allow her to find her own
path. 'For a woman to be truly independent, she must be
stronger than any man,' she had said. With her father, it was
just love. Never a cross word, never a row. A love that could
never be repeated, for it was as unconditional and absolute
as the sun setting over the sea. If she had disappointed him
or given him cause to frown, it had never been expressed.

All she had ever seen in his eyes was acceptance and a love to die for. He'd been one of those gentle giants. A man to turn to when a job needed doing. Not just on the farm but in the community, too. He always brokered a path forward when voices dissented. People trusted him and respected his opinion. As the snowflakes whirled about the graves, Kate smiled to herself. So many harsh winters had battered this town, and so often, it had been her father who led the call when the clean-up began. Fundraisers, community events. Rebuild the sea wall. Repaint the benches along the promenade. Reroof the old bandstand. Repair the boathouse. He'd been a force to reckon with, a powerhouse of a man, yet a gentle one. It was he who had the vision to acquire the lighthouse. He planned to keep the light alive, modernise it, and restore it to working order. Back then, nobody paid it any heed, but as the years went by, it became a thriving tourist destination, a symbol of the town's renaissance. Normally, she could see it from the graveyard, standing proud on the western clifftops, an indomitable stone monument to one man, but not today, not through this swathe of white.

As Kate looked down at her father's grave, thoughts of Peter came to her. It always happened. It was as if the memory of her father cast some ever-grey reflection over her husband that she couldn't lift and he couldn't leap. Was that what she'd really wanted, a man like her father? Maybe subconsciously, she had pursued the opposite. And if that had indeed been her subliminal goal, she had succeeded. The thought of Peter's arrival later that night sent a shivering dismay through her that even the frosty weather couldn't match. An end was near. To the secrets and lies. To the abuse. To their marriage? The hours to come would bring a long-awaited reckoning, but at what price and to whom? She reminded herself once more that with every end came a beginning. To what she didn't know, but a beginning, nonetheless.

Kate turned from the family plot and began making her way back towards the old stone church. Ahead, she spotted the familiar figure of Iris Brady. Kate had always been fond of Iris. She could be as irascible and gnarly as an old badger, but with Kate, she had always been caring and kind, even that time long ago when Kate had left for America, leaving Iris's son Dan behind. Then, Iris blamed Dan for not following her. Maybe that was the way of mothers, somehow seeking perfection in their children, finding fault when maybe the fault lay elsewhere. Iris looked up to see her and smiled a warm smile. Kate felt a small bolt of shock. It was as if Iris had shrunk since the last time they'd met. Her face was gaunt, the skin translucent and tight. She had lost weight. Kate moved to her side and greeted her. For some reason, she put her arm around the old woman's back and held her by the waist. Iris didn't pull away.

Kate looked at the graves beneath. Jim Snr and Jim Junior. She'd known Jim Snr, a local Garda sergeant. Dan had followed him into the force. Jim Junior nobody spoke of – a swimming accident when the boy was only five. Kate herself was but a baby at the time of the tragedy. Maybe that loss explained how quiet and withdrawn Jim and Iris had always seemed. They had never appeared to need others. Right up till Jim's passing, Kate would meet them on the cliff walk, just the two of them, arm in arm. Kate rubbed her gloved hand slowly up and down Iris's back. It felt to her that underneath the old woman's coat lay only skeleton.

'How are you, Kate?' asked Iris.

'I'm okay, Iris, but I've been better,' replied Kate. She never lied to Iris; they had hearts that could share truths. They'd always had that connection. 'I'm really not sure of much these days if I'm honest.'

Iris stared into Kate's eyes, into her soul.

'That man was never right for you. I'm sure I told you back then, and I'll tell you again now: some people run from happiness, others nurture it. Peter Kennedy is a runner. A lot of men are. They are never happy, never satisfied. With the right man, you can face down anything, without...' The old woman looked away, her mind back now in her own thoughts.

After a moment or two of silence, Kate spoke again. 'Dan seems happy with Grace,' she said. It came out sounding like a question more than a statement.

'I hope so. I hope she wants what he wants. He's too soft, that boy. He's always saving people.' Kate processed Iris's words. A mother's vantage. Who else could see better? All around, the graves were pristine, dressed in their best holy white. No weeds to be pulled, no flowers to change when covered by snow.

'What a vicious God, don't you think?' said Iris, catching Kate by surprise. She didn't agree but didn't say so. 'They say he takes the best ones young; how horribly cruel of him,' continued Iris, her eyes glistening with a fiery rage. Kate squeezed Iris's arm gently.

'Let's go, Iris,' she said softly. Together, the two women threaded their way carefully through the graveyard towards the church car park. Kate noticed that the old woman was limping ever so slightly, but it didn't seem to slow her down. She wondered if Iris had slipped in the snow.

'The weather is expected to get worse. Are you heading home now?' Kate asked.

'Soon, I have to visit Dr Hanrahan first,' replied Iris as she shuffled towards her small Fiat.

As Kate turned towards her car, a squawking jackdaw landed on the snow-covered wall. Kate remembered the owl from that morning.

'Amy and I saw a large snowy owl this morning in our backyard,' Kate blurted aloud as if she was an excited child again, revealing a secret to her mother.

'An owl?' replied Iris, turning her gaze back to Kate. 'Hmmm,' she sighed, unimpressed. 'Ruthless hunters, owls. They can smell death. The old folk thought they cried like a wolf. That's how they got their name. Howl. Owl,' she continued.

'Is that true? Goodness, I never knew that,' replied Kate. Iris arched her eyebrows and waved her hand with a gesture that seemed to suggest to Kate that today's generation knew little about much, but Kate took no offence. Instead, she marvelled at the old woman's tenacity and independence. Iris would rather die than seize up.

'Call me if you need anything,' said Kate as the old lady clambered slowly into her car and closed the door behind her. Kate waved as the vehicle eased slowly away in the direction of town. A thought lingered. When her time came, Kate longed to be one of those smiling, wistful old ladies, content with the life lived, hopeful for what still lay ahead.

Half-drunk mugs of coffee, uneaten slices of toast, the remains of that morning's aborted breakfast still sat on the kitchen table. The previous night's dishes lay piled in the sink. The Aga purred, and Król felt warmth returning to his toes, nose and hands. He glanced at a framed photograph on the wall. The happy couple, Grace Quigley and Dan Brady. What a fine, upstanding pair in the community: the schoolteacher and her policeman partner. Another picture hung next to it, a photo of Niamh when she was younger, maybe four or five years old. She sat at the bottom of a playground slide, an enormous smile lighting up her face as she glanced back towards the camera.

Król entered the hallway and then the master bedroom at the front of the house. He walked around the edge of the bed, peering down at the rumpled sheets. A damp stain was visible towards the centre of the bed. He leaned over, pinched the top sheet between his fingers and placed it covering the stain. He opened the bedside locker to the left of the bedframe and flicked through the contents. A bottle of perfume, a packet of mints, a few pens, a diary and a silver foil of tablets. He lifted the diary, sat down on the bed and began to leaf through the entries. Three distinct themes jumped from the pages. Grace's ex was a total jerk. Her daughter Niamh made life worth living. And finally, Grace was a dreamer, and better things lay ahead, and those dreams included Dan Brady. Król rose from the bed and made his way to the opposite side. On the floor sat an open suitcase. Loose garments lay on top of neatly folded clothing. A toilet bag was propped against the lamp on the bedside locker. He opened the drawers to find each of them empty.

Pictures of dogs and horses filled most of the wall space in Niamh's bedroom. Splashes of pink were everywhere – bedcovers, toys, dolls, there was even a pink rug on the floor. There were two single beds. One had been slept in, and Król wondered about the other. Did Grace have to comfort her daughter during the night? Was it for visiting friends? A crayoned picture was tacked to a bookstand. Two stick people, wearing skirts, both with long hair, walking through a meadow, around them misshapen cows and sheep. Król smiled and made his way out of the bedroom and down the hallway. At the far end, he opened the door to a small room that served as storage space. Files teetered in heaps on a desk. Some framed photographs lay stacked on a chair. He lifted one carefully as it appeared so old and delicate that it might break at the slightest touch. A faded colour image, turning to sepia, of a beaming middle-aged man standing proudly, his arm around the waist of the woman next to him. Behind them, this very farmhouse, its roof then thatched. In his right hand, the man held the reins of a horse that stood dutifully by his side. Between the two adults was a young girl of no more than seven or eight years, her head angled upwards, her eyes locked on Król. Król gazed closer at the picture, and for all the world, he felt he'd seen that young girl before. She was a double for Amy O'Connor.

Król made his way back to the spare bedroom where he had entered the farmhouse. The lace blinds still flitted up and down as an icy breeze whistled through the broken window. A dressed double bed filled the centre of the room. He closed the door behind him. His eyes hung as heavy as his heart. He hadn't slept properly in days. He dug out his pocket watch and flipped open the cover. There was time. He lay down on the mattress and retrieved the picture from the pocket of his jacket. There they were: he, his wife, and his daughter in the main square in Kraków. He sensed the lulling sensation of time looping over and over, wrapping itself about him, pulling him into sleep. Everything that was will be again, and again, and again.

11:45a.m.

Kate held on to the balcony rail at the top of the lighthouse tower. Even with the bar above chest level, she still felt nervous that somehow the gusts might lift her up and over. Below, waves rose in tumultuous swells before crashing into the cliff face. The ocean was a ferment of foaming white. Kate could feel her balance shifting with the wind. Standing exposed in the blizzard seemed foolhardy, yet she felt compelled to witness the tempest in all its glory. 'A once-in-a-lifetime polar storm,' the radio forecaster had announced. 'The worst to hit the country since 1957.' Kate remembered reading some of the old keeper's journals detailing shipwrecks and lost souls from storms of yore. The remains of long-forgotten vessels scattered the coastline, and countless others lay broken at the bottom of the ocean. She shivered at the thought of those harrowing ends. Behind her, the light rotated inside prisms of glass that reflected and magnified its beam, sending it out through the snow and far over the water – a 25-mile range in clear skies. If any poor souls were unfortunate enough to be on the seas today, the light would be of scant assistance.

Kate raised her digital camera and began to snap. It had been an early Christmas gift to herself. In November, she'd started photography classes, her aim, just this, to capture some of the breathtaking images these clifftops afforded: the never-ending skylines, the cascading seascapes, the teeming wildlife. Thousands and thousands of birds of every colour and species made these cliffs their home. Lapwings, kittiwakes, guillemots, gulls of every variety, even puffins – they were all to be found here. Most days, Kate would be greeted by the cacophony of the birds that nested on the craggy shelves beneath, but today, the roar of the storm drowned any screeches. The majority had already departed on their annual migration south, and for those that remained, it was batten-down-the-nests time.

Kate looked east, inland, towards town. She never tired of this place, this home, even when nature bared its teeth and attempted to tear it all asunder. Every other winter, sturdy seawalls were blown over as if made from children's building blocks. Slates from rooftops would go hurtling through the air like missiles. Summer furniture left out would end up in neighbours' gardens. And each time, with a hardened resolution not to surrender, the town's folk would rebuild, tidy up, and go again. In the summer, the city slickers would arrive, oblivious to the thought that winter might ever reach these shores. Then, it was dodgem cars, water sports and small children crying after fallen ice cream. They didn't understand the resolve required to live here all year round.

Kate could feel her nose begin to numb. She hated to leave the spectacle, but reluctantly, she retreated inside to the lantern room and made her way down the spiral stairs. One by one, she descended the six floors of the tower, down through the chambers that served as bedroom, kitchen and living quarters for the keepers through the years. Reaching the tower base, Kate faced the locked iron door that once was the only way in or out. Beyond it, stone steps cut into the vertical cliff face led downwards to the sea.

Kate opened the inner door that connected the lighthouse to her home and made her way along the corridor to the dining room and then the kitchen. She thought again of the summit that awaited with Peter. Thankfully, at least Amy wouldn't have to witness another row. Kate had waited for Christmas to pass, but now, with the New Year upon them, the time had come. Kate had always thought that she was just like her father: tough, determined, resolute. Cut from the same granite. Yet now, she felt lost, weak. Was she ready for what lay ahead? She hoped so. She had to be, for Amy's sake, if nothing else.

12:05p.m.

It was later than he'd hoped when Dan arrived back at the station. He'd been delayed by a multi-vehicle crash on the way into town. It had taken an age for the salvage guys to arrive, but thankfully, nobody had been seriously injured. Dan pushed through the door marked *Private: Garda Officials Only* next to the windowed reception area and entered the offices at the back. The station was a sixties building, and the ground floor had been recently redesigned to an open-plan style. There were four workstations, two of them hot desks, one office for the sergeant and then down a corridor to the rear of the building sat four holding cells.

Dan nodded hello to Edwards as he placed the cardboard box from the County Hotel on his desk. 'Sully here?' he asked, enquiring after his boss, Sergeant O'Sullivan. The sergeant rarely went by his first name, *Michael*, or by his surname, *O'Sullivan*, either, which Dan found odd. He never said it, but he found it a little bit silly for anyone over the age of twelve to encourage or even acknowledge a nickname.

'Yip, in his office,' replied Edwards. 'What's in that?' Edwards asked, pointing to the box.

'The remains of our missing man from the County Hotel,' said Dan, sitting into his leather swivel chair. Edwards sat up, startled. Dan laughed in a good-natured way. 'No, no, not his mortal remains, just discarded possessions.'

'Oh, I see,' said Edwards, a sheepish look now on his face. Edwards wasn't long out of Templemore Training College, and it showed.

Dan began lifting the items from the container, displaying them to Edwards as he did. 'Exhibit one: a Bible with bullet holes. Exhibit two: four passports, none of them Irish. Exhibit three: one used syringe.'

'Not your everyday travel pack,' said Edwards, whistling for effect.

'Yeah, a bit of a dark horse, this guy,' mused Dan as he tossed the passports and bagged syringe onto Edwards' desk. 'Ring the hotel and get the registration of his car. We'll need to run the licence plates through the system and also check if he's holed up in any of the other local hotels or B&Bs. Also, send that syringe for testing.'

Dan gazed at the clock on the wall. It was just after twelve. Next to the clock hung a mounted photograph of his father. Chief Superintendent Jim Brady decked out in his finest regalia, a broad smile lighting his face. It had seemed natural for Dan to follow in his footsteps and join the force. When Jim fell sick, Iris couldn't cope on her own, and Dan moved home to Blackcliff from his post in Dublin. His presence hadn't helped much. His father died within two months of his return. Top brass approved Dan's permanent transfer, a rare compassionate concession. Garda seldom served in their hometowns, too many conflicts. Dan never thought he'd return home, not for all the world, yet here he was.

'What was the problem at the hotel?' asked Sergeant O'Sullivan as he walked out of his glass-walled office and made his way to the coffee dock at the far end of the room.

'A missing guest left without paying. He left some odd stuff behind. Family passports. Drug paraphernalia. No sign of the woman or child in the passports. All a bit strange, really,' said Dan.

Sully raised his eyebrows. 'Gang related? Drugs?' he asked.

'I'm not sure. It's a peculiar one. There was also this Bible,' replied Dan, as he held the holy book aloft. 'Bullet holes!'

'Just what we need,' laughed Sully derisorily, stirring sugar into his coffee, 'a righteous nutjob on our hands.'

'Maybe,' replied Dan. 'Well, whoever he was, he certainly left in a hurry.'

The sergeant approached Dan's desk and then shot a pointed glance towards the cells at the rear of the station. 'That eejit Molloy is still in the back out cold,' he said. 'What do you want to do with him?'

'Let him sleep it off,' replied Dan. 'I'll drive him home later. I have a few calls out that way anyhow.'

'Okay,' shrugged Sully disappointedly, as if he had something else in mind. He turned and ambled back to his office, where Dan was sure he did next to no work

Edwards was talking to someone at the hotel, scribbling down notes. Dan entered Nicholas Król into the Garda Pulse database. Nothing popped up. He typed an email and sent it to Interpol, Dublin. They could check on any international cases or warrants. Until then, there wasn't much else he could do.

'Gotcha,' exclaimed Edwards aloud. 'Our missing man is driving a stolen car.'

'Is he now?' replied Dan, sitting up straight in his chair.

'It was taken nearly a month ago outside Ennis,' continued Edwards. 'No sightings since.'

'Okay, notify all stations immediately,' said Dan. 'Tell them to be on the lookout for the car and then get onto Ennis and establish the exact details of that theft. Get a copy of that passport out to all Garda stations in the county. I'm guessing our Mr Król has some tales to tell.'

12:3Op.m.

The operatic aria drifted in lilting waves, filling the silent spaces of the house. It was music that evoked memories of better times.

Cio-Cio-San's soaring voice sang of her lonely wait for the return of her American husband Pinkerton's warship into Nagasaki Bay. Kate could picture again the troupe on stage at La Scala performing Puccini's *Madama Butterfly*. The tickets had cost an arm and a leg, but Peter had insisted, arguing, 'Nothing but the best for my wife on her honeymoon.' They'd bought the CD in the foyer as they left. Kate knew the words to every part of the tragic tale. Outside, the stormfront rolled relentlessly across the clifftops. Snowflakes swooped and swooned like a murmuration of starlings. It seemed as if the mounting crescendo of the diva's voice was conducting the swarm, directing it back and forth in fluttering white sheets..'

How silly Butterfly had been, thought Kate ruefully, *crazy to have sacrificed everything for her wayward husband*. She poured a mug of coffee from the fresh brew and sat down at the kitchen table. She checked her phone. A text from the school: they *were* closing early – another one from Grace to tell Kate that all was well and the sleepover was still on. Kate phoned Grace but got no answer. She texted a thumbs up and an applause emoji. Kate had been in school with Grace's older brother, and many years later, when they sat reminiscing over a coffee, Grace had joined the pair, and immediately, the two women had hit it off. Later, when Grace was down on her luck and needed a place to live, Kate had let her stay in her parents' farmhouse. When she got the job at the school, Grace began paying rent, and, regardless, her and Niamh's presence instilled life and warmth back into the old place. The arrangement suited everyone.

Kate dialled Peter. The call rang out, no answer. She tried again. Still nothing. She shook her head in resigned frustration and looked at the screen. Six calls unanswered by him in the past two days. Closing her eyes, she listened again to the opera. Madama Butterfly readying herself to die, her blade to her throat, but thankfully interrupted by her son.

Outside, the snow continued to rise and fall in harmony. A tear trickled down Kate's cheek as she listened to sad Butterfly. On the kitchen table lay a bundle of letters bound by a fraying ribbon. Letters given to her on a beach by a stranger. Letters filled with the sweet language of love. She tentatively fingered the stack, poking it back, then forth. A few inches this way, a few inches that, as if it was a primed explosive. One false move and *kaboom*: it would blow her and the whole bloody lighthouse to kingdom come. Kate lifted her coffee cup, and with a sharp and sudden intake of breath, she sent it crashing into the opposite wall.

12:30p.m.

It was the children's laughter that woke him. At first, he had no recollection of where he was, but then the chill of the frosty air coming through the cracked window brought him back. He could hear them in Niamh's room, chatting, giggling, occasionally squealing. Król checked his watch; it was twelve-thirty, school was out early. He breathed in slowly and deeply. This was what he had planned for, waited for. This was destined. Reaching into his bag, he pulled out the loaded syringes and shoved them into his inside coat pockets. It was time to cross over.

Król crept to the door and opened it carefully. Silently, he inched down the empty hallway. He peeked through the gap in Niamh's bedroom door. The two girls were talking about a girl in their class named Lucy – a teacher's pet. Grace was calling from the kitchen. 'Girls, change out of those uniforms, put on warm clothes and then we can go outside and build a snowman.'

He heard Grace's phone ring, and she greeted the caller with 'Hi, love.' It had to be Dan. Król could hear her chatting as she moved about the kitchen. He stepped into the bathroom and closed the door behind him, leaving a narrow sliver that he could peek through. In his haste, he knocked a hairbrush that had been resting on the side of the bath, and it fell with a dull thud onto the tiled floor. There was a pause in Grace's conversation. Had she heard him? Król stood motionless. He moved to lift the hairbrush, and as he did, he clumsily toppled a half-empty bottle of shampoo into the tub. He stood frozen, silently cursing his awkwardness. All he could hear now was the ongoing babble from the girls down the hallway. After a moment, Grace began talking to Dan again, saying something about checking on the girls and that she'd call him back. Król ducked quickly behind the door as Grace entered the hallway. She stopped at the bathroom door. There were but inches of wood between them. Król held his breath as the door opened, and Grace peeked in. The hairbrush was back resting on the tub rim. One more step inward, and she would surely see him. 'Did you girls knock something over?' she asked aloud as she turned away, pacing down the hallway towards Niamh's bedroom. Król could hear denials coming from the children. He peeked out again. Grace was now standing in the open doorway to the spare bedroom, her back to him. She must have been staring at the broken window, the rumple in the bedsheets, calculating the negative possibilities, her heart beginning to pound faster and faster. Król hid from view as she turned and strode quickly up the hallway, lifting her mobile as she did. He had to move. She'd call Dan straight away, of that there was no doubt. As soon as she passed his hiding place, he sprang from the bathroom and was behind her in an instant, one gloved hand clasped tightly over her mouth, the other yanking her ponytail and thrusting her headlong into the kitchen. Grace wrestled aggressively, kicking her feet backwards and biting at his fingers. Król pushed harder; she was no match for his strength. She tried to scream, but his gloved hand stifled the noise. She felt light in his hands as she wriggled desperately for release. He pushed her across the room towards the armchair and shoved her firmly down into the seat. His hands were still cupped tightly about her head. It felt that he would crush her skull if he squeezed any harder. Releasing hold of her ponytail, his left hand still firmly covering her mouth, he held up his right index finger to his lips and turned his head pointedly towards the bedroom where the two girls were still changing noisily. His eyes told Grace what she needed to know – they could do this the smart way or the horrible way; he preferred smart. Grace seemed to understand, and she nodded in agreement. Slowly, he removed his hand from her trembling mouth. She made no noise as tears streamed down onto her quivering lips. Only the sound of the kids broke their deathly silence.

'Take everything. There's cash in my bag on the table,' she whispered breathlessly, 'my phone too. Take it all. Please, please, take anything. Then go!'

'That's not why I'm here, Grace.'

The utterance of her name sent an electric jolt through Grace's body. Król could see her computing the new variables as fast as she could. He lifted a syringe from his breast pocket. 'Oh Jesus, Jesus, no,' spluttered Grace breathlessly, her eyes bulging in panicked terror.

'It won't hurt,' he said as he pulled aggressively at her blouse to reveal her bare shoulder and upper arm. Grace shook her head, her eyes darting nervously, her body shaking uncontrollably.

'Stay still, or I'll go into the girls,' Król said, glancing again towards the room where the kids were changing. 'It's you or them,' he said blankly.

Grace knew, just as he did, that none of her choices were remotely good. She could try to fight, but she was no match for his strength. She could scream, but in the panic that would ensue, would they all die? He was her only hope. That he might be true to his word and that the children would be spared whatever fate awaited her.

Tears fell again from her eyes. She turned her forearm towards him. Król positioned the needle and injected it until the syringe was empty. 'Close your eyes, wait for sleep. It will come quickly,' he said softly.

'Rot in hell, you fuck!' spat Grace. Król counted down. Ten, nine, eight, seven. Before six, Grace's body had slumped sideways in the chair.

IV

We'd gone hiking in the countryside. Just my father and I wandering across rolling green fields that seemed to go on forever. It had started to rain, and we took shelter under some trees. I was only a boy, but I remember that smell to this day, like rotten eggs in weeks-old waste bins. The flies directed us to the source in the damp undergrowth. My father held me back as he treaded carefully towards the fallen carcass. 'It's a deer,' he said. 'Come see.' Filled with fear, I crept closer. Where eyes should have existed, there were now only holes. Maggots crawled through the empty spaces. I gasped aloud. 'It's okay, son, this is how nature works,' said my father. 'How did it die?' I asked. 'It may have broken a leg or fallen ill. If it cannot move, the game is up. Predators, insects and bacteria will break it down. That is the way of things. One dies so that another lives.'

I looked closer. The deer's stomach was a cavern filled with millions and millions of squirming worms and larvae. 'What is that smell?' I asked. My father rose from his squatting position and stood beside me, arm about my shoulder. 'When an animal dies, all the soft bits, the flesh and organs, they decompose until all that remains is skeleton. This process releases stinking gases. I think it's nature's way of sending a death notice to the field. One of ours has died.'

I struggled to comprehend how a large deer had been reduced to hanging flesh and bones. Where had it gone? 'These maggots devour it,' said my father. 'They will release its atoms one by one back to Mother Earth, from where they came. Every living thing has been formed by carbon and the universal elements. When we are done, it is to the universe we return. And on and on it goes.'

As we walked back across those fields towards the safety and comfort of our warm home, I couldn't take my mind off the deer. Did a worried family await its return? Had it suffered at the end? It was on that walk that I first understood my own mortality. The realisation that I, too, would someday return to Earth as my father had explained. I thought of my mother, already gone, and a deep longing set within me to be with her again. To tell her that I loved her.

3:10p.m.

Dan glanced up from his desk to the clock on the station wall: ten minutes past three. Soon, darkness would fall, and temperatures too. He dreaded the complications both would bring. The roads had been gritted, but with the continued snowfall, that measure was proving to be near useless. He looked to the list of all who lived beyond the

Cliff Road on the island. He had one last call to make, Kate O'Connor. She picked up straight away as if she'd been waiting for him.

'Hello, stranger, to what do I owe the pleasure?'

'Hi, Kate,' replied Dan, hesitating a little, 'how have you been?'

'Grand, you know, keeping busy,' she replied. 'Did you have a nice Christmas?'

'Yeah, great, I had a few days off, a welcome break,' he replied.

'I called Grace but couldn't get her,' said Kate. 'Will you thank her again for taking Amy?'

'Yeah, sure,' said Dan, 'I was chatting to her earlier, and it sounded like the girls were already having fun.'

'Ah, super, they'll have a ball in the snow,' said Kate and paused. 'Grace mentioned you've moved in. How's that going?'

Dan sensed something in Kate's tone that hadn't been there before. Judgement? No, that wasn't Kate. Maybe feminine curiosity, possibly even mild amusement. He could picture the smile on her face.

'Yeah, all good so far, you know how it is. Anyway, listen,' he said, changing the subject quickly, 'I just wanted to let you know that we may have to close Cliff Road if the weather worsens. It's too steep to drive safely if the snow gathers in drifts.'

'Oh, okay, what about the road from Ennis? Peter is flying into Shannon this evening.'

'A lorry crashed earlier, but it's open again,' he replied.

'OK, Dan, thanks for that. Say hello to Amy for me when you see her.'

'No problem, don't worry, we'll look after her. Take care,' said Dan, and he hung up.

'They've all been warned on the island now,' he said, glancing across the desk to Sully, who was stalking the coffee dock again.

'And how is our dear Kate?' smirked Sully, eyes glinting with mischief. 'Does she need Officer Brady to call up and take care of her while her husband is away?'

'Seriously, Sully,' replied Dan as he shot his boss a thinly disguised look of contempt.

'Can't seem to get a woman of your own, can you, Officer Brady?' crowed a voice from the holding cell at the back of the station. The dead had awoken.

'Shut up, Molloy, you thick shit,' coughed Sully angrily. 'What a big man you are, getting your courage from a bottle and bullying the poor mother of the child unfortunate enough to have you for a father.'

Dan looked again at the picture of his father on the wall and remained quiet.

'Just telling it as it is,' came a more hesitant retort from the back cell.

'Here's how it is,' roared Sully, standing up, his face now bulging and red. 'You were over the alcohol limit to drive. You trespassed on one of our good citizen's properties. If we press these charges, you are screwed.' Sully walked towards the holding cell, which had now fallen silent. 'You'll definitely notch more time, too,' he continued. 'I'd say there are a few boys inside who would like to see your face again, right, Tommy? So, listen carefully, asshole. Here's what you need to do. Shut up, go home, dry out. Then, keep a very low profile and make sure to give Grace Quigley a wide berth. Or else.'

A moment passed. Then came the dull, half-hearted retort. 'Or else what?'

'Or else something very bad will happen when you least expect it. It'll be your word against mine. Understand?' roared a red-faced Sully.

Dan shook his head disapprovingly. He couldn't help disliking the man who helped him get this job. The man who had been a friend to his father. The man who helped him carry his father's coffin. His dad had said once that some people were just fuelled by bad blood, or a need for drama, because they had nothing else. It made them feel that they were living. Others were just plain bad, no two ways about it.

'I need my inhaler,' crowed Molloy after what sounded like an exaggerated coughing bout. 'I can't breathe without my inhaler,' he continued to moan. Dan rose from his seat and grabbed his police coat. He, too, needed fresh air, even if it was frozen.

3:20p.m.

Król woke with a start. He felt that awful dread, the dull, sickening feeling that greeted him when he woke from rare sleep. It never left you alone for long, the knowledge that bad things had happened, bad things would happen. And there was nothing that he could do about any of it.

His hand touched something. He peeked through half-open eyes. Grace's clothed body lay next to him on top of the bed. She was motionless. Beside her, the two girls. The sight of them disturbed him. Innocents. Their limp bodies made him want to cry. How much time had passed? He wasn't sure. He rose to his feet, swaying dizzily. He breathed in and out slowly, holding his hand to his chest. It felt as if his heart might burst through his ribcage. He'd imagined these events so many times, and now it was truly happening.

He hadn't considered the horrible physicality of his actions nor the raw emotion that would engulf him. For a while, he could do nothing, just stand and stare, overwhelmed by all that had gone before, all that was yet to follow. Shrouded by the sadness that it had come to this. Tears formed and quickly turned to sobs. He steadied himself. He needed to be clear-headed. How little it had taken to transcend, to become the aggressor. There was still much to do. He could feel the pull towards darkness and the end.

He retrieved what he needed from his bag. It was awkward pulling the sleeping bag up and around Grace's lifeless form, but he managed. The two girls were easier. He went to the clothes cupboard in the hall and found some hats and scarves. He pulled a woollen hat over each of their heads and wrapped scarves about their necks.

The small outbuilding was beyond the courtyard in an unkempt field. The wild scrub and brush had grown as high as his shoulders in places. A week earlier, he had scythed a narrow path through the dense overgrowth to reach the shed. Only the black cawing rooks had noticed. Nobody came this way anymore, nor would they.

One by one, he carried them carefully. The woman draped over his shoulder. The children in his outstretched open arms as one might gently carry any child to tender sleep, their heads lolling backwards, their faces locked in wonder as white snow butterflies landed softly on their closed eyelids. The thorny bushes scratched and tugged like mourners unwilling to let the dead go. Inside the shed, he laid them next to each other at the far wall atop the bedding of straw he had readied. He ran a long chain through the holes he'd cut in the side of each of the sleeping bags and then through the gaps between their arms and their cuffed hands. He pulled the chain out through the other side and bolted it to a steel girder with a padlock. He paused to catch his breath and then lifted the homemade explosive device from his bag. He set the timer for 2:00a.m. and placed it on a shelf away from the bodies. He pressed the screen, and the countdown began.

His work done, he pushed the shed door closed and piled some loose overgrowth to help conceal the entrance. He looked at his stained hands, and for a moment, he was overcome. A rush of nausea swept through him, and he bent over and vomited, retching harder and harder until it seemed that the lining of his stomach might tear. The sour taste of acidic bile filled his mouth. At his feet, the snow melted under the sickly mess. He wiped his face with his forearm and then lifted his bag from the ground. He made his way back to the farmhouse.

Grace's large black leather handbag was still on the kitchen table where she had left it hours before. He turned the bag upside down, spilling its contents onto the tabletop. Banknotes, coins, receipts, make-up, sweets, an electricity bill, a doctor's letter, some tablets, a hairbrush, gloves, car keys and her pink mobile phone. He lifted the phone and tossed it into his holdall. He scooped up the car keys and made his way to the door.

Outside at Grace's car, he zapped the lock, opened

the door and sat in. The sight of a doll sitting on the passenger seat unsettled him. He tossed it into the back. Gazing around the silent yard and the desolate fields, he wondered what people would one day say about what transpired here. It mattered little. Over time, it would all count for nothing. The land would eventually swallow everything that had been forced upon it. It didn't care for human trifles. It was here before and would be here after.

3:30p.m.

Kate set the fresh mug of coffee down on the sturdy wooden desk. She didn't normally drink caffeine in the afternoon; however, she'd need the reserves for the long night ahead when Peter returned. The coffee-splashed wall downstairs had proven impossible to clean. Kate's futile attempts had only served to make things worse. Still, the brown smudge would serve as a reminder, if ever needed, of how life funnelled you down paths you never wished to travel.

The sight of the stain had begun to irritate her, so she'd moved upstairs to her study. She pressed yes to the prompt on the computer and frame by frame, the photographs began downloading from the camera to her laptop. Later, she would work on the pictures with the software package that had come free with the camera. You could alter anything these days, but still, she'd strive to retain the essence of the original images as much as possible. The best of them would be framed and added to the collection that already hung on her study walls.

To her left and right stood architectural tilt tables

that displayed an array of layered pencilled drawings. Cross sections, floor plans, elevations. Internal and external perspectives. All architectural projects she had once laboured over in her practice. Each infused with perspiration and inspiration, her goal was always to leave a structure that was functional, elegant and timeless. Now, other people spent their lives inside the buildings they had become. Offices, shops, homes.

The biggest sin of her profession was fashion. What was modern and cool today might be tomorrow's eyesore. She had always endeavoured to design with sympathy for both the past and the future. Above all, she designed for the land. Nothing could surpass nature's beauty, and equally, nothing should besmirch it. She had given it all up to raise Amy and support Peter's career, but every once in a while, a yearning to once more be at the creative coalface came and hung in the air.

The window before her gazed west over the Atlantic. On the other side of that vast ocean, she had learned her trade amongst the towering skyscrapers of New York. What remarkable feats of architecture, engineering and construction. Man's triumphant reach to the heavens. Kate cupped the warm coffee in her hands and breathed deep the rich aroma. Memories of the hours spent alone in the artisan cafes of Soho whispered on the delicate curls of steam. The early days had been tough. The work had been relentless, and the pace had been go-go-go. Yet, in the quiet hours, which were never truly quiet amid that city's constant symphony of ambulance sirens, alarm bells and beeping car horns, she had been homesick. She'd longed for the sea, for the green grass, for Dan. Their young romance had reached its end when she left, or so she had decided. It was either bells and rings or tears on the clifftop heather. She had chosen the latter and left Dan heartbroken. More than she thought he would be, which had surprised her. In those longing hours, alone in her shoebox studio on the Lower East Side, she had regretted that decision. But that was natural, wasn't it, to find it hard to move on. Something had to end for something new to begin.

Her father had acquired the old derelict lighthouse site and convinced Kate that she would be the best person to manage its restoration. Initially, she'd planned to do the work from New York, but each time, when she'd come home for just a few days, the magnetism of the land and her roots had tugged, and she'd stayed longer. Maybe that had been his plan all along, to bring her home. If so, it proved successful. She upped sticks and came back for good. Not much had changed except that Dan had moved to Dublin. She remembered her sadness at no longer having her dear friend near, but she had no right to feel sorry for herself, so she didn't.

Kate dived into the lighthouse project, preparing the technical drawings and managing the construction plan to restore the beautiful old beacon to its former glory. Most of the construction work her father undertook himself with the help of the countless local workmen he could call on for assistance. Kate's mother kept the family farm ticking over and, to her credit, never complained that she had too much to handle.

The Commission for Irish Lights had been happy to sell the site and retain the thousand-year licence to maintain the light itself. Kate's dad had the foresight to apply for planning permission to build four new cottages that would serve as tourist accommodation. The tower they carefully restored to its former splendour using architectural practices and building materials prevailing when the lighthouse had been constructed nearly two hundred years previously. Stonemasons, carpenters, plasterers, Kate always admired the skill and expertise of these tradesmen who had spent lifetimes perfecting their art. They even made good the three hundred and thirty-six weathered granite steps carved into the cliff rockface, leading from the sea inlet below to the summit and the iron door of the tower. Back in 1829, before any bridge had been built and when the tide submerged the causeway, that had been the only way in or out. The light itself was operated remotely from Dublin and had its own backup power supply. The keeper's bedrooms and living quarters they'd transformed into a tourist museum for the curious to step in the footsteps of the solitary men that once called them their sanctuary.

Kate had begun seeing Peter Kavanagh. He'd been charming and romantic, and, importantly, he gave her the space to complete the lighthouse project. Years later, after her father had passed and the lighthouse had been left to her in his will, Kate converted two of the four tourist dwellings into one family home and adjoined it to the tower. Peter moved in, and then came wedding bells and, finally, Amy.

Placing her coffee on the desk, Kate lifted the hardback book that sat beside it. *Blackcliff Lighthouse; Restoring History.* Two hundred pages that chronicled the lighthouse's past and detailed the intricate and painstaking restoration project that she and her father had overseen to bring it into the present. Her fingers ran over the authors' embossed names: Kate and

Michael O'Connor. He'd been annoyed at first when he saw his name on the final proof, but over time, he'd grown proud of it. In truth, she'd done all the writing, but he had helped with the ideas and the edits, and when all was said and done, the project wouldn't have happened without him. As she had written in the preface, in some ways, he had been the final keeper of the light, the one to keep it shining.

Kate thought of the conversation she'd had with Peter at Christmas when she'd mentioned her book. For the first time, she realised Peter had never really expressed any views on it. Never praised her writing style or the architectural drawings she'd included, never marvelled at the incredible old photographs she'd salvaged or commented upon the interviews she'd recorded with former keepers or the families of those who had passed on. He'd responded in an odd, distracted fashion, said something like 'yeah, it was great' and had changed the subject quickly. It was only then that it had dawned on her, for at the time of the book's publication she had been too helter-skelter to notice, that her husband had never even read it. It seemed that she had grown to know some of the keeper's lives better than she did her own.

3:40p.m.

A laughing couple exited Dolans Grocers, weighed down with supplies. Arms linked, they leaned into each other for support as they delicately negotiated the icy path. Next door, outside Byrne's public house, two young men in T-shirts, shoulders huddled and hunched against the cold, puffed on cigarettes and chatted about whatever was of world importance to them, oblivious it seemed that a storm was rolling in from the sea. Dan didn't recognise them. They seemed to detect his watchful stare, and they flicked their cigarettes and shuffled back inside.

He was grinding his teeth again. The bar shouldn't be open. Paddy Byrne, the proprietor, had no problem filling these lads full of booze but had scant regard for how they'd get home safely in a blizzard. The sky had turned charcoal grey in that late-winter-afternoon way, and the heavy snow showers were drawing darkness in earlier than usual. The light turned green, and Dan guided the police car slowly up Station Road. He glanced at the rear-view mirror to check on his passenger. Tommy Molloy sensed his gaze and met his eyes.

'Thanks for that waste of a day, Dan. I won't forget your hospitality,' he mouthed tersely.

'Glad to be of service,' replied Dan.

'You know we have old history, us two, don't you?' asked Tommy.

Dan drove on.

'It was your old man that got my da banged up, wasn't it?' continued Molloy eventually.

'I'd forgotten that,' lied Dan. He hated the term *Da*. Was it too much to ask for a dad, or a daddy or even a father? 'From what I remember, it was pretty much a special-forces operation, led internationally. My father was just a local uniform. He had no say in anything.'

Dan remembered his father nearly crying with laughter as he recounted the story to Iris all those years ago. Dan had been only fifteen or so at the time. He'd always listen to his father's tales from the beat, and he'd never breathe a word in school or to his friends. He knew there was a line you didn't cross; people's reputations were at stake. Nobody wanted their dirty laundry aired around the town. In those days, a local policeman was akin to a priest. The story about Tommy's father had been big news. A boat had been apprehended at a barren cove on the far side of the island cliffs. There'd been a tip-off that a shipment of drugs was being smuggled in from the Netherlands. A few local small-time crooks had been recruited to help facilitate the landing and to store the contraband until it could be moved on safely to the lucrative city markets.

The drug run had proved an enormous cock-up from start to finish. The vessel was supposed to arrive by daylight but lost its way. By the time the bungling amateurs righted their path and approached the rocky inlet, it was the dead of night, and a strong gale was blowing. None of the crew were seasoned sailors, and, as their bad luck would have it, they managed to run the boat aground. A jagged rock ripped a hole in the hull through which the cargo of sealed bags washed out to sea. Blackcliff was literally awash with cocaine. Two million quid worth, to be precise – at that time, one of the biggest drug busts in the country's history. The crew had to be saved by air to sea rescue as their vessel slowly capsized. Two local bandits, including Molloy Snr, got ten years for their part in the ineptitude.

'He gave evidence. He was part of the operation that put my da away for a long time,' continued Tommy, 'and now look at us two, fighting over the same woman. That's mad, isn't it?'

'Tommy. Seriously. We're not fighting over anybody. You and Grace were over a long time ago, long before I came along. You need to move on; otherwise, it's just stalking and harassment.' When Dan looked back, it wasn't acknowledgement or acceptance that he saw in Tommy's eyes. Instead, they burned with fury. Dan sighed deeply and drove on.

3:40p.m.

Król carefully manoeuvred the car up the tight country lane that led away from the farm. The wipers bashed back and forth in the swirling blizzard. Reaching the top of the track, he tentatively turned the car onto the wider road that led to and from the surrounding farms and homes. A few miles later, he joined the main road and continued at a steady pace towards town. This busier surface had been gritted, and keeping control proved easier. On the outskirts of town, traffic was backed up near the power plant. There was some kind of protest, and the cars had slowed to a near standstill as they passed. Some honked horns and others pumped fists out their windows. He froze. On the opposite side of the road, a police car was approaching. They were only ten feet apart, and he could make out the driver; it was Dan Brady. He inhaled slowly. In the back seat of the police car, Król recognised the man who had called to the farmhouse that morning. Król stared straight ahead as the vehicles slowly passed each other, never making eye contact. Had he been spotted? Had the policeman recognised Grace's car? It was still half covered in snow. He peeked in the rear-view mirror. He could now see the back of the police car, and incredibly, it kept moving in the opposite direction, further and further away from him.

Król steered the Micra slowly along Main Street. He wondered whether any eagle-eyed friends of Grace's would notice the new and unfamiliar driver of her car. The wipers swished the fresh snow across the windscreen. Some of it stuck to form a dirty scurf that obscured visibility. He tried the wiper spray, but nothing came except an empty buzzing noise. The tubes must have frozen.

Every few feet, he could feel the tyres slip, and all he could do was wait until they gripped onto the sparse gritting and gained purchase again. Both cars and people began to thin as he drove past the last few shops on Main St and continued west on the coast road towards the island and the cliffs.

Nobody saw the little Nissan cross the wooden bridge. Normally, the spaced boards would reverberate noisily under the weight of vehicles, but today there was silence. Snowflakes smothered the world, and before long, it was nearly impossible to see any further. Król made it to the base of the Cliff Road, and there he abandoned the car, leaving it parked tightly to the ditch. Soon, the elements would render it invisible.

Ahead of him, the road arced in a gradual rise towards the clifftops and the lighthouse. Slinging his bag over his shoulder, he began the ascent. After twenty minutes of arduous climbing, he paused to catch his breath. Below him, in the distance, two tall stacks rose high from the energy plant. Steam from the chimneys hung frigid in the arctic air. In town, the icy crystal antenna of the church spire glistened as it waited for a signal from the heavens above. He knew all it received was the microwaved static of the big bang. An electromagnetic message from the beginning of time to cement doubt for all the Thomases. Beneath the tall spire gathered the town's snow-covered rooftops.

Clad in utopian white, Blackcliff had become a vision of a world where nothing could possibly be wrong. Here and there, lights were being switched on, and these glowed yellow in the early evening grey. A memory came to him: holding his father's hand, wandering through a gallery in London. He'd stopped, entranced by the painting before him – *Hunters in the Snow*. High on a snowy hillside, hunters and their pack dogs are trekking home. Through a clearing in the trees, they see their welcoming village below and imagine the warmth that awaits them. He remembered being mesmerised by the painting's cold beauty. The sharp outlines. The simple yet vivid colours. The image had appeared so real, so heavy with winter. He remembered thinking that if he laid his hand upon the canvas, it would feel icy to the touch. Snow fascinated him. The incredible complexity of the crystalline structure, how intricate and spectacular, yet something so common. He loved this weather, always had. The cold brought brutal clarity. It was unequivocal.

On he climbed, slowly but steadily, digging his boots into the soft snow as he went. Twenty minutes later, he reached the summit. Ahead, the lighthouse came into view. With its white tower and red circled top, it stood tall and proud before the unending horizon. A sparrow hawk hovered overhead, having ventured from its hiding place amongst the hedgerows in search of whatever scant prey might be on offer. Slowly, Król circled the field behind the lighthouse until he found a sheltered nook. He crouched low near a clump of immaculate trees, newly attired in glistening white dresses. It was nearly time.

3:45p.m.

'Look at these losers,' blurted Tommy Molloy from the rear of the car. Dan stared ahead through the falling snow to the large gathering which had spilt onto the road at the gates of the power plant. Some held placards aloft; 'STRIKE.' 'NO SLAVE LABOUR.' Another read, 'NO ZERO HOUR CONTRACTS.' Dan slowed the car to a stop.

'Power to the people!' roared Tommy, punching his fist into the air. For the first time, Dan found himself agreeing with his passenger. Big business made his blood boil. It decimated towns like this. Ate them up and shat them out before moving on. Now, the workers were out demanding to be heard. Rightly so.

Dan flicked the switch on the radio and called into the station. 'Is Sully there?'

'Yes, hold on, Dan, I'll get him,' replied Edwards. Dan could hear a groan in the background and the scraping of a chair on the station floor.

A moment later, Sully snapped loudly into the speaker, 'What's up now?' Dan stifled the desire to tell Sully to get up off his ass, do some work and stop the eternal moaning. Instead, he spoke calmly but firmly.

'I'm out at the power plant. There's a strike. About fifty people or so are marching up and down, protesting. They are starting to block the road. We should send Edwards out to keep an eye on it,' said Dan.

'Fucking idiots,' Sully moaned aloud.

Dan could tell that his boss was about to launch into another tirade that he wasn't willing to endure, so he wrapped up the conversation quickly. 'Gotta go, Sully. I need to deal with something here.' Dan flicked the off switch and drove slowly past the group as they hooted and hollered. After a mile or two, he turned left onto a narrow road that led to the estate of small bungalows where Tommy lived on the outskirts of town.

Dan indicated and pulled the car to the kerb outside the Molloy home. 'Here you go, Tommy, returned safe and sound. And I didn't hear you coughing once for that inhaler you needed so badly.' Tommy didn't reply as he climbed out of the car. Tommy's mother, Maggie, stood in her open front door, an exaggerated expression of annoyance painted large across her face. Dan was about to reverse when a notion entered his mind, and he turned off the engine and climbed out. He reached the porch just as Maggie was about to close the door.

'Hi, Margaret, how are you?' he asked.

Maggie Molloy was a frail, wiry, tobacco-skinned woman. Although she looked well into her sixties, Dan guessed mid-fifties. Wary feral eyes scanned him up and down. A cigarette hung preposterously from her lip as she spoke. 'And what's it to you, Garda?'

'Just checking that you have all you need with the storm coming in.'

She eyed him coldly, maybe trying to turn him to stone. 'We don't need any help from the pigs.'

Charming. If Tommy was the apple, here was the rotten tree. 'Tell Tommy to go easy, keep out of trouble, for his own good, you know,' said Dan.

Maggie's face distorted in resentment. 'You can go now. You pigs have caused enough problems around here.' Tommy had heard the chatter and had returned to stand behind his mother. Dan went to leave but stopped, turning to face the pair again. 'By the way, Tommy, that's a fancy set of wheels you were driving earlier. The social must be paying well these days. You know I can get a revenue inspection started in your name if you'd like. This morning, you were drink-driving. You were harassing a law-abiding citizen. I can give the benefit of the doubt and be accommodating, but hear me clearly when I say this: don't push your luck too far, or someday I'll come down on you like a tonne of bricks. You got it?'

Tommy's mother turned to her son and gave him a lightning-sharp clip around the ear. 'I told you to keep your nose out of trouble, didn't I?' Tommy backed off sheepishly, rubbing his ear. 'Now fuck off and leave us alone,' roared Maggie as she slammed the door in Dan's face.

Dan trudged back to his car. What chance did any of these kids have growing up like this? As he drove away, he immediately regretted his tough-guy outburst. These idiots never listened. He'd been talking to himself, making himself feel better. He hoped Tommy Molloy wasn't going to become a thorn in his side.

4:25p.m

Kate nibbled on a piece of grilled chicken and then toppled the remainder into the green salad. She covered the carved wooden bowl with clingfilm and placed it on the kitchen table next to the bottle of Rioja she had bought in the smart new wine shop in Ennis the day before. She closed her eyes to let the opera fill her senses. Then the phone rang, and the moment was lost. Expecting Peter or Grace, she was surprised that it was Dan Brady again.

'Can't stop calling me, eh, Dan,' she said jovially.

'That's right, Kate, you are always on my mind,' he replied in a mock-serious tone. 'I'm just ringing with an update. We'll be closing Cliff Road from the base of the hill at 5:00p.m. It's already pretty much impassable. Have you everything you need? Is Peter home yet?'

Typical, thought Kate. *She had planned to have this night with Peter, just the two of them, face to face, and now he probably wouldn't make it back at all.* An incoming call alert flashed on her phone, but just as she was about to ask Dan to hold, the call rang off. It had been Grace. Damn, she really wanted to say a quick hello to Amy and make sure that she wasn't nervous at her first sleepover. She knew Amy would want to hear her voice, just for reassurance. She was growing up, yet in many ways, she was still only a baby.

'That was Grace trying to call me. I'll ring her back,' said Kate.

'Ah, sorry about that,' said Dan. 'I'm sure all is going well with the kids, don't worry.'

'Thanks, I hope my wee rascal is behaving herself. Yes, I've plenty of supplies here, just no daughter and no husband. Home alone! By the way, if Peter's flight does get in, will the road into town still be open?'

'Probably. It's had more traffic and has been gritted, so it's still passable, but who knows for how long.'

'Okay, thanks, Dan, you take care, bye.'

A very brief silence followed – a moment when it seemed Dan was going to say something else, but he didn't, and then the line went dead. Kate stared at the phone, lost in thought, lost in the past. She dialled Grace's number again – three more tries, still no reply. Outside, the last of the cold winter light was fading fast.

4:25p.m.

Król eyed the lighthouse through his binoculars. Only the swirling snow obstructed his view across the walled gardens and through the large, illuminated kitchen windows. He recognised Kate's graceful profile. For a second, she stood motionless, gazing out to the world. She seemed to sway, her eyes closed, until something broke her spell, and she moved out of vision. Soon, she returned with the phone to her ear. Without hesitation, he immediately put down the binoculars and lifted Grace's pink mobile from his bag. No passcode needed. *Not smart, Grace.* As quickly as he could, he dialled Kate's number and then lifted the binoculars again. He saw Kate look at her phone to check who was calling her. He killed the call. Kate continued to look at her phone, and then she put it back to her ear and carried on her conversation. Król switched Grace's phone to mute and returned it to his bag. He smiled contently. That would buy him some time.

From the corner of his eye, he spotted something: a slight movement, a shift against the stillness. Ten feet away, a fox stood watching him. It stared warily, eyes scanning, ears alert. A kindred spirit. Surviving, protecting, hunting.

There, in that moment, they were joined as one, complicit in their stealthy silence as darkness descended like a cloak around them.

V

I was born the day my mother died. Complications with the birth. Internal bleeding. One life for another. All part of the greater scheme, as my father said. God's will, nothing we could do. Initially, I accepted it all, like most kids do, but then I questioned: Why would God not want me to have a mother? She who gave the warmth of her womb for the cold of the grave. What kind of scheme was that? Where was the 'greatness'? Why would he insist on such sacrifice, the burden of which I've carried all my life?

Each weekend through my school years, my father and I would carry a fold-up table and chairs up the hill to Mum's graveside. Dad would have a picnic prepared. Meat sandwiches, dumplings, biscuits, tea. Lemonade in the summer. I loved those evenings. He would tell me stories about her, about himself. How his family moved to England from Kraków before the outbreak of the Second

World War. How they settled in Oxford, starting anew. How my grandfather had fought for the British in France and returned a war hero. My father would talk and talk until nightfall.

Then, he would take his prized possession from its protective case. A vintage telescope given to him by his father upon his graduation. In that heavy darkness, away from the lights of the town, the stars glittered in all their glory. He showed me the Milky Way, the Constellations, the Pillars of Creation, and the solar fires. 'Every star, planet, galaxy that we can see above us, they are all exactly where they are supposed to be,' he said. 'There is no chance in the universe, no random event. Everything happens because it is meant to happen. These are the laws of nature, the laws of physics. These laws lead every event, every moment, onto the next. The past, the present, and the future are all mapped out, each moment, each action, leading inescapably to the next. Time. Stretching into space, filling the void as it tumbles over and over onto itself. We have little choice in any of it. The vast expanse of time ticks by design. It is all predetermined.'

He believed our very being spoke of something unique and wonderful. Tuning, finely calibrated to the billionth degree, somehow allowing, amidst the cauldron of an exploding and expanding universe, for humanity to exist. To be. There could be no luck involved. A fraction change to any of these constants and life would have proven unsustainable. Any closer to the sun, we could not survive the heat. Any further, we'd freeze – irrevocable proof of design. 'We are the universe, and it is us,' he said.

I think he felt this idea of a grand plan would make me feel better about my mother. Our conversations nearly *always came back to her. How much he had loved her, and she him. How excited she was to have me and how much she had loved me even before I arrived. He said she was somewhere out there waiting for us and that one day, we would be with her again. It was meant to be.*

I don't sleep much. Sometimes, in those lost hours, I feel the dead near to me, like I might touch them, join them. When I am gone, when all that had to happen has happened, and when the ghosts are at rest, people will ask why I did what I did. Why? The question that dogs us all the way to the grave. And if I was to answer, I might say that it was written in the stars.

4:35p.m.

Kate switched on the radio to catch the latest weather updates. The bulletin recounted tales of woe from every corner of the country. All across the land, schools, shops and workplaces were shutting down. The extreme conditions were causing mayhem, and the unseemly reporter sounded overly excited as he kept toll of the damage. In Dublin, two children had fallen into a river after the thin ice they were playing on cracked. One was rescued, but the other drowned. *Where had the parents been?* wondered Kate. Were they there in the final moments? She felt ill at the thought.

In the Midlands, an old lady drove her car into a tree and died at the scene. Up north, two hikers were airlifted off the Mournes after getting into trouble. That one annoyed her. She wondered what type of person would go up into the mountains in this weather. *Who was sufficiently removed from the world to have missed all the impending storm alerts? Or did they just not care?* Nothing bad would happen to them, they thought; it only happened to others. They were the type of people who would recount stories the next day of how they never stopped for any storm and would ask others what all the fuss was about. Attention-seeking narcissistic fools.

Kate was only half listening as her mind drifted. She stared at her kitchen wall, its soft pistachio paint marred by the brown coffee stain and the subsequent failed attempt to clean it. She kept thinking of the parents of the child below the ice. Not a minute of their lives would ever be the same. Ever. A tear came, and she wiped it away. Life could be so cruel.

She'd always prided herself on a glass-half-full mentality. She had somehow passed her days in a state of happy contentment. She knew full well that she was privileged in so many ways, but all the same, she believed it was more her personality and outlook that kept her positive, not her fortunate position or circumstance. True, her status in the community had been assured before she was even born. Her family were respected and successful. She had married into achievement, too. Peter had practised as a lawyer initially, then entered politics, like his father before him and was elected to Dáil Éireann. Years later, he was on his way to Brussels to become a Member of the European Parliament. So, Kate understood when she detected the envious looks and whispers behind her back. She knew that no matter what she said or did, some would form the view that she believed she was better than them, *a snob*. But prejudice ran both ways. Indeed, it ran all ways. She had resolved long ago not to let any of that change who she was. When she lived in her studio in New York, with hardly a bob to spare, she was still happy. She loved life itself. Yet recently, she could feel the joy ebbing. Fault lines fissuring beneath the smooth surface.

Kate's mobile buzzed on the table beside her. She snatched at it. Peter, at long last. She answered, peering at the time: 4:35p.m. Outside, the daylight was nearly gone. 'Hey, how are you? Are you stranded?'

'My flight's been delayed, and I'm stuck here in the city until I get further news. Nothing seems to be leaving for at least a few hours yet,' Peter replied.

'Oh, okay,' said Kate. She felt her mood lift a bit. She had no desire to face what was coming. Maybe it was best to put things off and let the earthquake arrive naturally, of its own volition.

'How's Amy?' asked Peter.

'She's having a sleepover tonight at Niamh's. I told you a few days ago.'

'No, you didn't,' Peter replied, his voice raised. 'You never bloody tell me.'

Kate held the phone away just a little.

'I'm sorry, I was sure that I'd told you,' she said, annoyed now at how defensive she sounded. 'Will you make it home? We need to talk.'

'Talk about what?' Peter rasped.

'Well… everything. You, me. Amy.'

A moment's silence followed.

'All we do is talk,' said Peter, 'over and over.'

'Well, this time, we need to find some agreement,' replied an exasperated Kate.

'Do we?' said Peter tersely. 'Look, I'd better go. I'll call when I have news.' And without a goodbye or a love you, the call went dead.

Kate had forgotten to mention that the road might not be passable, but first things first. She rang Grace again to check on Amy. Still no answer.

4:40p.m. (Brussels 5:40p.m.)

Peter placed his phone down next to his coffee and gazed out the large window to the snow-covered cobblestones of Place du Luxembourg. The square bustled with commuters making their way home from work. He raised his hand and hailed Bernard, the café's manager, gesturing to his cup as he did. '*Un autre.*' Bernard was busy at the coffee machine, so he clicked his fingers to the waitress next to him and pointed to where Peter sat.

It always seemed an unnecessarily loud business to Peter. The ear-grating grinding of beans. The banging of filters as they were yanked off and pushed onto the espresso machine. The steaming and frothing of milk. Hiss, bash, wallop. Could it all not be accomplished with less noise? The orgy of sound seemed designed to convince the customer that it was a serious art perfecting the ideal coffee. This is why we charge you five euro per cup.

After what seemed an age, the girl arrived with his order.

'*Bonjour*, Adelle,' said Peter, smiling broadly.

'*Bonjour, monsieur,*' she replied with a quizzical arched eyebrow. Peter pointed to the name tag pinned to her black waistcoat lapel. 'Ah, *oui*,' said Adelle, smiling as she placed his coffee on the table. '*Cinq euros, monsieur, s'il vous plait.*'

'Here. Keep the change,' Peter said, placing a ten euro note into her hand. 'You are new?'

'Oh, *merci, monsieur.* Thank you! *Oui*, this is my first week,' she replied in hesitant English, brushing a long wave of dark hair over her shoulder.

'*Ah, bon.* Let me guess. Université Libre?'

'*Oui.* I am in my final year studying *économie.*'

'Very good, my area of expertise, too,' said Peter, as he lifted a business card from the breast pocket of his suit jacket and handed it to her. He pointed out across the square to where the enormous façade of the European Parliament buildings loomed high behind the train station. '*Je suis un Minister – Irlande.*'

Adelle glanced at the vast glass-clad structure and then back to Peter. As he scrutinised her delicate, blemish-free face, he wondered if she was impressed by his status. It was hard to know with these younger ones; not much enthused them.

'If you are free later, I can give you a tour.' *No time like the present*, he thought, holding her gaze confidently, then allowing his eyes to wander ever so slightly.

The girl blushed a little and smiled. 'I cannot, *monsieur. Je suis désolée.* I must study.'

She held his business card out as if he might need it back. 'Keep it,' Peter insisted. 'Call me. You might need work experience or something.' He watched her turn and walk back to the till at the counter. She was as exquisite from behind as she was face to face. He'd return to chip away until, hopefully, she relented. Slow and gradual invariably worked for him, particularly with the students. Convince them that they'd nothing to lose. He didn't want anything but fun. They could enjoy all his experience, not just the flustered grabbing of youth. He was a man worth knowing – he could help them up the ladder someday. As his father had always said, 'It's not what you know, it's who you know.'

His thoughts drifted to his conversation with Kate. Maybe he wouldn't go back to Ireland at all this weekend? The idea of flying and then driving through the snow for a summit with his beloved wife didn't appeal. A flight cancellation would be perfect – no excuses needed then.

He scanned his phone for updates and then called his secretary. She informed him that, albeit delayed, the airline had confirmed that his flight was still scheduled to depart. *Bloody typical*, he thought. Swallowing the coffee and biting down the last piece of his Danish pastry, Peter pulled on his dark woollen overcoat, lifted his briefcase and reluctantly made his way to the door. Bernard waved, and he nodded back. Adelle had vanished.

His feet crunched on the icy pavement as he proceeded to the line of taxis. 'Airport?' he asked of the driver at the head of the queue. The driver put down his newspaper and grunted something in French that Peter couldn't make out but which seemed to suggest a begrudging acceptance of the transaction. Peter levered himself with some difficulty into the rear of the small car. He was a little heavier these days and not as agile, either. The driver had not adjusted the seats properly, and the space was cramped. The cab smelt of stale cigarettes and musty body odour. He rolled the window down a little and then settled back awkwardly into the seat and closed his eyes. A quick nap might help him endure the snail crawl to the airport and the likely chaos that would ensue.

He had hardly closed his eyes when he heard his name being hollered. He glanced to his right and spotted Wagner waving to him as he negotiated the icy white steps that descended from the train station down to the square. He seemed to be coming his way. Peter pretended not to have seen him. Wagner's thin smile faded as Peter rolled the window up again, and the taxi moved away. Wagner could wait; Peter didn't want to renew their discussion of that morning. He would call Tanya when he got to the airport, see what that business was about and why his name was the talk of strangers. His brow furrowed with anxiety as he stared at the passing buildings. Can nothing ever stay buried?

4:55p.m.

The phone call with Peter had annoyed Kate. These days, most exchanges with him did. Beneath his words lay selfishness, arrogance and contempt. It was *The Peter Show,* and nobody else really mattered.

She bent down and lit the fire she'd set that morning. She rested back into one of the two brown leather armchairs that faced the hearth as the dry kindling crackled into life. They'd bought these chairs years ago: one for Peter, one for her. These days, Amy insisted on sitting there too, so now they operated on a first-come, first-served basis. On the mantelpiece sat a photograph of her father and mother standing proudly side by side outside the family farm. The same farm she now rented to Grace. The same farm that her childhood sweetheart Dan Brady had moved into and was now calling home.

What advice would her father offer if he was still alive? He'd always been a quiet man, but in his silence, he had said everything he needed to. The gaps between his words were filled with support, love and pride. For her, for her mother. She remembered cuddling up beside him in his rocking chair as a small child. To her, it had seemed huge, but he filled it like a king. She would climb into it when he was gone, but she couldn't muster enough strength or momentum to keep it moving back and forth without him. She would wait for him to come in from the fields so that the fight for possession of his throne could commence. He always won, but she would sit on his lap until dinner was ready, and he would listen to her tales from school – who was nice and, more importantly, who wasn't.

As an only child, she'd grown up in the constant company of adults. From an early age, she'd contributed through hard work: milking cows, feeding the animals, cleaning out barns. Sometimes, she felt that her childhood had passed her by. Yet, she'd always been happy. Kate looked again at the picture. Both were now gone. Their faith had been unshakeable to the end. Heaven awaited. Were they there now? She hoped so.

In the fireplace, the flames licked higher, and a damp log barked loudly, spitting hot sparks onto the granite stone. There, they burned bright, ebbed and died. The smell of burning wood began to fill the room, a scent she had always loved. She stared deep into the fire and wondered how her parents had managed to stay together for all those years. Had their love remained as strong as it looked? Had they ever strayed to others or wanted more? If so, she had never detected it.

She thought of Amy and phoned Grace again. Still no reply. Probably out playing in the snow and refusing to come in, she guessed. Kate rose and changed the music. Just as she was settling back into her armchair, eyes closing, the doorbell rang, startling her. A minor wave of alarm rose within her. Who would call in this weather? Maybe Amy had given up on the sleepover and insisted on being brought home. *Poor Grace*, she thought, *how had she managed Cliff Road?*

Kate rose, walked into the hall and opened the front door. The frosty air bit hard at her skin. A man stood in the doorway dressed head to toe in black. Windswept cheeks, nose flushed red, he stood tall, his feet set apart as he brushed snow from his coat. Slung over his shoulder was a large black holdall. Kate felt light-headed. For a moment, her breathing stopped. 'You?' she stammered.

'Hi, Kate, may I come in?'

'Why are you here?'

'Can I come in?' he repeated.

Kate felt her stomach knotting.

'We agreed we wouldn't see each other again.'

'I know. I'm sorry, I'd nowhere else to turn.'

A feeling of helplessness washed through her. She opened the door wider and beckoned the man in.

Dan breathed a sigh of relief and pushed the last of the administration files to the side of the desk. He always seemed to leave the paperwork to the last minute, but somehow, he got it done in time. Court filings, licence applications, identity verifications, accident reports, the variety and volume were infinite. He swivelled the chair to face the desktop computer. His visit to the County Hotel had been playing on his mind all the while. He keyed in the name Nicholas Król. Plenty of *Króls* popped up, but after a quick scan, none seemed to be his missing hotel guest. Most links were of Polish origin, and one page explained that the surname Król meant superior or king. Dan logged into the Garda Facebook account and entered a search for Nicholas Król. Once more, plenty of Króls but no exact matches. He entered Judyta Wojcik. At last, what looked like a possible fit. Dan lifted the passport from the desk and compared the photo to the on-screen image. He couldn't be absolutely sure, but the two pictures bore a strikingly close resemblance. Dan sat up and pulled his chair closer to the screen. He scrolled the account profile. Born in Chrzanów. Moved to Kraków to attend university at the Jagiellonian. Achieved a major in marketing. Married to Nicholas Król. One child. Dan browsed through the photographs that had been posted through the years. Pictures of Judyta with what must have been her mum and dad on a farm. Judyta in the college library. Photos from her wedding day. Her husband, Nicholas, a clear match for the man in the two passports. Further down the wall of snapshots, a baby arrived, and then she began to grow larger and larger. *Theia* he saw written atop a birthday cake. Dan lifted the child's passport and held the picture up to the screen images. There was no doubt he had found his family. He didn't understand the Polish written entries, so he continued to flick through the many, many photographs: school plays, sports days, Christmas dinners. If a picture equalled a thousand words, then the tale that these images told was one of family happiness. Then again, who posted miserable photos?

On a hunch, Dan entered a new search – Nicholas Król and the Jagiellonian University together. Maybe Judyta had met her husband at college. What had Nicholas studied, and what was his background? He scrolled down the list of search results. An old article from the *Sunday Observer* titled "Safe Haven in Oxford" piqued his interest, and he clicked on the piece. It outlined a potted history of Professor Konrad Król and his family. The professor's father, Tomek, served on the board of directors of the Jagiellonian many years before. With the outbreak of the Second World War imminent, Tomek, his wife and his toddler son Konrad moved to Oxford, where Tomek took up a teaching role.

Later, Konrad would follow suit, becoming dean of the astrophysics department at Oxford University. Dan read how Konrad Król married and then sadly how his wife died giving birth to their son, Nicholas. Dan pressed the print button. Was this the Nicholas Król they were searching for? The son of an Oxford professor. His grandfather connected to the university in Kraków. His own wife, Judyta, a student there many years later. It seemed to tie together. It would explain the British and Polish passports.

Dan searched for Nicholas Król and Oxford University, but only the professor popped up. Nothing about his son. It seemed the rest of the family had lived, studied and worked, but not Nicholas. It was as if he had never existed. Yet, his passport and his stay at the County Hotel proved otherwise.

Dan checked the professor's Wikipedia page – heart attack at the age of fifty-two. Dan clicked on a video of the late Professor Król presenting a symposium on his new book *Copernicus and the History of Astronomy* to a crowded lecture hall. Dan put on his headphones and pressed play. He'd heard the name Copernicus before but couldn't recollect why or where. If Professor Król's oration was to be believed, then Copernicus was responsible for establishing both a meaning and a home for the human race.

As Dan continued to listen, the professor explained how, in 1543, Copernicus published his life's work, *On the Revolution of the Celestial Orbs,* which, for the first time, correctly mapped the orbit and movement of the planets. Copernicus argued that Earth was not stationary but instead was a moving sphere and that it and the other planets orbited the sun. A bold and radical thought. Heresy, even. Back then, the accepted belief was that Earth was the centre of the universe and that the sun and other planets orbited it. The Catholic Church had declared it so, for we earthlings were the chosen children of God; it could be no other way.

Dan listened to how the publication and distribution of Copernicus's ground-breaking book was suppressed. Yet, the seed had been sown, and from that plant of knowledge, Galileo, Kepler, Hubble and Einstein would blossom. At last, mankind knew that it was not the centre of all things, that we were only a speck on a huge and ever-spinning kaleidoscope. All our knowledge and perspectives had to be recalibrated. The professor finished his speech by explaining to the audience that in writing the Copernicus story, he had built a bridge back in time to his homeland, Poland, to his hometown of Kraków and to the university where his father and Copernicus himself had studied. Lastly, he pointed to the front row of the audience, and the camera turned its gaze upon a young boy. The professor introduced his son, named after the great man himself, Nicholas. Dan paused the video to catch a glimpse of the kid. He looked about twelve or thirteen, and he stared in what seemed a mix of awe and embarrassment at his father.

Dan sat back into his chair and swivelled from side to side, his mind dizzy from the unexpected journey through space and time. He was astounded how one man, who existed more than five hundred years before Dan was even born, had managed to pinpoint humanity's place in the universe, how one man had changed all that had been previously thought and believed. It was chastening, yet emboldening, too. Now, he needed to learn more about the professor's son, Nicholas. Why had he turned up in Clare? Where was he now? Where were his wife and daughter, and why on earth had the son of an eminent professor turned to crime?

5:05p.m.

The man stepped inside. Kate surveyed in wonder the transformed world from which he had come. The garden

98

wall, the low hedge, the driveway, and even the road itself had blurred indistinguishably into white. A muffled hush hung densely across the land. No revving car engines, no chattering people, no barking dogs, no chirping birds, just serene silence and the soft ultraviolet glow of the snow in the early evening dusk. She closed the door and studied the visitor she knew as Król, the stranger who had called her name on the strand.

He kicked his boots together heel to toe, shaking off the powdery snow onto the doormat.

'I said I'd call you,' said Kate.

Król shrugged his shoulders but said nothing.

Kate stood silent and still, waiting.

'Can I take this off?' he asked her as he began to unzip his dark coat.

'I guess so,' replied Kate.

Król proceeded to remove his snow-covered coat along with his black hat and gloves.

'I'll hang them in the boiler room to dry,' Kate offered, reaching her hand out.

'Thank you,' he replied.

When she returned, he was standing by the circular table in the centre of the hallway, awaiting her invitation to encroach further into her home. This small show of manners gave Kate heart. *This might just go okay*, she thought wishfully.

'You have a beautiful home,' he said as he gazed from the hallway into the large dining room and on into the kitchen. 'You are very lucky.'

'Thank you, we are very grateful to have it,' Kate replied, sensing ever so slightly the hint of a judgement lurking somewhere within the man's words.

She gazed into his face – a map of coarse terrain and harsh ravines leading to two turquoise pools. There, cat-like eyes penetrated, never leaving hers. Not a blink. Beneath them, layered furrows had set. His cheeks were stubbled and dark, greying hair swept back over his head. His face had thinned a little; his jaw was narrower. It seemed that he had aged years in the mere weeks that had passed since she first laid eyes on him. He started to speak again but stopped.

Kate wrapped her woollen shawl tighter to her neck and chest. 'So what brought you up here in this awful weather?' she asked. In truth, she didn't really want to know. She had been very clear with him the last time; she needed time and would call him when she had more news. He shouldn't have come, not to her home. A mix of emotions washed through her: annoyance, anger, fear. Curiosity, too. He still intrigued her. Strangely, she also felt some form of an obligation to him, as if she owed him something. Maybe she did. A reason? An apology? She wasn't sure. Perhaps it was he who owed her.

'I needed to talk to you,' he said.

'Were you hoping to stay over?' said Kate, laughing as she pointed to his bag, but Król didn't react, didn't return her smile.

'Just some personal things. I didn't want to leave them in the car. I had to abandon it.'

'Jesus, that wasn't very smart, driving in this snow.'

'I know, but I needed to see you. Are you alone?'

'It's just us,' Kate said, and even as the words passed her lips, she regretted them. Only after Amy was born did she worry about living in relative isolation up in the lighthouse. When it was just her and Peter, she hadn't even thought about it, not even when he was travelling, and she was left alone. At this moment, though, she felt very distant from the rest of the world.

'...for now. Peter will be home soon. You can't be here when he gets home,' she added hurriedly.

'It's okay, I'll be gone by then,' said Król.

Kate hardly recognised him from their last encounter. Was he sick? There was something different she felt. The mood? The look in his eyes? Something was off. The voice was the same, southern English, not too posh but certainly well to do and with a hint of something else. A Polish lilt she had eventually discovered.

She'd never forget the first time he spoke to her. That Sunday morning in December. It was one of those fresh winter days when all seemed right with the world. The biting cold breeze and the warm glow of the sun combining to alchemise the senses and jump-start the soul. You could walk forever through days like that. She and Amy had gone down to the water's edge. Their feet left cushioned imprints in the wet sand as they ambled hand in hand. She could sense somebody walking behind them, but she paid little notice. After a short while, she realised the presence was still there. Too close to them on the broad expanse of sand. A shadow over their shoulder. Then he spoke. It was a question.

'Kate?' he'd asked. She'd held Amy's hand tighter and turned to look at him. She had never seen him before that morning. Up on the promenade, people were out for their Sunday morning exercise, and everything appeared normal in the world.

'Yes,' she had replied casually, without concern or awareness that she had reached an intersection, a junction where the trajectory of one person's journey intersected another's, their paths from that point forward forever tangled. Since that unforeseen encounter, layer by layer, her life had started to unravel. Now, as they stood side by side alone in the lighthouse on the clifftop, Kate wished for all the world that she'd never laid eyes on this man.

5:10p.m.

Kate motioned for Król to follow her into the kitchen. 'You must be freezing. I'll make something warm to heat you up,' she said, as she crossed the tiled floor to the range and placed an old cast-iron kettle onto the metal hob.

Król gestured to the wooden kitchen table that dominated the centre of the room. 'May I?'

'Yes, of course,' Kate replied. 'Coffee?'

'Yes, please,' he replied.

Kate scooped ground coffee into a cafetière, and then when the water had nearly boiled, she filled it two-thirds and placed it on the table. She cut a homemade brown loaf and arranged slices on a wooden platter, which she laid on the table along with some butter in a dish. She buttered a piece and took a bite. 'Please, help yourself. I've got to make a phone call. I'll be back in a moment when that coffee has brewed.'

Kate went back to the armchair in the dining room where she had been sitting. Her mobile should have been there but it wasn't. Maybe it had slid down the back of the cushion. She poked around, but there was no sign.

She looked on the coffee table, then the mantelpiece and by the CD player, but still nothing. When she returned to the kitchen, Król was still sitting quietly at the table. Kate searched the countertop and rummaged around some of the jars and cereal boxes. 'That's so annoying,' she said, in an exasperated tone, 'I had my phone just a while ago, now I can't find it!'

'Do you want me to call your number?' Król enquired, fishing his mobile from his pocket.

'No, no, that's okay. It's got to be here somewhere. I was only using it before you arrived.'

Król placed his phone on the table and poured some coffee, heaping two large spoons of sugar on top. 'Will you have some?'

'Yes, please,' she called back from the ongoing hunt, which had circled back to the dining room. 'I'll use the landline instead. Just give me a few minutes.'

The house phone was on a table in a hallway that serviced the kitchen, the downstairs bathroom, the boiler room and the stairs to the bedrooms. Kate lifted the phone and began to punch the numbers, but nothing happened. No beeps, no dial tone, it was completely dead. She cursed to herself and returned to the kitchen. 'It's not working,' she said, her voice faltering just a little.

'Maybe it's the storm,' Król suggested. 'I know some of the lines are down around town. One of the telephone poles along the bay was blown over. I still have your number – I'll ring it.'

Kate sat down opposite him at the table. He dialled and put the phone on speaker. The call went to Kate's message minder. Now, that didn't make sense at all, she thought.

She was sure her mobile had been on and fully charged – she'd only had it in her hand less than twenty minutes ago. Kate stiffened a little as a small tremor of dread shook through her.

5:20p.m.

Snowflakes floated like tiny feathers over a near-deserted Main St. Ahead at the kerbside, Dan spotted John Hanrahan, the town doctor, waving at him to slow down. There was a time when Dan wouldn't have stopped and instead would've ignored the doctor and driven on. They'd been in the same school year together but had shared little in common. Hanrahan had gone to college, excelled, and taken over his father's general practice when he came back home. He'd married the prettiest girl in town. He had it all. Dan, all the while, had struggled to make his mark. It embarrassed him to admit it, but for a long time, he'd been jealous of Hanrahan, but that had changed.

A few years previous, he'd been called out one evening to investigate an unidentified car parked down a private laneway on Tom Findlay's estate. Findlay had money and plenty of it. He was a retired judge from the Clare Circuit Court. He'd shared with Dan his fear of being targeted by revenge-minded criminals. Dan had listened, but privately, he had felt the judge was a little precious and self-obsessed. That night, he'd driven out anyway. The car was where Findlay had said he would find it, parked up along a path about a kilometre from the manor house. The tail lights were off, but as Dan approached, he detected movement inside. One of the internal lights glowed dimly through fogged windows. Dan recognised the vehicle. It was John Hanrahan's white Mercedes.

Dan tapped on the driver's window, and after what seemed an age, the glass lowered, and the doctor greeted him – in the passenger seat sat a much younger man whom Dan didn't recognise. Dan asked the doctor what had brought him to Judge Findlay's land on a dark winter's evening. The doctor muttered something about the two men needing privacy to talk about a family matter, and with flushed cheeks, he apologised for any misunderstanding. He hadn't realised it was private land. Dan shone his flashlight into the face of the doctor's passenger and asked him if he had anything to add to the doctor's account. The young man shook his head sheepishly in return. Dan remembered the awkwardness of the scene, the slow realisation that had dawned on him. And that had been that. Dan never revealed to the judge, or anybody else for that matter, who had been parked up that lane or why. He'd reported it as some teenage kids acting out. In some ways, it felt to him now as if the encounter had never happened. In the years since he had developed a cordial friendship with the doctor. The episode had taught him never to assume or judge the lives of others. We never truly know another living soul.

Dan eased on the brake, and the police car came to a slow halt. He climbed out and trudged over to where Hanrahan was waiting on the footpath, a crown of snow already settled on the doctor's full head of dark hair.

'Hey, Dan, good to see you. This is quite the weather, eh.'

'It sure is, John,' said Dan, shaking the doctor's hand. 'I hope your work is done.'

'I wish. I'm heading out to Margaret Boyle's.'

'Oh,' said Dan, 'is everything okay?' Margaret lived twenty minutes north of town. She was pregnant with her first child.

'I hope so, but it's always hard to know exactly what's what over the phone.'

'Well, shout for help if you need it.'

'Yes, yes, of course, thanks,' said the doctor. He paused for a moment as if unsure of what to say next, and then, finally, he spoke again. 'I saw your mother today,' he said slowly as he pushed his circular-rimmed glasses further up his nose.

'Did you?' replied Dan. 'She never tells me anything. I'm actually on my way to see her now.'

'Indeed,' said the doctor. 'An old woman and her secrets. Like an Egyptian pharaoh; proud, majestic, but very, very silent.'

Dan tried to read the doctor. Was he conveying a cryptic message to him? 'Anything *you* can tell me, John?' he asked. The doctor stared at Dan, a warm and caring countenance moulded naturally upon his face. The kind of expression that you'd want a doctor to wear. A look that spoke of empathy and compassion.

'Have a talk with her,' he said, and with that, he made his way cautiously across the ground to the driver's side of his Mercedes. Looking back, he called, 'Soon, okay.'

Kate squeezed two knuckles hard into the bridge of her nose in a futile attempt to relieve the painful scraping in her forehead. She didn't get them often, but when she did, her headaches were excruciating. She'd felt the dull ache arriving that morning, and here it was in all its glory. She fished out some strong painkillers from the press: two plus an extra one for luck might do it. The tablets fizzed away in the glass as she gazed out the window. The lull hadn't lasted long. Earlier, she had marvelled in awe at the irresistible beauty of the storm, but now, as it blew hard and conspired to cage her in, the spectacle was losing its lustre.

She eyed Król as he sipped on his coffee. He'd been pretty dumb to come up here in this weather. He'd said he needed to see her again. Why? To have sex? She was sick of fragile men and their endless need for mothering. They communicated best with their dicks. That's when you felt their love or their anger most, or, as she had grown more accustomed to of late, their distinct disinterest. She'd read somewhere about female snakes who could breed without males. Sometimes, they chose to, even when the slithery lads were present. "Virgin Births", the headline had proclaimed – a vision of hope for the future.

Król prodded the batch of letters resting on the table, lifting his head slowly to meet her eyes, his poker face betraying little emotion. 'So, you kept them.'

'Yes, I'm sorry, I would rather have burned them,' said Kate.

Król started to say something and then stopped, all the while pushing and poking his finger at the bundle as if tempting them to bite.

'I'm sorry, too,' he said after a while.

Sometimes, it seemed to Kate that everybody was sorry. All the time. And if they weren't, they should be. Sorry for hurting others. Sorry for hurting themselves. The human default condition seemed to be destruction. Maybe this storm was coming to purge them of their follies. Mother Nature's reminder that she was more powerful than all of them and all of their foolishness.

VI

Some events crawl under your skin and never leave. You wish they'd never occurred, but there's no changing the past or what it makes of you. I was about twelve, I think, on the verge of knowing things and shaping my own ideas. One night, I woke to a hand clasped over my mouth. My father hushed me. There was an intruder downstairs. When my eyes adjusted to the darkness, I could see that in his other hand, he held his father's revolver, a war memento. He told me to stay where I was, and he crept down the stairs. I heard loud voices: angry at first, then quieter. For once, I disobeyed his authority, and I rose and followed him. I approached the kitchen and peeked in, heart in my mouth. I could see him talking to a young man, both sitting at the table. Everything seemed ludicrously normal. My father's hands were resting on the wooden top, palms down. One calmly held the gun, barrel pointed directly at the stranger's chest. My father told the intruder that he could have some of the money he had come to steal, but he would have to work for it. Our burglar was invited to come back the following week and earn his reward honestly. To encourage his involvement in the scheme, my father took some ink from his writing press, all the while holding the gun. He dabbed the man's forefinger and took a fingerprint. I watched on, flabbergasted. Their pact agreed, my father ushered the man from our home. I tried to sneak back up the stairs without detection, but he saw me. After a rebuke for not heeding his instructions, he explained to me that what he had done was the right thing. That there was strength in forgiveness and rehabilitation. I remember falling asleep that night filled with pride for the man who had raised me.

A week later, our fingerprinted burglar was back and earning an honest living doing odd jobs at the university. My father's plan had worked. A lesson had been learned, or so we thought. Unfortunately, about a year or so later, I saw our intruder's face again, this time on the front page of the Oxford Chronicle. He had broken into an old woman's home, and in the ensuing horror, she had passed away. Police confirmed that she had been brutally beaten, raped and then left to die. Three hundred pounds had been taken. The paper reported at length upon the old woman's virtue. A life of helping others. A devout churchgoer with a heart of gold. I never told my father that I read that story. He, of course, had heard the news; it was everywhere. In turn, he said nothing to me. We lived silently with our shared knowledge. I could hardly look him in the eye and witness his realisation that there were no rules. Regardless of whether he played by the book, it didn't assure anybody else did, for there was no *book. Only the strong survived. The hunter hunts and the prey dies.*

5:40p.m.

What was done was done. Kate couldn't change it, nor could her uninvited caller. Nobody could. Had he come here to stir things up? She sighed. It was time to move forward, to begin again, and not look back in need of masochistic self-punishment. When would these bloody painkillers kick in? Her head was still pounding. She longed for the turbo-charged ones that the hospital gave her after she'd given birth to Amy. She'd needed an emergency C-section. Afterwards, the pain had been excruciating. One nurse – Mahalia, a young woman from the Philippines – was especially kind. She made sure that Kate had enough chemical assistance to get her through. People talked about C-sections as if they were a trip to the dentist – they should try having one and then caring for a newborn as the scars healed. Every twist or turn tearing at the wound. Her parents had proven invaluable in the weeks after. Taxiing her back and forth, arranging shopping, cooking meals, giving her a chance to breathe, to ease into a new life in which every day from that point forward would summon the responsibility of assuring the welfare of another human being. Peter had pressing business in Brussels, and it couldn't be helped. He had to leave the day after they arrived back home. He promised a nanny, but Kate didn't want one. Amy was her child – she'd do whatever was needed herself. And she did. Now Amy was eight, and the time had gone by in the blink of an eye. Besides Amy, what did she have to show for those years? No promotions or awards. No public acknowledgements. No statue erected in the town square – just an absentee husband and time spent alone on the clifftop.

Kate sat down at the kitchen table opposite Król. He stared at her. The same way he had done before. Unblinking, penetrating. It was as if he could see deep within her. Feel her emotions. Think her thoughts. She realised with some annoyance that she felt arousal. It was an involuntary reaction driven by instinct, memory and possibly absence. Her body instinctively responding to something, someone it had felt before. Her mind wandered to events she could hardly believe happened. She was back in his hotel room. He was behind her. With every push, she'd felt the exhilaration, the freedom. With each delicious and illicit thrust, she'd escaped further and further away. In those reckless moments, nothing else mattered. She had wanted to be taken, to be used. She'd been disappointed when he finished; she'd wanted more. She'd pleasured him until he was ready again. It had been so long since she had been desired like that. When both had no more to give or take, they lay back and allowed their blissfully aching bodies to recover. They'd hardly spoken. They hadn't needed to. They'd both understood what had happened and why. There had been an instinctive inevitability to it. Caring and sensitive at first, wounded animals easing each other's pain. Then carnal, visceral, a frenzied exorcism of the flesh. Bodies screaming rage. She'd sworn that it was a one off, but it hadn't been. She'd gone to him again and had given everything once more. Done everything. More than she'd given or done with any man. Things she thought she didn't like, but in the excitement and the fever, she'd revelled in their baseness. After, she nearly drowned in the guilt. Yet the very existence of her husband brought her up for air, and again, she breathed – the long-drawn breath of the dissatisfied.

And now he was here, sitting at her kitchen table. She laughed so she wouldn't cry. Kate cursed Peter for his inadequacies and his frailty. It was his fault for bringing this sordid debacle to their home. Her father was too decent a man to say it in plain terms, but Kate had always detected his disappointment in her choice of husband. With good cause, she now knew.

'So come on, tell me, why did you come?' she insisted.

'I wanted to see you again,' he replied but without much emotion. Kate didn't believe him.

'You really shouldn't be here. It's madness, you know we can't.'

Król sat up straighter in his chair; she'd hit a raw nerve. Then his posture softened, and he waved his hand in a sardonic gesture towards the wooden serving dish and the bottle of red wine next to it. 'Of course, I wouldn't like to be getting in the way of the happy family, would I?'

'Don't you judge me,' snapped Kate. 'Things are not always what they seem. I'm dealing with all of this as best I can.'

'As am I, Kate. That's why I wanted to see you, to talk to you. To decide the best way forward.'

'Where is your wife?'

'She's gone; it's just me now.'

The news was a surprise more than a shock, but still, it hit hard. The gusting wind whistled through the eaves. The storm wasn't going away, nor was this mess.

6:00p.m.

Dan rested his hands on his mother's shoulders and crouched low to kiss her head. His usual greeting, his way of saying, 'I love you.' Was it so hard for him to say those words aloud? He couldn't remember the last time he had. It seemed that beneath her cardigan was bone and very little else. He felt a pang of alarm.

Iris shuffled to the stove, enquiring as she went, 'Tea?' She moved slowly. Slower than usual, carrying her leg slightly.

'What's wrong, Mum, are you okay?'

'Ah, nothing, it's nothing, don't be worrying,' she replied. 'I just slipped in the graveyard this morning after Mass. I'm not sure why I even go. To Mass, not the grave. You know I don't believe any of it anymore. This is what I get for my stupidity.'

Dan remained silent. There was nothing to say. He didn't believe in God. Or, as his mother would proclaim, he didn't believe in anything. In many ways, the reverse was true. He believed in everything, everything but God. He believed in humanity and its ability to be God and the Devil in equal measure. He'd seen it with his own eyes. God certainly hadn't been there for his father. Not at the end, as he gradually faded, cancer devouring him from the inside out. Soiling himself, wrought by pain, suspended on deathly hooks by an assortment of drips and drains. Unable to say goodbye to his loved ones when the time at last came. He hadn't even looked like his dad. In truth, he was dead long before he died. No, there'd been no sign of God in that hospital room.

He'd never met his brother J.J. He'd died before Dan was born – a drowning accident at the Pollock Holes. Somebody got distracted and wasn't paying attention to the children; he never knew who, and it wasn't a conversation he and his parents ever had. God had been busy that day, too.

'I can't believe there even was a Mass today. Does Father Murphy not follow the news? Does he not believe in storms?'

His mother still attended Mass every morning since his father died. Even if her faith was waning or gone, as she declared, he knew she would never let her friends rejoice in her absence. She wouldn't give anybody the pleasure of saying she'd given up. If there were a competition for who put in the hard prayers and devotion for the departed, his mother would not be found wanting by her whispering peers. So, whenever he did hear her castigate God for his careless absenteeism, it was when she was at home, away from the prying ears. Anger seemed to be her fuel in these golden years. Funnily, though, he preferred her arguing to the times when she said nothing at all and just stared forlornly into the distance.

'Is it bad? You should have it checked,' he said, looking down with a concerned look at her leg.

'Sure, it's only a little bruise,' she replied. 'Doctor Hanrahan said it will be fine.'

'I bumped into him this evening. You were with him today, I heard,' said Dan, leaving an unasked question hanging in the air.

Iris said nothing, ignored it, and just kept busying. She refused to tell him anything about her health. She even denied her age. She would never admit reliance of any sort. That would be a display of weakness, and that wasn't allowed, not even before her son. Dan both hated and admired this hardwired tenacity, particularly at her age, but it didn't excuse foolishness.

'Is everything okay with your health?' There, he'd asked the question.

'Of course, don't be silly,' she replied, waving him off. 'Did he say something?'

'No, no, he didn't,' said Dan as he wondered what more he could say or do to penetrate the will of this iron-clad woman.

'Will you please stay indoors until this storm passes? It will get worse before it blows out.'

She had her back to him making the tea and one arm lifted in the air in an all-too-familiar motion, waving off this suggestion as nonsense. Dan went outside to the car and shuffled back in with a cardboard box filled with groceries. 'I got these just in case you were stuck. There's some milk, tea, bread and eggs.'

'I have plenty here. Take them with you,' she replied tersely as if insulted at the thought that she couldn't keep herself. Dan ignored her protests.

'Have *you* eaten?' she asked. 'You don't eat enough, always too busy running around after everybody else to look after yourself properly.'

'I'm fine. I can't stay. I just wanted to check you were okay. I'll come back tomorrow.'

'Get that eejit Sully to do some work. He does nothing. It takes three of you now to do what one man did before – it's a disgrace.'

Dan didn't reply. He'd never shone favourably in the halo of his father. Stepping into his shoes had sentenced him to a lifetime in the shade.

'I haven't seen you for over a week, and now here you are, going already. What has you so busy? Has that Grace got you hooked on a line? You probably should just settle and accept what you've got. You're no catch anymore.'

Maybe he wasn't. Maybe he had never been. Regardless, it always staggered Dan how many hurtful words could be delivered wrapped in the cloak of love. His thoughts drifted to that morning. He could tell his mother how he felt about Grace. He could tell her that this time, he believed something good was happening but that it was complicated and that he was easing his way through it as best he knew how. He could tell her that Grace was a much better person than Iris gave her credit for. He could tell her that he loved Grace. He could tell her that he remembered sitting on her lap as a child, in front of the fireplace, listening to her talk to his father. He could tell her that he missed Dad. That he missed him more than words could ever say. That he wished he'd met his brother. She might respond by telling him that she loved him. No matter what, unconditionally. That she'd always been proud of him, she was his mother. They said none of that. They said nothing at all, and instead of words, a lifetime of compounded silence hung heavy between them.

Dan opened the door to leave. He waved goodbye and reassured her he'd be back tomorrow. He didn't turn to see the look in her eyes. That expression he knew all too well. The one designed to fill him with guilt. He could never quite pinpoint its precise essence or discern exactly what message it was conveying, but if you stirred together equal measures of disappointment, pity and sadness, that's the look she gave.

6:05p.m.

Kate combed high and low for her phone but to no avail. She wondered how Peter and his delayed flight were fairing. Had he tried to contact her? She switched the radio back on. The only news was storm news. Things sounded much worse in the East. Workplaces were shutting down, and public transport had ground to a halt. All schools were now officially closed. Another death was reported. A car crash in Carlow. Kate thought of Amy, longing to talk to her, to hear a voice that spoke from pure love. Maybe Grace had called. *Where was her bloody phone?* It couldn't have just vanished into thin air. She sat down at the table and poured another coffee.

Król seemed lost as he gazed trance-like out the large kitchen windows to the snowstorm. There was something feral about her visitor. She had felt it before, a furnace burning beneath the cool exterior. Had she expected him to make a move on her? Probably. Did she want him to? She wasn't sure. It dawned on Kate that Król never initiated conversation. Instead, he waited and drew out his opponent as if engaged in some high-stakes poker game. She didn't mind. She'd little to lose.

'Will you stay in Kraków or move back to England?' she asked.

'There's nothing in Poland for me now,' he replied. 'Maybe I'll settle here in Blackcliff.'

Kate's eyes widened. Surely, he was teasing her. He didn't believe that they could have something together in Blackcliff? She'd never suggested that could ever happen. Did he want her to leave Peter for him? Had she misjudged this man altogether?

'I can read your mind,' he said, smiling. 'Don't worry. I'm not asking for anything,' he said, holding his palms face out in conciliatory fashion. 'It was wrong of me to come, to add to your stress. I only wanted to see how you are.'

It was, thought Kate, but she didn't say so. Men hurt like little children. She'd learned to tread cautiously with her words. 'I'm sorry, but you being here, in my home, it's just strange. It feels wrong,' she said. 'I know this has been tough for you too. I understand how you must be feeling.'

'Do you?' he asked tersely. 'I doubt that.'

The sudden change in tone took Kate aback.

'Yes, of course I do. I've been hurt as much as you. My husband wrote those awful letters,' said Kate, gesturing to the stack on the table.

'To my wife,' he replied curtly.

For a moment or two, they just stared at each other in silence – the jilted spouse's club.

'So, what about you? And Peter?' he asked eventually.

'I don't think there will be a me and Peter. That scares me, you know.' Tears began to well. She didn't want to cry in front of him, to be so weak, but she couldn't help it.

Once the dam had been breached, there was no stopping the flow. He came around the table and knelt by her chair. He held her head to his chest and stroked her hair. She could smell his scent, a mix of sweat and cologne. With his thumb, he wiped the tears from her cheeks and the hair from her face. She remembered he'd done that before, a relationship formed from tears. Then he kissed her eyelids, one by one. She let him. Then, her cheeks. Then, her mouth. She still let him. She kissed him back, gently at first but then a full kiss, a lustful kiss, pushing her tongue into his. He pulled at her clothes. Then he stopped.

'Where's your bedroom?'

'We can't,' Kate said.

'We can. Come,' he said, taking her hand. She rose, and he led her from the kitchen and into the hall. Together, they climbed the stairs, she first, he behind. She showed him into her bedroom. He sat on the bed. The bed where her daughter was conceived. The bed where only she, Peter and Amy had ever lain. He began to undress. She shut the door behind her.

6:30p.m. (Brussels 7:30p.m.)

Delay after delay arrived in waves of rolling red that washed across the departure board. Occasional green letters offered hope for the lucky few. Peter's flight was one. Shannon, 6:30p.m. He should be somewhere high over the UK by now. A new departure time flashed for 8:05p.m., along with a message to go to the gate. *They needed to open the check-in desk first!* Peter's breast pocket began to vibrate, and he reached inside his coat and retrieved the phone. Damn. Some numbers delivered only bad news. Peter cursed under his breath and answered.

'Mr Kavanagh, how are you, my good sir?' a man's voice enquired in an overly friendly tone.

'What is it? I'm busy,' Peter replied.

'Oh, sorry to disturb you, but I have some news,' said the caller.

'Listen, our business is finished. We have nothing more to talk about,' said Peter.

'I had hoped that might be true, Mr Kavanagh, but I am afraid that things have changed. There are new problems. We need to meet.'

Peter felt like flinging the phone along the queue of bedraggled travellers waiting in line for a desk that showed no signs of opening. 'No way! You must be joking. We are done.'

'Oh, well, that is a shame, Mr Kavanagh. I will have to try and deal with this problem myself,' said the voice.

'What problem? What the hell is it now?'

A few nearby passengers looked around to see what the fuss was. Peter shot one of them a dirty look and then left the queue to find a quiet corner.

'A man has come asking questions, looking for information. I think he's a private investigator. I can hush it up, get rid of him, but it will need more money, I'm afraid.'

'More money? No way! Who is he?' Peter replied loudly. Too loudly. More bored passengers were beginning to take notice. Peter walked out of the terminal and stood on the icy footpath in front of the taxi drop-off location. The line went momentarily silent.

'He didn't say, but he knew something. That much was very clear.'

'Fuck,' Peter said. 'Listen, Inspector Kowalski, I've no more money. I can't do this anymore.'

'Okay, Peter, I understand. I will need to look after it here. I can't make any promises, though. You do understand—'

'We agreed that this was over. I paid what you asked,' Peter insisted. He struggled to think of any leverage he might possess to end this recurring nightmare.

'I know, I know,' said the voice, 'but circumstances change. This will be the last time. I will destroy everything I have this time. I promise.'

'You said that before. What's different now?'

'You will just have to trust me, Peter. That is all I can offer you. I, too, have other things to be doing. I, too, have my reputation.'

Peter didn't believe a word the policeman was saying, but he had no counter to this argument. 'How much this time?'

'Ten thousand.'

'Fuck off. Seriously? You must be joking!'

'I wish I was.'

Peter inhaled deeply. *What a fuck-up.*

'Leave it with me, and I'll see what I can pull together, but listen, Kowalski, know this. I've recorded this conversation. If we go down, we go down together.'

Peter hung up.

He scrolled down his list of callers until he found her contact. He tapped the screen and waited. No answer. Fuck. He dialled again. This time, she answered.

'Hi, Tanya, we need to talk.'

'I don't want to talk, Peter. I'm busy,' replied Tanya Wagner.

'I'll be quick, okay? It's very important. Please.'

Tanya hesitated, and for a moment, Peter thought she might hang up.

'What is it?' she asked, each word ladened heavy with disgust.

'You spoke to a man outside the office last week. My name was mentioned. Why?' Peter asked.

'How do you know that?'

'Your father overheard your conversation. He told me.'

The line went silent for a moment, and again, Peter feared that Tanya would end the call.

'He warned me not to talk to you. He was very serious, Peter,' said Tanya, the tone of her voice shifting from anger to worry.

'He won't know I spoke to you,' said Peter softly. 'What did he want? Did you tell him anything?'

Peter could hear Tanya crying on the other end of the line.

'I didn't need to. He said he knew everything,' she spluttered, sobbing aloud. 'I don't know how, but he seemed to know all about us. He said... he said...' It sounded to Peter that the words she sought were choking her and that she was unable to cough them out, but eventually, she did, and then he wished she hadn't.

'...he said that we had blood on our hands.'

Peter's skin flushed hot from the rush of fear that coursed through his body. He looked forlornly about the exterior of the terminal as if some answer to his problems might miraculously materialise like a genie from the swirling snow. All the while, Tanya's words were nestling deep into the queasy pit of his stomach. *Blood on our hands.*

'What did you say?' he asked.

'I told you. I said nothing. Peter, I'm so scared. I'm not talking about this anymore, okay? I have to go.' And with that, she hung up.

Peter immediately called her number again, but he got an engaged tone. 'Fuck!' he exclaimed aloud and walked back inside towards the departure desks.

The Shannon queue had by now started to shuffle forward, the only line moving amongst the throng of immobile and irate travellers. Peter wondered who else here was dealing with the world of shit that he was. You could spend your life doing good, but fuck up once, let the guard down one time, and that's it, you'll pay forever.

He looked up at the departures board. Bangkok. Manila. Bali. He could lose himself in any of those places and start again. He'd enough money hived away in his Swiss bank accounts to afford him a comfortable lifestyle. The thought had entered his mind before, but this time, it lingered long and slinked around.

7:05p.m.

Mirror, mirror on the wall, who is the most screwed up of them all? The reflection staring back at Kate provided the answer. Ruffled hair, bloodshot eyes, her cheeks flushed and streaked. She pulled some tissues and wiped tears from her face. She'd aged. Crow's feet. Fallen mouth. Thinner lips. Her tummy bulged under her top, ever so slightly, but enough. Her breasts beginning to sag. All gradual, all unhurried, but all very real. Permanent frown lines furrowed her forehead. She'd avoided becoming one of the Botox generation, and now she wondered why. The young and the beautiful always win.

She was still attractive, wasn't she? It had been said to her before by a man, that women never know if they are beautiful or not. They didn't see what a man saw. When her daughter looked at her, did she see an old woman? Kate remembered her parents had seemed from another world when she was growing up. Their clothes, their conversation, their proximity to death. She thought she'd never be like them, yet here she was.

She could hear Król coughing hoarsely downstairs. At least he'd had the good grace to leave the scene of the crime. Sex was one thing; pillow talk was a whole different matter. The idea of sharing intimacies and secrets while lying side by side didn't bear thought. She wondered what his wife looked like. Was she younger? Prettier? It wasn't just youth that made men stray. Her father had warned her that some men need to prove themselves over and over. It was a Genesis thing, Adam and Eve.

The woman in the mirror kept gawking at her, demanding to be seen. Look at me, she cried. Truly look at me. Sadness filled her eyes. This wasn't how it was supposed to be. Thirty-eight years old, and now it was time to restart. Square one again. For God's sake, how did everything fall apart so quickly?

What were their finances like? She hadn't worked since Amy had arrived. How would she survive? The house was in her name, but what else? She left the en-suite bathroom and slipped quietly into the bedroom. She crossed the room and locked the door. She hadn't wished for any of this. Why Peter had lost interest in her, she couldn't tell. She thought again of her father and mother. Expectations must have been more reasonable in their day, or did they just suffer each other? Took what they got. Was that why half the country were alcoholics? But wasn't this man's wife a mother, too? With two children? What had Peter found with her that he was missing at home? She felt anger, no, not anger, detachment. Detachment was an emotion Kate could use. She would nurture it.

Kate lay on the bed and curled up in a ball, draping the duvet over her as she did. Her head was groggy from too many painkillers. From the exertion, too. The covers were still damp. She wanted to forget about Król. She wanted to forget about Peter. She closed her eyes and listened to the comforting cry of the storm. Oddly, it made her problems seem small, inconsequential. Before long, she succumbed to sleep.

She and Amy were walking hand in hand through a park. They stepped out of their sandals and trod barefoot through the lush green grass. The golden sun warmed their cheeks, and their laughter hung on the soft breeze. They set a blanket for a picnic, laid down and closed their eyes. When she woke, the skies had darkened. She turned to wake Amy, to tell her they should go home, but her child was missing. Now, only an empty sun-scorched plain stretched to the horizon. Kate shivered. Whichever way she looked, Amy was nowhere to be seen.

Peter shoved his cabin bag forcefully into the packed overhead locker and went to take his seat. He sighed loudly to be heard. Someone was sitting there already, a portly older woman. Peter turned back towards the front of the plane and spoke to the young air hostess who was approaching. Rebecca, her badge declared. She was a pretty, petite girl, but she wore an undisguised fatigued frown that spoke of irritation and annoyance. Well, he was worn out and not a little stressed, too, and he was paying for the pleasure.

'There's a woman in my seat,' he said and flashed his boarding pass at her. '6C.'

'Oh, Mr Kavanagh, yes. We are aware you are allocated that seat, but with this being our only flight out of Brussels today, we are overbooked. That lady is travelling with her daughter, and they hoped to sit together. If it's okay, there's a seat free in the row behind.'

Rebecca's tone suggested that somehow it was he who might be the problem. That he should take what he could get for boarding last.

'An aisle seat?' asked Peter in an exasperated tone, not wanting to assist but too tired for the hassle.

'No, a middle seat, sir.'

'No, no, I'm not having a middle seat,' Peter replied. He refused to sit in middle seats. They were so narrow and uncomfortable, the airline should pay the passengers to suffer them. 'Listen, I'm a platinum member. I book ahead. I choose my seat so I can board last and get off first, and so I have a little bit of legroom while I endure the flight.'

'Oh, we know who you are, Mr Kavanagh, we just thought that—'

'No, no thinking. I just want my seat. Will you arrange that for me, please?'

'Okay, of course, sir,' said Rebecca as she flashed him a smile that could kill.

After what seemed an age, finally, the woman rose with the maximum of huff and puff and proceeded to take her original seat in the row behind. Peter could hear her tut-tutting and could feel dagger eyes aimed at the back of his skull as he settled into the seat that was rightfully his. Peter wriggled and squirmed. The cushion was warm.

The flight was a nightmare. No doubt, to emphasise how ungracious Peter was, the woman's daughter insisted on leaning over and talking loudly and continuously to her mother behind. Then, when Peter ordered coffee, Rebecca practically threw it over his lap. They could all go to hell. He was in the right. He would be penning an official letter to the airline about their *insolent little Rebecca* when he returned to Brussels. For now, he'd bite his tongue. Peter closed his eyes. Sleep fell like a tender duvet over his tired, frazzled mind.

VII

After tucking me into bed as a child, my father would lie beside me, and we'd look up to the painted polystyrene planets that we'd diligently made together and then hung from the ceiling. He would tell me that we were going on a magical journey to the stars above. We would drift upwards hand in hand, sailing past the moon and floating out into deep space. He told me of the acid rains of Venus, the red lunar landscape of Mars, Jupiter's moons, Saturn and its dust rings.

Further and further we went until we'd left the freezing blue gases of Neptune and the ice rock of Pluto behind. On we soared, right to the edges of the solar system, and there we gazed into far-away galaxies and nebulae. He painted pictures of exploding supernovas, gargantuan solar clouds and cascading meteor showers. Then he said we must stop. We could go no further, for ahead lay a dark monster – the

black hole. If we went too close, crossed an invisible line,
it would pull us in, never to escape. We turned and glided
slowly back towards Earth, orbiting for a while as the moon
tugged us in its wake. I rarely made it all the way home,
having drifted off to sleep on the journey.

As I lie here now, all these years later, I still sense it,
the constant movement of the universe whirring above, the
earth spinning beneath. The turning of time. I think of that
black hole. I can feel it. The vengeful weight of a dead planet.
A pitch-black spectre swallowing everything that crosses its
path. Those colossal gravitational forces pull at my fibres,
stretching my skin. It waits for me in the inky darkness. It
waits for you. For us.

8:10p.m.

Kate bolted upright in the bed. She hadn't intended
to sleep, but somehow she had drifted. She rose and
crossed the room to the table by the window. Outside,
the blizzard had waned, and a full moon lit fluorescent
the fields that descended from the lighthouse to the
sea and the town beyond. The amber lights of clustered
houses glowed in the dark just as they had that morning.
The tall chimney of the power plant blinked faintly. To
the west lay the deep rolling darkness of the Atlantic.
Kate checked her watch and swore; she'd been asleep for
nearly an hour. She quickly tidied herself and made her
way downstairs.

Król raised his head and opened his eyes as Kate
entered the kitchen. For a moment, he looked confused,
as if he, too, had woken from a deep sleep. Maybe he had.

Wasn't that what men did when they'd done the deed? What had happened upstairs was the final nail in the marital coffin. Each time with this man was a step closer to something. What, she didn't know for sure. A reckoning? An end? A beginning? She walked to the sink and filled a glass of water.

'The queen has arisen,' said Król.

'Was that what you came for?' Kate asked.

'Don't say things like that, Kate. It just happened, and it's natural, given what we've been through.'

He was right, but it still felt wrong. Using her body as a weapon against her husband. Was that what she had come to?

'Don't overanalyse it,' he continued, leaning back in the chair, arms folded across his chest. 'We are not the guilty parties here.' Kate wondered to herself about that, about who decided innocence and guilt but decided to say nothing.

'Look what I found,' he said, lifting a book in his hands to show her the cover. A black and white photograph of Blackcliff Lighthouse taken in the late nineteenth century. 'Very impressive work,' he continued. 'You must miss him? You two must have been very close.'

'I do, and we were,' said Kate, but she offered no more. She didn't know this man well enough to allow him anywhere near the safeguarded memories of her father. Król muttered something she couldn't make out and dropped the book on the table. Kate wondered what else he had been snooping through while she slept.

'So, what now?' she asked.

'Are you going to leave Peter?'

'I'm not sure. I think so, but it's not easy. What difference does it make? We can't keep doing this. I told you before. There is no *us*.'

'I'm offended, Kate,' Król replied, but he didn't look offended at all. A smile momentarily crossed his lips. Briefly, she felt the urge to cross the room and slap his face. Was it trouble he was after? A confrontation with Peter?

He lifted the letters in his hands. 'Did you read them all?' he asked.

Kate didn't answer the question. Of course, she'd read them all.

'Your wife, can you make it up with her? Do you want to?' Kate asked him.

'No, there's no way back,' he said, and in his face, she saw an expression of pained finality that sealed his words. He bent down and reached into the holdall, which sat by his feet.

'Here, Kate,' he said, holding aloft a cream-coloured envelope. 'This is why I came. Peter's final letter to my wife. You should have it, not me.'

Kate gasped. Jesus, there was yet another one. Her face flushed hot. She couldn't take any more of these repulsive notes.

'I'm sorry, I didn't want you to have to see it,' Król said quietly. He took a sheet of paper from the envelope, which he unfolded and held aloft. He began to read.

I promise with all of my heart that I love you and that I am only yours. I will leave my wife, I promise. It will be just us two. We can start our own family.

Kate felt like retching. She placed an involuntary hand over her tummy. She thought she was done with these horrible letters and their words of lust and betrayal. 'You shouldn't have had to hear that, Kate, but this is who Peter is. This is the man you are married to.' Król pushed the note in front of her. Kate lifted the handwritten note and read it, tears falling from her eyes as she did. She tossed it back on the table.

'So when will Peter be home?' he asked her.

'In a few hours,' said Kate, but she wasn't really listening to him, her mind fleeing in all directions.

'Maybe I should wait for him at the bridge, hail him to a stop and then drive him and his Range Rover into the water. He'd freeze in minutes. Everybody would blame the storm,' said Król, grinning. 'What do you think? Everyone wins.'

'This isn't a joke!' Kate shouted aloud. 'None of this is funny.'

'I'm sorry,' he replied with exaggeration. Yet, something he had said had jarred with her. Maybe it was nothing. 'How do you know Peter drives a Range Rover?' she asked.

Król looked at her, still grinning. 'Oh, I just guessed he would. Peter likes things big and bold; he's not exactly the subtle type, is he?' he said, raising one eyebrow in an arch. 'Am I wrong?'

Kate said nothing.

A serious expression returned to Król's face. 'Do you want me to stay here until he arrives? Sort this out together.'

'No! No. You must be crazy,' said Kate with a wave of her hand, 'I don't need any help dealing with my husband.'

'Okay, okay, don't worry, I just thought... I'll leave soon,' replied Król.

But Kate was worried. The sooner this whole sordid business was over, the better. Even her daughter had sensed that her marriage was failing. Why had she hung on this long? Somehow, it had felt like if she ended it, all structure, everything she had worked for, would collapse. So, she'd kept convincing herself that all marriages floundered on the rocks now and again, that she should keep going, they could work it out. She'd done everything for Amy's sake, hadn't she? Or was that just a convenient righteousness to hide behind? *I did it for the kids* – kid, in her case. No second child was offered to her. Kate suddenly felt quite frail and useless. She wasn't prepared for this ugliness to take root here, inside her home.

8:20p.m.

It was long after eight by the time Dan pulled into the station. He'd checked on as many of the old and vulnerable as was possible. Most had family keeping tabs on them, but some had nobody. It wasn't his job, per se, but then again, ultimately, he was here to help. That's how he'd always seen it. All he could do now was hope that the impending storm showed a little mercy. He was hardly through the station door before Sully was whingeing aloud.

'You'd think they'd call a bloody truce up at the power plant. Who the hell goes on strike in weather like this?'

Dan walked over to the coffee dock and filled himself a cup of black porter that a mouse could trot on.

'That idiot Edwards can't control them. They're out on the road blocking the traffic. He can't budge them. It's dangerous enough out there without these loonies trying to get themselves run over,' continued the chief.

Dan sat back at his desk. He opened his inbox and began to check his emails. Sully was now on the radio barking out orders to Edwards. Whatever the young Garda was saying in reply seemed only to make Sully angrier and louder. Dan silently conceded that Sully had a point about one thing: this was the worst possible night to be causing a disruption.

'Bloody immigrants, the scourge of this town,' Sully snorted. It was a refrain Dan had heard more than once. He feared if he left Sully to deal with the strike, it would degenerate into an *us vs them* dispute, and all hell might break lose.

'I'm sure anybody who is determined enough to be on a picket in this weather must feel very strongly about their cause. They have rights. Their livelihoods are at stake,' said Dan, not because he thought Sully might listen but because it needed to be said, regardless.

'Rights my arse,' beefed Sully. 'I'm heading up there soon. I'll give them rights. They either go home or spend a night in that cell back there. That's their choice.' It seemed clear to Dan that Sully was simmering for a fight, but what more could he do? There was no stopping a bull at full steam.

'I'll drop by and help after my last calls,' Dan offered, but Sully wasn't listening anymore. Dan glanced at his phone. Grace still hadn't called him back. Maybe some of the phone networks were down, and his messages and calls had been lost to the maelstrom. The desk phone rang. Dan answered. It was the ElderCare Alerts Scheme. Dan listened to the anxious voice on the other end. He placed the receiver down, grabbed his car keys and jumped up from his seat. 'It's Bobby Kirwan,' he mouthed to Sully. 'He's triggered his distress alarm, muttering something about a fall.'

8:25p.m.

Król turned the crown on his watch. He hadn't noticed how often he played with it until Kate pointed it out. A poker tell. It didn't matter. He'd be laying all his cards on the table soon enough. He liked Kate. She had character, poise, and beauty, too. She listened, and she observed. It had felt natural to become one with her; it had also served his purpose. Oddly, though, it nagged at him that somehow it was a betrayal. Yet, whom could he betray now? He'd never met Peter, but few in Blackcliff had good words for him. Big shot. Arrogant. Ignorant. Poor choice, Kate. Beware the road's fork. We must travel the paths we choose.

'Can I use your phone, please?' she asked him.

'Do you still love your husband?' he asked abruptly, ignoring her request.

'I really need to use your phone,' she demanded.

'OK, but answer my question first,' he replied.

'The truth? No, I don't think I love my husband. I don't think I've loved him for quite some time.' There, it was out. Her whole body seemed to exhale deeply. Kate wept gently into the vacuum that followed her admission. She'd declared it unequivocally and out loud, and nothing had happened. The walls hadn't started to crumble. The lighthouse tower hadn't toppled into the sea. The earth kept on spinning, and outside, the snow kept on falling.

'The phone?'

'Are you the same person you were when you were younger?' he asked her.

'Can I just have the bloody phone?' said Kate irately. His charms were wearing thin, it seemed. It didn't bother him.

'Yes, in a moment,' he replied. 'Are you,' he persevered, 'the same?' He took his phone from his pocket to placate her.

'Jesus, alright, I suppose I am,' Kate replied, 'I haven't thought about it much.' He could see the doubt in her eyes as she considered his question.

'Have you heard of the *Ship of Theseus*?' he asked.

Kate said nothing.

'Theseus was a legendary Greek hero. After he died, his ship was preserved in the bay in his honour. Over time, it fell apart. Oars were lost, and the timber rotted. Yet all the while, the locals repaired it bit by bit until, eventually, everything original had been replaced. Then they asked, "Was it still the *Ship of Theseus*, or had it become something new?" He paused for a moment, then asked, 'Do you see the dilemma?' He handed his mobile phone to her.

'I'm like that,' he said. 'So much has changed, I can't work out which bits are me and which aren't.'

8:30p.m.

Dan darted to the police car, zapping the lock as he ran. The tyre chains bit into the snow as he accelerated out of the parking lot. The radio crackled into life.

'No news from Kirwan's. Nobody answering the phone,' said Sully.

'Okay,' replied Dan, 'I'll call it in when I get there. Get Dr Hanrahan on the end of a line. We may need him.'

'Okay, we'll have him on standby.'

Dan pressed the pedal to the floor. Bobby Kirwan was one of Blackcliff's characters. Ninety-one years old, yet he hardly looked a day over seventy. He'd drunk whiskey and smoked cigarettes all his life, and he'd swear to anybody who'd listen that the combination had preserved him. Maybe it had. Only since he'd entered his nineties did he seem to be slowing. Bobby had seen some things in his time, and whenever Dan could, he'd visit and let the old man regale him with stories of the bygone days. Bobby's father had fought in the civil war. Bobby himself had fought in the Second World War with the Irish Fusiliers. He'd even survived Dunkirk.

A few years back, he'd been attacked in his own home. Two men had tied him up, beaten him, and then defecated in his kitchen before leaving empty-handed. Bobby had steadfastly refused to tell them where his money was hidden. He said he had none, that he'd drunk it all. He'd lied. Many would have withered after that, but Bobby didn't let it beat him. He soldiered on, attending book clubs, bingo, seniors' dances; you organised it, and Bobby was there.

These days, he had a panic button that linked him to the Elder Care Alerts Scheme. Dan had organised a fundraiser that assured all the town's older citizens were connected. A few local businesses had chipped in, and Dan was proud that it provided peace of mind to those who needed it most.

Dan swerved the car into Bobby's driveway and broke

hard. He cut the engine and jumped out. He ran across Bobby's snow-covered lawn to the porch. Bobby had no doorbell, so Dan banged hard on the wooden door with his fist.

'Bobby, Bobby!' he shouted.

Again, he banged on the door. No answer.

The phone started to ring inside the house. Thankfully, Bobby hadn't closed the curtains, and Dan could see clearly into the well-lit sitting room. The TV was playing some sitcom. A plate of food lay on the coffee table. Dan's radio crackled again.

'Still no answer, Dan,' said Sully.

'I know,' said Dan. 'I'm outside, and I can hear the phone ringing out. I'm going to go around back.'

Dan made his way around the side of the property. A six-foot-high gate leading to the backyard was locked. He turned a waste bin onto its side and, carefully balancing on top, he managed to haul himself up onto the wooden gate until his legs straddled both sides. He swung his right leg over and landed on the soft snow on the other side. Dan could see footprints leading from the back door across the yard towards a barn. He quickly followed the steps. At the open metal door, Bobby Kirwan's body lay prone on the ground. Dan crouched down by his side. His face was scratched and bloodied. Bobby's cat, Mussolini, appeared from nowhere, leaping onto an oil barrel near the body.

'Bobby, Bobby, can you hear me?' Dan asked.

Dan bent low to check for breath from the old man's lips. The lightest wisps of exhalation rose on the frozen air. *Thank God*, thought Dan. *Bobby was alive.* Still, the old man looked terrible. His nose was red from the exposure, and his ears and face were freezing to the touch. Thankfully, he wore a large overcoat and a woollen hat. They'd probably saved his life. It was now nearly twenty minutes since he'd activated his buzzer. That was an eternity in these conditions. Mussolini looked on from atop the rusty barrel. Was it the cat that Bobby came out after? Bobby did love that cat. The little dictator was probably his closest companion on the planet.

Dan gazed past the cat to a car that was parked up in the rear of the barn. Something about the beat-up vehicle nagged at his mind, but he couldn't figure out what. Dan pulled out his phone and called the station.

'What's happening, Dan?' asked Sully.

'I've got Bobby. He must have fallen when he went outside,' said Dan. 'I'll call Hanrahan so he can tell me what to do.' Dan hung up. Bobby appeared to be drifting in and out of consciousness, but most importantly, his breath still came. A trickle of red stained the snow beneath his head. The old man moved just a little, and he mumbled something unintelligible. 'It's okay, Bobby. I'm going to get you help,' said Dan, not knowing if Bobby could understand what he was saying. Dan dialled Dr Hanrahan, who answered immediately.

'What's the situation, Dan?' asked the doctor.

'Bobby's fallen outside. He's been exposed to the cold for, I'm guessing, twenty minutes or so. He looks and feels frozen, but he's alive. I can see a head injury, an open gash. He can't seem to move.'

'Okay, Dan. I am home now. It would take me nearly an hour to get there. We may not have enough time. Can you get him to the hospital? I've already checked with Ennis, and all their ambulances are on the road. You'll have to drive him there. Can you?'

'Yeah, sure,' Dan replied.

'Good, good. Lie him on the back seat. Wrap him in a blanket. Cover the wound if it's still bleeding. Keep him as warm as you can. I'll ring ahead. They'll be waiting for your arrival.'

'Okay, Doc, keep the phone on.'

'Of course, and good luck.'

'Thanks,' said Dan and hung up.

Dan ran back to the house. He made his way quickly through the rooms. There was no sign of any intruder. Everything seemed pretty much as Dan had seen on previous visits. He switched off the gas fire in the sitting room and checked that the cooker was off in the kitchen. Dan scooped a duvet from the bedroom and made his way back to the door. A set of keys sat on the hall table. Dan unlocked the front door, carried the duvet to the police car, and laid it over the back seat. He returned quickly through the house and out to the barn where Bobby still lay. Carefully, he hooked an arm around Bobby's neck and slowly raised the frail yet surprisingly heavy frame up and over his shoulder.

'Hold on, Bobby,' Dan said aloud. 'Help is on the way.'

Dan carried the old man through the house and out to the police car, where he positioned him gently onto the back seat. Thankfully, the wound on Bobby's head had stopped bleeding. Bobby grunted at Dan, but, again, no discernible words came. Dan draped the rest of the duvet over him and then trotted quickly back to Bobby's front door and pulled it closed. Back in the car, he turned up the heat and pulled speedily out of the driveway, switching the police radio on as he did.

'I have Bobby. We're on our way to Ennis Hospital. Hanrahan can't make it. He called it in. Will you make sure they are expecting us?'

'Will do, Dan, Godspeed,' replied Sully.

Dan flicked the beams and put his foot to the floor.

8:45p.m.

Kate quickly tapped in the digits of Grace's number and held Król's phone to her ear, hoping at last to talk to her baby. 'Christ,' she exclaimed in exasperation, 'it just rings out. What is happening with the phones today?' She killed the call and went to hand the mobile back, but as she did, the screensaver changed. She froze momentarily, then gathered herself and glanced up at Król. He took the phone from her, peering at the image as he did. A gravestone. Three names etched in granite. Kate hadn't seen it long enough to discern any details. Król said nothing as he stared into her eyes. An uneasy feeling was settling in Kate's stomach. What did she truly know of this man? He was, to all intents, a stranger. She'd been told fragments of his story, but there was so much she didn't know. Storm or no storm, he needed to go, and soon.

'I'm not feeling well. I'll be back in a few minutes,' said Kate as she walked hurriedly from the kitchen. She made her way to the boiler room. She lifted Król's black jacket from the warm pipes. The house was eerily quiet but for her heavy breathing. Opening the coat, she began to search the pockets. She dug out a folded sheet of white paper. It was a page from a notepad headed the Clare County Hotel, the same hotel that she had visited him at. Kate gasped aloud as she recognised a handwritten address on the paper. 118b Rue Montoyer was Peter's apartment in Brussels. This mess was descending into madness. She put the paper back and lifted the coat, gloves and hat. She felt a bulge in one of the coat pockets. Kate reached in and fished out an empty plastic vial with a pink lid. She opened the lid and sniffed. It was a strange smell. Sweet but acrid, too. What on earth was that? Medication would explain her visitor's erratic behaviour. She closed the lid and put the small bottle back into the pocket.

'All okay, Kate?' came Król's voice from behind her.

Kate swivelled in shock, closing the jacket as she did.

Król stood at the door, a wry smile creasing his face.

'God, you frightened me,' she said.

She steadied herself and handed Król's clothing to him.

'These are dry. It's best you go now,' she said sternly.

Król nodded his head slowly.

'It's time to be honest with you, Kate' he replied.

'What do you mean?' asked Kate.

'I came here to confront Peter. I have no intention of leaving until he comes home and we sort it out, man to man.'

Kate could feel the blood draining from her body. She was shocked to see excitement in Król's eyes as he spoke. Did every man have a want for damage? They were like toddlers, always needing to tear everything down. Never the smart way out.

'No way,' Kate said, 'not a chance. That's crazy! It's the absolute wrong way to deal with this.'

'It's the only way, Kate.'

'Well then, if you insist on staying, I'll go. I'm not waiting here to watch you and my husband rutting your fucking antlers.' Kate walked past him and then turned her head and glared back.

'What do you think you'll get? An apology? I'm sorry for screwing your wife. What difference will it make?'

'Closure,' Król replied after a pause. 'That's what they call it. Closure.'

'Fuck closure!' Kate spat angrily. 'I'm not staying for these boys' games. I'll be no part of it.'

'But you are part of it, Kate, very much part of it.'

'Let's see about that,' roared Kate as she marched in fury up the stairs.

9:00p.m.

Kate stood, eyes closed, back tight against the locked bedroom door, her heart pounding uncomfortably in her chest. She'd allowed herself to wallow in her own misery. She'd allowed this man to take her. And now it wasn't some random country hotel; this was her home. She hardly knew him. That's what a marriage of neglect did to you. It allowed weakness and doubt to seep into your pores, corroding clarity and clouding better judgement. What was that screensaver? She hadn't had time to make out the names, but she was sure they were Polish. Why did he have Peter's address in Brussels? Kate felt more vulnerable now than she'd ever felt in her whole life.

Kate crossed to the table and opened her laptop. If the

phone line was dead, the Wi-Fi no doubt was, too. She tried anyway. No connection. She cursed silently under her breath. Then she remembered the old dial-up dongle they'd used before broadband was rolled out in the county. She searched frantically in the desk drawers until she spotted it under a mess of old cables. Thank God.

Kate inserted the dongle into the USB slot and dialled up the connection. The blue indicator light flickered, which at least was a sign of life. The connection seemed to take forever, but at last, it bit, and immediately, Kate felt her spirits lift. She clicked into her email account and waited for it to load. It seemed to take an eternity. She breathed a deep sigh of relief when it finally opened and updated. She clicked on *new message* and frantically started to type.

Hi Grace, missed your call. I can't find my mobile, and there's a problem with the landlines, I think. Sorry for the late contact. Hope all is OK with u guys and that Amy is being good and behaving herself. Tell her I love her. Email me please when you get this, Tks Kate.

She pressed send and then hurriedly began typing an email to Peter.

There's a man here in our house. You had an affair with his wife!!! He won't leave. I think he's looking for trouble. Stay away. I'm going to try to hike to Grace's. What an absolute fucking disaster. Thanks for destroying my life!

Finally, she wasn't fully sure why, but Kate typed in D, and Dan Brady's email address popped up. She assumed he still used it. Was she overreacting? Probably, but still, a nagging hunch made her write.

Hi Dan, a man arrived uninvited at the lighthouse today. I know him, but not very well. He was stranded, so I let him in. Now he won't leave. I'm worried. All the phone lines are down, and my mobile is missing. Peter is still due to come home late. I'm going to try to make it to Grace's on foot. Not sure why I am sending this, but just in case. Tks always, Kate.

Kate clicked the send button for the third time. She went to the bed and hauled out a plastic storage box from underneath. On top sat a travel guide for Switzerland. An assortment of yellowing, tattered tickets, receipts, menus and photos were lodged between its pages. Evidence of happier times. She hauled out her snow boots and then her weatherproofs. Behind the box, lying directly on the floor, were two ski poles, which she grabbed too.

She squeezed into the waterproof pants and laced up the snow boots. In the wardrobe, she found a heavy knitted jumper, put it on over her clothes and then pulled on a hiking jacket. She stuffed a hat and some gloves into the pockets. From the drawer beside her bed, she lifted a torch and, beside it, a set of fresh batteries. Kate never left a torch with the batteries inside weeping and corroding. She marvelled at her own efficiency.

Kate crossed to the door and turned the key. Silence. Had he gone? She stepped quietly onto the landing. Down the carpeted stairs. No creaks despite the clunky snow boots. She looked left down the corridor to the kitchen. Nothing. She slowly descended the final few steps. Ten feet to her right was the back door.

She inched her way cautiously and quietly towards it, but then, behind her, his voice stopped her in her tracks. 'Leaving me alone?'

She turned and faced Król. He stood silhouetted in the dark hallway, the light of the kitchen behind him.

'I can't stay here if you won't go. None of this is my doing. You said it yourself.'

'Nor mine, Kate,' he replied, shaking his head slowly.

'Please, before you go, I need to show you just one final thing,' he said, gesturing for her to follow him into the kitchen.

Kate looked at him warily. She'd seen enough already, too much.

9:10p.m.

Król stood by the fireplace, staring into the framed photograph on the mantelpiece. It was Kate's favourite picture in all the world. Her father, Amy, and her sailing on the Shannon. Amy at the wheel of the cruiser, her grandfather's hands on her shoulders. Kate with her arm around her dad. She could picture the gentle wake as the boat eased its way through the glassy water, the golden summer sun high in the sky above them.

Król slowly traced his finger down the picture along the outline of Amy's face. Kate felt light-headed, unable to breathe, the earth's spin grinding to a halt. She wanted to say something. *What? Don't touch my daughter?* Amy smiled back at her innocently. Unaware that this strange man was in their home. Unaware that the thing she called family was disintegrating. Unaware that her mother's uneasiness was mounting and mounting. Then Król lifted his hand and moved away from the picture and across the room. Once more, the world began to revolve, and air entered Kate's lungs. She needed to end this.

'So, what is it you want to show me?' she pressed him, her voice as stern and commanding as she could manage.

'You can't go, Kate. I need you. It will be you who makes the final decision when the time comes. Who lives and who dies.'

'What the hell are you talking about?' she cried incredulously.

Król dug a pink mobile phone from his pocket. Kate watched on as he fiddled with the device for a moment. They both lifted their eyes in unison as suddenly a phone began ringing noisily in the kitchen. Kate ran through the open doors and scanned the room. There, where it hadn't been before, lay her phone vibrating on the kitchen table. She raced to it and picked it up. Grace's name flashed on the buzzing screen. Kate answered.

A man's voice spoke. His voice. Her heart stopped beating, and she froze, suspended in an eternal second of cruel, deadly knowledge. The blood drained from her face as she listened.

'Hi Kate, at last, you've found your phone,' said Król.

Kate walked slowly back into the dining room, her legs shaky beneath her. There he stood, waiting for her, talking into Grace's phone, talking to her.

'Unfortunately, Grace cannot be with us. She sends her best wishes,' he said and ended the call. Kate reached out to a narrow table along the wall to steady herself. It felt like her heart might explode at any moment. What was happening? How did this man know Grace? How on earth did he have Grace's phone? How did Kate's missing phone just suddenly turn up?

'I have your daughter, Amy,' said Król. 'Grace and Niamh too. Amy is alive and well, for now, in a location that only I know. Do exactly as I say, you get her back safely,' he continued. 'Don't, you will never see her again.'

Kate could hardly process what she had just heard. None of it made sense. Rage boiled over. She took a few steps forward and slapped Król as hard as she could in the face. Her hand recoiled in pain. She lifted it to repeat the blow, but he snatched hold of her wrist before she could strike.

'That's allowed, Kate, but enough. Now we work together. You help me, I help you.'

Kate grappled to free her hand, but she was no match for his iron grip. When her fury subsided a little, and she stopped resisting, he eased his grip and let go of her wrist. He walked into the kitchen with Kate hurrying after him. He crossed to the drinks cabinet and lifted a bottle of Middleton from the shelf. He proceeded to pour himself a large measure and then turned to her, bottle raised. 'Whiskey?'

'What the hell is going on?' Kate screamed in fury. Król ignored her and downed his whiskey in one gulp.

'What do you mean you have my daughter? Where is she?' Kate roared aloud. 'Why? What have you done to her?'

'All in good time,' Król retorted calmly.

'Now, listen and do as I say. Ring Peter and tell him

that I am here waiting for him. Tell him what I just told you and tell him to hurry on home like a good boy. There is a bomb, it will detonate at 2:00a.m.'

'A bomb!?' screamed Kate. 'Oh my God, are you crazy?'

'Just tell him what I said. No police, or I blow them up! We sort this out tonight ourselves.'

Tears tumbled down Kate's cheeks. Her body trembled in violent convulsions. It was as if every shred and fibre of her being was being ripped asunder.

The phone nearly fell from her quivering hands as she made the call.

'There's no answer,' she said.

'Leave a message, and then give your phone back to me,' Król instructed, as he poured himself another shot.

VIII

Waves of black moved back and forth between the kitchen, sitting room and back garden. I wore brown, his favourite woolly jumper. I floated through the crowd, speaking to faces I recognised. I wanted to do the right thing as the host if that was what I was. I wanted to represent him, his essence, what he was. What was that? A man who read books, who wrote a book, who lectured from books. The man who spoke to me about stars, planets and black holes. About Boltzmann, Einstein and Schrödinger. About life and love and loss. About the woman I never met. The woman he never replaced. The man who gave himself to me alone.

In truth, I felt embarrassed to be the centre of attention. I had no idea what to do or say. I was just nineteen, still a boy becoming a man. My father's writing desk was pushed back against the wall. I could still hear the sound of that typewriter clacking me lowly to sleep. It was gone, and in its place, large pots of tea and coffee bookended rows of cups and saucers. There was wine and liquor for those who needed something stronger. His fellow professors nodded respectfully at me. Some touched his familiar jumper as I passed, smiled, and offered their condolences. Faces bore pained looks and strained expressions to show that the wearers understood and shared my loss. Occasionally, a hushed apologetic laugh would be heard over the murmuring din of reverent voices. His closest colleagues seemed particularly shocked by his premature passing. None of them had seen it coming, nor had I. A heart attack at fifty-two made no sense.

She'd been observing me, listening as I chatted with the mourners. She wore an elegant knee-length black dress topped by a black cardigan. Demure, respectful. I guessed early forties. It was hard to tell; her eyes were a little red and puffy from crying. For a second or two, we caught each other's gaze, and then she moved towards me. She offered her hand and introduced herself as Helen. 'Your father always spoke so lovingly of you. It is so nice to meet you at last. You look like him, just younger,' she said. I was surprised to hear this. I'd never noticed, and nobody had ever remarked.

I learned that she and my father had collaborated on different projects. She was a horologist, an expert in the measurement of time. Like many horologists, she was also a watchmaker. From the Egyptians with their obelisks and shadows, the Greeks and their sundials all the way to Galileo's pendulum clock, she explained how she'd helped my father with research for his book. As I listened, I realised how easy it would have been for my father to like this woman. For no reason, I opened my pocket watch and began to fiddle with it. Her eyes lit up. 'I restored that for *him,' she exclaimed excitedly. 'He wanted a keepsake that he could pass on to you, something special and unique. It's from Toruń in Poland, where Copernicus was born. It's very old. Can I look at it again?' she asked. I handed it to her, and she took hold of it softly and reverentially within her cupped hand. 'We repaired it as best we could, modified it where needed,' she said. 'He had the astral map etched on the back from Copernicus's illustration of the orbiting planets. I know he would be so proud to see you holding it now.' I remember crying, and she hugged me, and I hugged her in return. We held each other for what seemed an eternity, and then she left, and I never saw her again.*

9:20p.m.

Peter breathed deep the chill air as he walked from the terminal building into the frosty night. The bracing cold was a relief after the cloying, claustrophobic somnolence of the flight. He checked his phone. He had missed a call from Kate. The screen told him that twenty-one new emails had arrived since he had taken off. No let-up, not even in this weather. He lit a cigarette and slowly exhaled as he made his way gingerly through the snow to his Range Rover in the nearby surface car park.

After five minutes of clearing snow and scraping ice, Peter finally sat in the vehicle. He opened his email inbox and scanned the names of the senders. Most were work matters that could wait till the morning. Then he noticed one from Kate, which was odd. She preferred to text. He read the message. Head spinning, heart racing, he read the email again. Peter hurriedly checked his voice messages to see if she'd left a message. A tsunami of panic washed over him as he listened to his wife's alarmed voice.

Peter clambered out of the vehicle and paced back and forth frantically, not sure of what to do next. The last passengers from his flight streamed from the terminal. Some made their way to empty snow-covered cars while others were greeted by loved ones and a lift home. He wished for the first time that he could be one of those passengers and not Peter Kavanagh. He began to cry. The portly woman and her daughter from the flight passed near him, and both shot him dagger stares. Another passing woman enquired if he was okay. Peter had no capacity to respond. She asked again, and whatever he said to her made her trudge away, shaking her head. The 4x4's exhaust fumes had formed a cloud in the dense air. Peter sat back into the car, his mind capsizing beneath the weight of a million horrible thoughts.

Peter reread Kate's email. A stranger was at the lighthouse. No mention of Amy. He listened again to Kate's tear-choked voice as she faltered over the words. '*There is a man here in our house. He knows you. You had an affair with his wife. He says he has taken Amy. She's hidden somewhere. There's a bomb that will go off at 2:00a.m. Get home quick! If we do what he wants, we get Amy back. No police, Peter. Do you hear me, Peter, don't get smart! No police! Otherwise, he says we will never see her again.*'

He called Kate, but there was no answer. Peter had never felt so scared. How could this be happening? None of it made sense. Through the tears and the coiled anger, Kate had spoken with a focus and clarity that he knew to respect. This was real. She'd left no room for second-guessing. It felt like some malevolent force was squeezing his heart and that, at any moment, it would just stop.

He pulled out of the parking lot and made for the exit road. The M18 should be manageable as far as Ennis, he hoped, it was a main artery. From Ennis to Blackcliff would be treacherous. He fumbled a text to Kate:

> Landed. Got your message. I'm on the way.

9:20p.m.

Król poured another shot, downed it in one gulp and then filled another. When times were good, he'd quit the bottle and took back control. He'd wanted to, for his wife. He never needed it when he had her beside him. God, how he had loved her. Now, there was no reason for restraint, not tonight. Wasn't that it? If we knew that nothing really mattered, that there were no repercussions, wouldn't that change everything? Then we'd do anything, be anything. Unfettered freedom. Anarchy. Humanity thrived for structure and meaning, for the application of order to inherent disorder, but there was the fallacy. We were always doomed to failure. Eventually, everything broke down – the entropic destruction to our quantum state.

Kate was quiet, but he could nearly taste the revulsion in her stare. She'd asked him question after question, screaming and roaring as she did. Then she'd tried the softly, softly approach. It hurt him, it did, but he refused to engage, not until Peter arrived. He'd already told her what she needed to know. Amy was alive, and she was with Grace and Niamh. Play by the rules, and you get her back. Don't, and the bomb detonates at 2:00a.m. He could tell that just sitting and waiting was driving her crazy, but Kate was smart; she knew she had no other choice. Reluctantly she'd changed back out of her snow gear. Now she was whispering to herself, head lowered in her hands.

'What's that?' he asked.

'I'm praying,' she replied barely audibly.

He shook his head. 'Kate, I thought you were smarter.'

She ignored him and kept whispering her useless prayers. Did she really think someone or something was listening? 'Listen to me, Kate, your God sacrificed his only son. Allowed him to die nailed to a cross. That's a bit fucked up, isn't it? Do you really think he's about to help you or Amy?'

'I think you'll find that it was Jesus who sacrificed himself for mankind,' Kate replied angrily.

Król started to speak but paused to consider her words.

'Fair point, Kate, fair point. That was heroic, noble. To sacrifice your life for others. Can you do that? Give your life. Or Peter's? For Amy's, let's say.'

Kate's face paled. If she hadn't known before, he could see that she did now. The realisation: this nightmare was real. Then came hatred, her eyes blazing savagely.

'This is what I'll do, you sick fucker. I'll rip you apart and leave you for dead if you've harmed even one hair on my child's head.'

Król laughed and clapped his hands. 'Good, that is what I want to hear. Keep that anger, Kate. It might prove useful.'

He felt sorry for her despite her brave words. She was struggling to hold it together. He could nearly hear her mind whirring, trying to work it all out. She was used to making things right, but that wasn't going to work this time. It was he who was in control. This was his stage.

Earlier, watching Grace and the two children, the light receding from their eyes as their lids grew numb and heavy, he had felt it, the transformation. He had ascended into this new dimension, and whatever had existed before, whatever he had been, it was gone. And that was okay. What else could he do? He, too, knew sacrifice and its price. He owed them – the dead.

9:30p.m.

More than once, the police car had nearly slid sideways off the road. Dan was driving too fast, but what choice did he have? Now and then, Bobby groaned, but for the most part, he seemed to be out cold. Dan breathed a huge sigh of relief when they passed the sign for Ennis Hospital. The porters were waiting at the entrance to the Emergency Department when they arrived. Without delay, they whisked Bobby away into the heart of the hospital. Dan waited anxiously for an update, and when it came, it was good news. Bobby's vital signs had improved. He had some frostbite, but the headwound wasn't too serious. It had been stitched and would heal. There didn't seem to be any cognitive issues, and a full recovery was expected. They would keep him in for a few days to build his strength and monitor his progress. He'd spoken, too. It transpired that he'd been trying to cajole Mussolini to come back inside as the cat flap had frozen shut. The nurse assured Dan that he would be well looked after and that she'd keep him updated.

Dan shuffled back out into the cold night, glad to leave the overcrowded Accident and Emergency Department behind. He felt good, euphoric even. He thought of Bobby and Mussolini, and he grinned. He thought of Grace, and he felt that warm rush again. He sat into his car, placed Bobby's house keys into the glove compartment and then drove carefully out of the hospital parking bay. The streets around Ennis were busier than Blackcliff, and traffic was backed up. Red lights and exhaust fumes hung in the cold air. Dan drove slowly over the bridge by the mill and proceeded past the myriad of hotels and shops until he'd left the town behind. At the ring road roundabout, he took the exit for the West and Blackcliff.

The cars faded one by one until only Dan's remained. Lost in thought, he cruised through the deserted, dreamlike landscape. He called Grace's mobile. Still no answer. It was very unlike Grace not to answer. Had he said something wrong to her? Had he offended her? He couldn't think what it had been, but it wouldn't be the first time he'd put his foot in it without even knowing. Anyway, he'd be home soon, and he'd make it all good. Suddenly, it struck him. He knew why the parked-up car in Bobby's barn had bothered him. He could see the vehicle again in his mind. A Corolla. It was dark, but he felt sure it had been blue. It must be the missing car stolen by their mystery hotel guest, Król. On Dan drove, his mind now a swirl of unanswered questions. First, he'd check on the strike at the power plant, and then he'd return to Bobby's to take a closer look at the Corolla. Why had it been abandoned there, and where was its driver, Mr Król?

10:00p.m.

Amy had nearly been lost before leaving the shelter of her womb. With the pregnancy at full term, the umbilical cord had positioned itself below and around the foetus. Not only was it blocking the baby's exit, but the child was also losing oxygen. Continued loss would lead to irreparable lung or brain damage. The doctors had to act quickly. Two hours later, Amy entered the world, surgically extracted from her mother's splayed form. The procedure floored Kate, and she only met her daughter for the first time days later. When she did, she was startled to see that her little girl was all but hidden beneath a mass of snaking tubes and sensors. A ventilator assisted her weak lungs until they grew stronger. Kate couldn't even hold her. They touched through an opening in the glass incubation box, Amy's whole hand grasping her mother's smallest digit. After years of trying, her hopes often hanging threadbare, Kate's dream had come true.

Since then, with Peter away so often, she and Amy were like two peas in a pod. As close as a mother and daughter could be. Kate had wanted more children – two, three, maybe even four. Amy would want siblings too, a family to share her life with, to be there when her parents were old or gone. But Peter refused. He seemed to be missing the parenting gene. Time and again, he obstinately snubbed any discussion on the matter. Kate had considered secretly ditching her birth-control pills, but she knew that would result in the end of their relationship, and she hadn't wanted to pay that price, not for her or Amy's sake. As time passed, she began to feel differently about another baby. She would never admit it, but innately, she knew that she didn't want to carry another child of Peter's. And then she'd had to read how her husband was offering his future children to a new lover. All the while placing her Amy in peril. The storm had blown a reaper to her door, and he threatened the one thing she lived for, the one thing she would kill for.

10:05p.m.

Peter held the cold metal of the diesel pump in his gloved hand. His teeth clattered involuntarily. Shock and fear had thinned his blood to water. Snowflakes fell in swirling descents over the deserted forecourt. He'd passed Ennis and was now on the road to Blackcliff. He'd driven this road a thousand times, but as he looked around, nothing appeared familiar. He could be in the middle of anywhere or nowhere. Any recognisable features were hidden under a blanket of white. The road ahead was a neon strip that narrowed and arced in a bend through an overhang of luminous white tree limbs until all was smothered by the black horizon.

Peter shuddered at the prospect of what might face him at the lighthouse. He knew that from this moment forward, nothing would be as it was. This night would define the before and the after. Dread clung like a leaden veil. He couldn't explain it, but for some time, he had sensed a reckoning coming – an untouchable presence skulking in the gloom, waiting and waiting. And now, here it was. Fate? Karma? Whatever it was, he had failed to escape its clutches.

Peter replaced the pump and stared back from where he had come. There was nothing. Not a sign of life in this desolate limbo, this place caught between his past and his future. He trudged towards the door and entered the garage. An old man sat behind the counter. Empty rows and shelves suggested the garage sold fuel and not a whole lot else. It hadn't caught up with the new shiny multiples yet. By the appearance of the old man, he might not know they even exist. At least it was open. A calendar on the wall showed the wrong year. Another time. A better time.

'You look familiar,' said the old man. 'You local?'

'No,' said Peter.

'Hmmm, very familiar indeed,' the old man continued in a broad Clare accent. Wispy hair protruded from behind his ears. On top, there was none. His sagging face creased when he spoke, and his open mouth betrayed discoloured teeth. Laser eyes fixed on Peter, reading him. 'You know where you're headed?' asked the old man.

'Yes.'

'West?'

'Yes.'

'Well, okay. It's bad that way. I hope you make it. People will die tonight. Not a doubt about it,' the old man declared solemnly. 'In a storm like this, the weak get punished. The old, the stupid, the sick, it's nature's way.'

Peter was taking a strong dislike to this idiot. Was he senile? What did he know, sitting here, rotting away in this dump?

'Sure, sure, nature's way,' babbled the old man in his sing-song voice as he rang up the charges, all the while peering at Peter from over the rim of his spectacles. 'You may be going the wrong way, you know.'

'What makes you think that?' said Peter.

'The road west is snowed over. I'd say there's nothing good in that direction. If I were you, I'd turn myself around and go back to where you came from. Go east. Find a place to stay; start again tomorrow.'

Peter wanted to tell him to stick his advice where the sun didn't shine, but he hadn't the will. He felt beaten. Leaving enough money on the counter, he turned his back on the old man and made his way towards the exit.

'It was the last big storm we had here, you know. A man very like you came through. It was the dead of night. I think that's who I was remembering. I thought he was you for a minute, but that couldn't be. It's just that you looked similar. It was a long time ago. He insisted on going west. Big mistake. You know, somehow, it's like this all happened already, isn't that crazy? The mind. It plays tricks on you. I could have sworn it, though. I could have sworn it.'

'What happened to him?' Peter asked.

The old man was lost in thought, not listening.

'What happened to him?' Peter repeated, louder this time.

'Who?'

'The man in the storm.'

The old man gazed past Peter out to the snowfall, piecing together the memory as if somehow the traces of it still lived on outside in the gloaming. 'The car went into the river. They never did find him. Not a trace.' The old man shifted his weight and slid off the stool. Then he shuffled slowly to the rear of the station. Peter stared after him until he was gone.

He turned and left the garage. Walking to the rear, he opened the boot and groped around inside. He spotted Amy's bear – Buster – and lifted it out. Buster lived in Peter's 4x4, always there for her when they went on a drive. He held the bear to his face, smelt it, kissed it. He lifted a monkey wrench and closed the boot. Peter started the engine and steered gingerly onto the icy road, Buster and the monkey wrench next to him on the passenger seat. In the rear-view mirror, the garage lights faded until behind him lay only darkness.

IX

Sleep never came easy for me as a child. Back then, the psychiatrist suggested I might be of a nervous disposition, that I worried more than I should. What age was I? Thirteen, I think. My father whispered the word 'melancholic' as they discussed me. I didn't know for sure what it meant, but I remember liking the sound of it. Mel... an... cho... lic. It felt grown up, adult. I never saw myself as nervous or even melancholic, for that matter. It was more that I couldn't switch off. That's the problem when you have too much time on your hands: you can't silence the noise. The same thoughts come visiting, loops, playing continuously, over and over.

After he died, I fell very low. I would lie for days on my bed, unable to move. Once, he told me how stars die. When they become too dense, too heavy in mass, they pass a threshold, the Chandrasekhar Limit, I think it was called.

The stars can no longer bear their own weight, and they fall inwards in a violent explosion, a supernova. That was me. I was collapsing in on myself, imploding. My heavy head sinking into my body, pulling me down through the floor into the earth.

When I did rise, I drank a lot. Drugs, too. Ecstasy, speed, acid, anything really. The executors of my father's estate paid me a monthly stipend. We'd lived in one of the professor's lodges that overlooked the quadrangle. The university said I could stay until the start of the next academic year, then the new professor would move in and life would move on without us. Then, I received a phone call from the executors to go to Kraków, Poland. There, I would stay with my uncle Maciek. He and my father had co-owned some property holdings, which were now to be sold. My father had stipulated that I should travel and assist with the sale and that his share of the proceeds would be settled on me.

It's odd. I'd never considered Poland to be a part of me, nor me of it. Yet, as the aeroplane cut through those clouds, a peculiar sensation began to overwhelm me. The long-lost DNA of my grandparents and their grandparents and their grandparents before them somehow was awakening in my marrow.

10:20p.m.

Kate ran the cold tap in the kitchen sink and splashed water on her face. She gulped some of the liquid from her cupped hand. Her child, her only child, was in mortal danger, and she could do nothing to help her. Some things in this world you will never truly comprehend, not fully, not until they have happened to you. Only then do you realise that all the other stuff you've spent your days worrying about is nonsense. Nothing mattered now but Amy.

Kate couldn't help thinking the worst. She turned and squared Król dead in the eyes. 'How do I know that you've got... Amy?' she asked, barely able to say her daughter's name aloud. He gazed at her silently, contemplating a response. Then he spoke.

'I talked to Amy at the school the other day. She was in the yard playing. She remembered me from the beach. Mammy's friend she called me. Niamh was with her. They told me about the sleepover that was planned. Kids will tell you anything.'

Kate's chest tightened; the air was being squeezed from her lungs, burning its way up her trachea as it left her body. Król rose from the table and came towards her, reaching into his pocket as he did. He dug out a small object and handed it to Kate. She recognised it immediately, holding it in her hand like she would a rare and delicate flower – Amy's orange hairclip.

'Why, why?' Kate cried, the tears streaming down her face. Król walked back to the table.

'You know I'm not lying. We understand each other now,' he said.

'Don't fucking flatter yourself. You don't understand anything about me!' Kate shouted, wiping the tears from her eyes. Internally, she chided herself. It was time to wake the hell up. She needed to dispense with emotion, to be ice-cold and determined. She had to see this out and get her baby back. She had to win this game.

'Did… did you harm her?' she asked, the words struggling to leave her lips.

'No, no, that's not what this is,' Król replied immediately. His words sounded genuine, but what did she know? What did anybody know of another person and what they would or wouldn't do?

'Why did you take her?' she spluttered.

'I'm sorry, Kate, but when Peter arrives, you will understand,' said Król, holding his hands up in a request for her to stop, as if somehow that would appease her.

'I don't want to understand! I want to know where the hell my daughter is,' Kate shouted.

'They are safe, but nobody will find them without me. If you follow my rules, you will get your daughter back,' he said. 'Amy is alive.'

Again, for some bizarre reason, Kate believed him. She had no choice but to. It was only then that she thought of Grace and Niamh. They were suffering just as much as Amy. She had been consumed by her own loss and had spared no thought for the others. Thank God Grace was with the kids. Grace was a fighter, she would find a way.

10:45p.m.

'Welcome to Blackcliff,' announced the sign. Peter exhaled a long breath. It had been a hazardous journey, but somehow, he'd made it. His new four-wheel drive had barely clung to the road. He'd been fortunate that another driver, obviously as mad or as desperate as he, had driven the road not too long before him, leaving helpful tyre furrows to follow.

His mind raced, searching for solutions, reasons, and hope. Was this whole mess about money? It had to be; wasn't everything when it came down to it? If so, then how much? He had about twenty thousand euros in the safe at home and could probably muster that sum again within a day if given the chance. Would that be enough? Kate knew the code. Had she paid up already? He wiped the tears from his cheeks and wondered where his poor baby girl was. He'd kill anyone who harmed her, not casting a second thought.

The power plant loomed large to his right. At its gates, all manner of chaos seemed to be unfolding. A queue of three cars sat motionless ahead of him, dense exhaust fumes clouding above them. Further on, blue police lights illuminated the darkness. In this weather? At this time? 'For fuck's sake!' Peter swore aloud. He couldn't believe his eyes. He slowed to a halt behind the last car in line. A crowd was marching up and down, chanting slogans and lofting placards. Hot mist rose from the heads and bodies of the protesters.

Typical Blackcliff, he thought, *worst snowstorm in years, so let's call a strike, block the roads and cause anarchy in the middle of the night. And the Gardaí just sitting there, letting the whole thing happen, practically encouraging it.*

He spotted Dan Brady. Peter had no time for Dan. Not now, not back then. Dan was moving along the line of cars, talking to each driver. Behind him, Sergeant O'Sullivan was arguing with one of the protesters; both their faces snarled and agitated.

Fuck this. Peter wasn't stopping for anybody. He had no choice, not tonight. He turned the wheel, eased his foot down on the accelerator and steered his vehicle up the wrong side of the road. It was all or nothing now. If somebody stepped out, he wouldn't be able to stop in time. He moved steadily past the log-jammed cars and past Dan Brady, who was waving and calling for him to stop. Shit, he could hear Kate's voice warning him, 'No police!' He kept going, ignoring the cacophony of horns as he did. He steered past the stop sign, through an opening in the congregation of protesters and back into the correct road lane. In the rear-view mirror, he could see Dan gesticulating after him. 'Fuck you,' Peter mouthed and drove on faster towards town.

The Range Rover zoomed up Main Street and then out along the coast road. He continued over the wooden bridge, but soon, his journey came to an abrupt halt. At the base of Cliff Road, two large signs blocked further progress. ROAD CLOSED was announced in bold white letters on a red backdrop.

Peter parked into the side and climbed out. Quickly, he removed his suit jacket and pulled on his navy overcoat, black woollen hat and gloves. His polished brown Italian leather shoes were hardly the footwear for this trek, but what could he do? He grabbed the monkey wrench and slid it into his inner breast pocket. Then he began the slow ascent home. Nearly a foot of snow covered the narrow road. To the sides, it lay much deeper. Within fifty paces, his feet and socks were soaked. The bottom of his long overcoat hung heavy and sodden as it dragged through the drifts. The recent fall hadn't compacted, and the footing was soft and manageable. One foothold propelled him on to the next. It was an arduous climb, but the adrenalised mix of fear and anger drove him on.

Hollowed footprints were visible. He swallowed hard and followed in their wake. The wind cut sharp at his exposed face. He thought again of Amy. Was she alone? Was she cold? He vowed that if his family survived this night, he would change. He knew full well this was the clarity of the scoundrel, a 20-20 vision that always focused too late, but this time it would be different. It had to be. He owed it to Kate and Amy. If they'd have him.

10:50p.m.

Dan stared after the red tail lights of Peter Kavanagh's car until they were lost from sight. Dan must have been only minutes ahead of him on the road from Ennis. While he was glad to see that Peter had made it back to Blackcliff safely, that stunt he just pulled would have to be accounted for. On another night, he would have gone after him. Politician or not, everybody had to play by the same rules. He'd deal with Peter Kavanagh tomorrow. For now, this crowd had to be disbanded.

Dan trudged past a horde of protesters, acknowledging the faces he recognised as he went. Those who knew him greeted him in return. From the back came a heckle or two, but that was to be expected. These were good people stretched to breaking point. Dan reached Sully, who was locked in an animated discussion with the group's leader by the roadside. The striker was a Polish man named Czarek, Czarek was a foreman at the plant and one of the union representatives. Dan knew

170

him from the GAA club and had always held him in good regard.

'How goes the UN negotiations, Sully?' asked Dan, squeezing between the two of them.

'I've given one last warning,' Sully puffed. 'This mob needs to break up and go home.' Dan pretty much agreed with that, but he also knew that unless they could prove a disturbance of the peace, they had little authority. Without diplomacy, barking orders wouldn't work.

'Czarek, good to see you,' said Dan, turning to the strike leader and shaking his hand. 'How are you holding up in this weather? How are Agnes and the kids?'

'We are good, Dan. We get by. But not now. If I lose my job, then what do I do? Look around you; we need these jobs.' Dan scanned the worried faces around him. 'We need to be treated equally. That's all, you know.'

Dan could hear the earnestness in Czarek's voice, see it in his eyes.

'I'm okay with all of that. I agree completely with your stance, but listen, tonight is the wrong night for this, we need to get these good people home safely and quickly,' said Dan, gesturing to the strikers along the line. 'They can come back when the storm blows through. They listen to you, Czarek. Can we agree on a compromise? Please?'

Czarek grimaced a little. The group cheered him on with the same chanted slogans: 'No slave labour!' 'Equality!' 'Worker's rights!' Dan could see that Czarek didn't want to give; he was probably tired of giving.

'Let's say one Garda stays here with you for another thirty minutes, and then, for safety reasons, you go home and come back tomorrow? It's getting late, Czarek. We don't want any of your good folk getting hurt on their way home.'

Czarek rubbed his chin with his gloved hand as he surveyed the scene about him.

After a long pause, he at last took Dan's hand and shook it. 'Okay, okay, we do as you say it.'

'That's great, Czarek. I owe you one, thank you,' replied Dan.

Czarek started to make his way along the line, shouting out the new plans in Polish. Dan walked back to Sully, who had stepped away and was now climbing into his police vehicle.

'I'm calling it a night, Dan. It seems you have this under control,' said the sergeant. Dan could sense that Sully was a bit miffed by the successful peace negotiations, but for once, he wasn't making a fuss. 'Yeah, I think we're good now. I'll wait a few minutes until the crowd disperses, and then I'm heading out to Bobby Kirwan's. I think I found our stolen Corolla abandoned in his barn.'

'That's some coincidence,' replied Sully.

'Let's see,' said Dan.

'What about Peter Kennedy?' asked the sergeant.

'We'll sort it out tomorrow. He's not worth it tonight,' said Dan.

Sully nodded in agreement, started his engine and drove away towards town. Dan plodded his way back towards Czarek, who was waving goodbye to some frozen souls who looked more than happy to be escaping the storm. Dan, too, was keen to get home to Grace, a warm fire and a nice glass of red wine.

Kate could hardly contain her fury any longer. Shouldn't she be doing something? How could she just sit around when Amy was out there in danger? If she made her way to Grace's, could she find some clue of where her daughter was being held? Could she manage this alone? Only Król knew what she needed to know. What was there to do but agree to his rules and wait? For Peter and whatever might happen when he arrived.

She thought of the email she had sent earlier to Dan. What had she said again? All she could remember was her apologetic, embarrassed tone. Was it panicked enough to stir some alarm?

Król poured another tumbler of whiskey. He had taken reign over her home and also now her family. Kate resisted the urge to lift the whiskey glass that he'd laid before her and shove it into his face. He flipped open the pocket watch that he'd left resting on the table. Kate had never felt it so acutely. Time. Ticking relentlessly by. Every minute was another minute that Amy was missing, another minute closer to his 2:00a.m. deadline.

'Is she sheltered from the cold?' Kate asked.

'Yes, she's wrapped up. Indoors. She should be fine so long as we finish this tonight,' Król replied.

'Should be? What the hell does that mean? Is she okay, or is she not?'

'I said she's okay, Kate. For now. We're all waiting on your beloved husband, Peter.'

'This is your responsibility. Don't you bloody hide behind Peter.'

'Like you've done, Kate. Hiding up here in your lighthouse while your husband roams wild. Aren't you culpable too?'

'Fuck you,' she replied, her blood boiling over with rage. She spotted the rack of kitchen knives by the sink. His glance followed hers. Instinct took over as she lunged to the counter and grabbed the largest one. Even as she did, she regretted her actions, but it was too late. She whirled to confront him, waving the knife back and forth wildly. It now acted as an extension of her fully outstretched arm; the blade probing inches from his face.

He stood statuesque, staring at her. No fear, no panic. Ice-cold. Without hesitation, he moved unflinching into the path of the weapon. Lifting his chin high and with his head tilted backwards, he allowed the tip to graze his neck. Kate's hand trembled as a trickle of his blood fell along the sharp steel. She fought to control her thoughts, to formulate a plan of action, to avoid the temptation to plunge the knife deep into his neck.

'Do as I say or I... I will kill you,' Kate stammered. The words didn't sound convincing even to her. 'Where is my daughter? Tell me!'

Król looked at her for a moment, and then he spoke. 'Please don't, Kate. Don't make this mistake. Not because of me but for Amy's sake. Grace and Niamh, too. Remember what is at stake here. Use your head. I don't care if you push that knife into the back of my skull. Honestly, I'd welcome it. But what then? You won't find Amy until it's too late.' He lifted his arms until they were fully outstretched by his sides, resembling some crucifixion martyr waiting for another jab of the spear. 'I'm ready,' he said with disturbing calm.

Kate had to decide her next move, but she couldn't. There was nothing.

'Okay, enough of this bullshit,' said Król, lowering his arms. 'Hand me the knife.' Kate relented and did as she was told. Król moved closer to her, the knife down by his side. Kate retreated backwards as far as she could until her hips met the worktop and could go no further. He closed the gap and raised the knife to her face. Lifting his other hand, he slowly ran his thumb along the razor-sharp edge, drawing a thin, beady line of red to the skin. He then traced the oozing thumb slowly down her left cheek to her mouth, leaving a red trail as he did. 'Now, Kate, you have my mark. You can have all of my blood if you wish, but it won't return Amy.' Król placed the knife down on the counter beside her.

'Don't break the rules again,' he warned sternly. 'I am ready to kill every fucking last one of us if I need to.' Suddenly, as he turned his back to her and walked towards the kitchen table, all of the lights went out.

11:15p.m.

Dan was about to pull away from the power plant when the radio crackled into life. 'Dan, the power has gone off on the island. It must be the bloody strikers acting up; I thought we had a deal with those guys. Will you see what the hell is going on?' said Sully.

Dan shook his head wearily and replied that he would. He stepped out of the car and plodded back towards Czarek. 'The power has been cut out on the island, Czarek.'

The man looked genuinely surprised at the news. 'I don't know anything about that, Dan. I doubt it's any of our guys,' he replied.

'Can you get it fixed?' asked Dan, in a tone that left no doubt that he was growing tired of the whole debacle.

'Of course, give me a bit of time to work out what the problem is,' replied Czarek. Dan walked past the straggle of remaining strikers to where Edwards was standing by his patrol car. 'Keep this lot in check and make sure they are all gone within the hour,' said Dan. Edwards nodded in the affirmative.

Dan sat back into his car. He closed the door with a thud and started the engine. After about five minutes, Dan turned off the main road and continued down the narrow country road that led to Bobby Kirwan's isolated house. He used the old man's keys to enter. Dan had a quick scan to see if anything had been disturbed since his departure. It didn't seem so. He switched off the TV. Mussolini gazed on quietly from the sofa. Bobby's half-finished dinner was now fully gone. It was no surprise that the cat looked so content. Dan left some food and water out for when it got hungry again. He emptied the trash into the outdoor wheely bins. He gave the cat flap a deft kick, which got it open and working again. He left the lights on, closed the curtains and with the house sorted, he made his way out to the barn.

The Corolla was unlocked, which was no surprise given the last driver did not possess a key. Dan pulled on a pair of evidence gloves and sat in. It seemed clean bar the usual items: a half-empty bottle of water, an empty packet of gum, the butt of an apple. Dan rummaged around under the seats for anything that might have fallen. There was nothing bar a few coins. He would return tomorrow to do a more thorough search and to lift some fingerprints. He climbed out of the car and made his way to the rear. He hesitated. He thought of the woman and the child in the passports, and an eerie sensation crept through him. Dan popped the trunk, half-holding his breath. A replacement tyre and a few empty shopping bags were all there was. He closed the trunk and walked back towards the house.

Out front, Dan shut the main door and locked it top and bottom. He'd greet Bobby on his return with his keys and some hot food. Dan puffed his cheeks and sighed aloud as he walked to his police car. How easy for a life to pass. One moment, Bobby was calling for Mussolini and the next, he might have been gone forever. Yeah, he was old, but nobody woke up that morning, not expecting to make it to the end of the day.

Dan thought of his mother. He was sure something was up with her, but she wasn't telling. Dr Hanrahan had all but said as much. He'd ring her to say goodnight when he got home. Then, he'd drop by tomorrow and begin again on a better footing. He'd follow Grace's advice: more tolerance and patience. Dan thought of the hearty fire that awaited at home. He could feel Grace's fingers running through his hair, his weary frame stretched across the wooden boards, his head resting on her lap. She: watching the news or some current-affairs programme on TV. He: falling serenely into sleep. These thoughts lifted his spirits as he turned on the engine.

Dan phoned Grace to tell her that, at last, he was on his way home. Still no answer. She must have busted her phone. He opened his email inbox to find five new emails. Dan scanned the names with the unread blue dot beside them. One was from Kate, sent hours earlier. He tapped on it. An uneasy feeling crept through him as he read and reread the mail. A man had arrived at the lighthouse unexpectedly, causing problems. Kate was going to try and make her way to Grace's. Was that why Peter Kavanagh had sped by? Dan called Kate's mobile, but there was no answer. The phone went straight to messages. Where was she now? Had she gone to Grace's? Dan called Grace again, but still no answer. Was something wrong? Dan glanced back at Bobby's house and the barn to the rear, and he thought of the abandoned car and the man from the hotel. Grace's farm was only a few miles from Bobby's. He forwarded Kate's email to Sully with a message saying that he'd deal with whatever it was and set off on the short drive home.

Dan knew Grace, Kate too. They were both responsible and strong-willed women. They wouldn't just go off-grid like this, not at the same time in different locations. It didn't make sense. Who was the man Kate had referred to? Dan sped up as much as the road allowed. He eased the car down the laneway towards the farmhouse. It seemed like a lifetime had passed since he'd driven away that morning with Tommy Molloy. He remembered Grace's expression as he left, her face a sea of concern. She'd been worried that the ugliness of Tommy Molloy might somehow drive a wedge between them, that Dan might decide her skeletons made more noise than he could handle. *No chance.*

Ahead, amber-lit windows glowed welcomingly in the inky night. He drove through the open wooden gates and around to the rear of the house. The yard was empty, and

Grace's car was gone. Where had she left to? With two kids in a storm. Had she spoken to Kate and gone up to the lighthouse instead? How? The Cliff Road had been closed since five. Maybe she'd gone to a friend, but why hadn't she contacted him or Kate for that matter?

The kitchen door was ajar. A bolt of alarm washed through Dan. What the hell was going on? Warm light spilt out, illuminating the flurry of snow swirling about the yard. Dan jumped from the squad car and darted towards the open cottage door.

11:15p.m.

Peter passed the old schoolhouse. He was half a mile from the summit. Without warning, a black shroud fell over the island. The faint orange street lights and the dim glow from distant houses and farms all suddenly extinguished. Ahead, the lighthouse stood tall, dark and silent. In this complete darkness, it was reborn. Every twenty seconds or so, its proud beacon beamed far and wide over land and sea. Lungs full of cold air, Peter lumbered forward in the tracks of the one who had come before him. Tracks that proved, if proof was needed, that this was no nightmare to wake from; it was as real as an electric jolt. He thought of Amy, and his heart sank. He had to keep going for her.

At last, Peter stood at the door to his home. He tentatively turned his key in the latch and opened the door. Nobody came to greet him as he edged nervously through the hall and into the candlelit dining room. He stopped abruptly. It was as if he'd interrupted after-dinner drinks at a country mansion. A fire blazed in the large hearth to his left. Before it sat two people in armchairs, both with glasses in their hands. A bottle of whiskey rested on the coffee table. Opera filled the room.

Was this some cruel joke, he wondered, Kate's revenge? Would Amy come running towards him at any moment? Instead, it was Kate who rose from the large armchair that faced him. Opposite her, with his back to Peter, sat the intruder. The man didn't turn around, and all Peter could see was the dark hair that swept in long strands from the top of his head down to his neck. Kate walked to him, her eyes wide with fear, her cheeks smeared with blood and tears. She raised her trembling hands upwards and held his face. 'He has our baby, Peter,' she stammered. 'He has our little baby. You've got to fix this.'

'Jesus, what's happened to you? Are you okay?' Peter asked in shock.

'He has Amy, Peter. We must do exactly what he says to get her back.'

Peter could see that look in her eyes. That look that said don't even think about messing with me, that look that said she would fight the world and everyone in it.

'And so our hero returns,' said Król, as he rose from the chair and came towards them. Peter didn't recognise him. He'd never seen him before. What he did recognise was the violence simmering beneath the façade. It brimmed with visceral hate and savagery.

'Where the hell is our daughter?' Peter demanded aloud, confronting the threat. 'What have you done with her?'

'She is safe, for now,' Król replied, his voice even, not betraying any emotion.

Peter reached quickly into his coat and yanked out the monkey wrench in his clenched fist. He waved it threateningly inches from Król's face. 'Where is our daughter?' he shouted. Unfazed, Król edged closer to Peter, only stopping when they were face to face. Peter could smell the whiskey on his breath. Król lifted his left hand towards Peter's head. Peter froze. In the stranger's grip was a gun.

Slowly, Król nuzzled the barrel into Peter's temple. 'Mine's bigger than yours.'

Kate jumped desperately between the two of them, shrieking, 'No! Stop, stop!'

'Quiet!' Król shouted. And, turning to Peter, he mouthed, 'Who is the boss here?'

Peter felt his knees buckle. He looked at Kate, and her eyes told him what to say.

'You are,' Peter stuttered.

'Yes, I am,' agreed Król. 'Hand it to me.'

Peter handed over the wrench.

'Now, both of you, sit,' said Król as he tossed the wrench onto the coffee table with a bang. Peter sat down deflated, and Kate followed. 'Is your car at the bottom of the hill?' Król asked Peter.

'Yes, why?' replied Peter.

'It's just a question of time, that's all,' said Król, turning away.

Peter swallowed hard. Who was this fucking maniac? Was he really a vengeful husband that he had wronged? Had his selfishness delivered this anarchy to their home? Kate gazed wild-eyed at him, terror writ large on her face. Her stare screamed the unspoken words: 'This is on you, Peter. Sort it out!'

'Grace?' called Dan aloud, 'Grace?'

Silence.

Dan entered the farmhouse slowly. Dishes were propped on the rack by the sink – the bowls and cups they'd used that morning at breakfast. The Aga had been cleared of pots. An array of items were spread haphazardly across the kitchen table. Bank notes, a coin pouch, some receipts, and a pair of pink woollen gloves. Next to them lay Grace's upturned handbag. Dan lifted it, looking inside. It was empty. A newspaper lay neatly folded and unopened on the table. Dan opened it out and checked the date – that morning's *Independent*. 'Storm Warning' announced the headline. Grace bought the paper daily in town. She called it her shield. She could read on her coffee break if she wanted to avoid the other teachers. Two bags of sweets lay next to the newspaper. Dan lifted them. Again unopened. Kids didn't leave sweets lying around for long, that he knew. Fear coursed through him. These were bad signs, really bad signs.

Dan shouted the kids' names. No reply. Two school bags had been flung by the sofa in the adjoining sitting room, books half spilling onto the floor. Dan moved quickly down the hallway to Niamh's bedroom and turned the lights on. School uniforms lay tossed and strewn on the bedclothes. Dan peeked into the main bedroom. It looked as it did when they had left that morning. He could feel a current of cold air. It was coming from the unused bedroom at the end of the corridor. Dan moved to the door, wary of who or what might be behind it. He pushed it open slowly and was met by a frosty draught. Dan entered the room. One of the windowpanes had been broken. Small shards of glass lay on the carpeted floor below the sill. The duvet cover on the bed was ruffled, and a shallow depression had been left on the side nearest the door.

Dan pulled out his phone and called Sully. There was no answer. The 'leave a message' prompt came, and Dan spoke as calmly and with as much authority as he could manage. 'There's been a break-in at Grace Quigley's farmhouse. There is no sign of Grace, her daughter Niamh or Amy Kavanagh, who was staying over tonight. The dog is also missing. Something is very wrong. Kate O'Conner sent an alarmed email earlier. She said she was coming here to Grace's cottage. Neither she nor Grace have been answering any calls. The burned photograph from the County Hotel bedroom, I think I know who that is. I'm sure it's Peter Kennedy. That stolen car was left not too far from here, either. Bobby Kirwan's place is only a few miles away. I don't know how any of these things are connected, but they must be. I'm going to check the outbuildings, and then I'll make my way up to the lighthouse to see what the hell is going on. I think Grace may be there with the children. Send Edwards out here to do further searches and take prints.'

Dan ended the message and hurried back down the hallway to the kitchen. On the floor next to the Aga lay Rocky's silver dog bowls. One for water, the other for food, both still full. He went to the back door and called the dog's name into the night. Only the bawling wind replied. He called for Grace – still silence. Suddenly, Dan heard the movement of feet behind him. He swung about to face the intruder, instinctively ducking low as he did, but not low enough. He was stopped in his tracks by a ferocious blow to the side of his head. Dan felt or saw nothing more as he crumpled to the floor.

X

Four billion years Earth has spun on the thread of time, my thirty-six years but a shallow breath on these ageless solar winds. No sooner have we arrived than we are leaving. Time, but a wily deception. Never to be held or touched. No here, no now, we are never present. Am I, too, merely illusion? At a quantum level, I am indistinguishable from you. Electrons, particles, atoms, stardust. Molecules adrift in a shifting sea. Whatever I am, whatever I am made of, I can feel it slowing to a halt, breaking apart. I have grown weak. My energy is nearly spent. These last acts will see me transform and return to the past, the future, the eternal. To rest. Equilibrium.

Yet, there is something real. I held it once. I felt it rush in my veins, burn a fire in my belly. It lit a flame in the darkness. You couldn't see it under a microscope. It didn't consist of atoms or molecules. It knows not of time. It led me here. When all is done, and you ask why, know this. It is, and always will be, the only answer. Love.

11:45p.m.

Król had waited an eternity for this moment, and finally, it was here. He poured three glasses of whiskey and prompted Kate and Peter to lift theirs. Reluctantly they obeyed. He stood between them and lifted his own. 'I propose a toast. To our children. May they live to see us die.'

Król smiled at the expression of horror that appeared on both of their faces. Still, they lifted their glasses dutifully and sipped their whiskey. They were learning the new non-negotiable house rules. 'Good, good,' he said approvingly. 'Kate, some more opera. Verdi's *Rigoletto* please. The CD I sent you for Christmas.'

Peter stared quizzically, first at Król and then at Kate. Kate rose and did as she was instructed. 'How the hell do you know each other?' asked Peter.

'Silence, Peter,' Król ordered. 'All the fun and games in good time.'

A vision of Król's father came to him. Half-moon glasses resting on his nose, face in a book or typing on his typewriter, opera playing in the background. Always Verdi.

'Listen, my friends, listen to the tragedy. Poor Verdi knew first-hand about loss, two of his children dying young and then his wife too. He wrote from the heart. Do you know Rigoletto's story?' he asked as the female soprano sang *Caro Nome*.

Neither Kate nor Peter answered.

186

'Rigoletto is the court jester, a clown for the duke. The duke is a Casanova. Together, they conspire to lure the town's women to the duke's bed. Rigoletto mocks the poor husbands who have been left alone. However, a curse is sworn on both their heads. When Rigoletto's daughter, Gilda, falls for the duke, she is struck down by the curse and dies. A tale of lust and deceit, with the innocent paying the price.'

The room was silent but for the soprano's voice. Król saw the look of repulsion in Kate's eyes as she processed his words. Upending his glass, he sent the fiery liquid coursing into his bloodstream.

'You look worried, Kate. Once you do as I ask, you can prevent any further suffering of the innocent. Understood?'

'Yes,' Kate said immediately.

'Peter?'

'Yes,' muttered Peter. 'Yes.'

'Good. We are ready. Let us commence. I have your daughter Amy. I have Grace and Niamh, too. They are alive. You need me, to find them in time. If you both do as I say and these matters are resolved, then you get Amy back. If not, then a bomb has been set to explode at 2:00a.m.'

'Jesus Christ, are you fucking crazy?' said Peter aloud.

'Jesus can't help you with this one, Peter, and yes, I guess I am a little crazy. Regardless, that's not the issue at hand.' Kate looked at Peter as if admonishing him, and then she spoke. 'We will do as you ask. Will you switch off the bomb, please?' She was crying as she spoke, desperately trying to hold it together.

'It cannot be defused remotely. You need to enter the

correct number on its keypad. Push the wrong one, and it detonates. Get there later than 2:00a.m., and it detonates. So, we are wasting time, your daughter's valuable time. Can we proceed?'

Kate nodded yes immediately. 'Yes,' said Peter.

'Do you understand natural law? The concept of crime and punishment?' Silence greeted the question. 'I'll take that as a yes,' said Król. 'Let me explain why I have come here. I seek justice for certain wrongdoings. Retribution for crimes committed. These matters will be resolved tonight. First, we must establish whether the crimes have indeed been committed. Then, we ascertain guilt or innocence. Lastly, we decide on a suitable punishment for the guilty. We will hold a court of sorts. It will be a democratic court with a decision by jury. You two will hold the jury majority. I will be your judge.'

Kate and Peter looked at each other with a mixture of fear and bewilderment. They were on trial in their own home.

11:50p.m.

Król lifted an upholstered chair from the corner of the room and positioned it to face the two armchairs occupied by Peter and Kate. Then, he opened the gold-plated cover of his pocket watch and placed it next to his glass tumbler on the table. Kate sat to his left, Peter to his right, the burning fire behind him. In his hand, he held a Luger pistol, a war relic of his grandfather's, a reminder to him that some people will always believe their lives are of more importance than others. In the hearth, the wood crackled and spat. Król could feel the heat on his back. It seemed to fire the whiskey in his bloodstream, emboldening him to act. He began.

'Tonight, we will hear the trials of two men.' He looked to Peter and then to Kate, wagging his index finger in warning. 'It is important that you bring honesty and dignity to these affairs. I warn you that I will not tolerate lies or contempt.' He paused for a moment so that they could fully digest his words and then continued. 'Tonight is about truth. Those accused will be afforded all reasonable opportunity to defend themselves. A verdict will be based upon a majority, two out of three. Should one of you abstain from voting, I, as judge, shall have a casting vote. If found guilty, we will observe the rule of natural law and also any precedents set by this court to determine punishment. All sentences will be executed tonight.'

Król pointed to the timepiece on the coffee table. 'It is late. Matters of life and death are at play, and time is of the essence.' He looked solemnly at both of them. 'Do you both understand the rules of this court?'

Peter laughed derisively. 'This is not a court that I recognise,' he said. 'It's a sick fucking joke is what it is.'

'Why so, Peter?' asked Król. 'It is a court of your peers ruled by a majority vote. You and your beloved wife possess that majority. To what do you object?'

'It is a military court by reason of that gun in your hand,' Peter replied. 'You have abducted our daughter. We have no idea what you have done with her or where she is. We are at your mercy and will do whatever you want and vote in any way that you wish. So please don't insult us with your bullshit.'

Król studied Peter's angry face. Peter held his gaze for as long as he could, then broke and looked to Kate. Król rose from his seat and walked the few steps to Peter and pointed the pistol directly between his eyes. Peter went ashen, his lower lip trembling involuntarily. Tears began to stream from his eyes as he closed them. 'Open your eyes,' ordered Król. Peter did as he was told. Król took the gun in his other hand, turned it about and offered the butt to Peter. 'Take it, but please be careful: it is loaded. Now, you have all the power. Be wise, though. Power is a precarious thing.'

Peter put out his trembling hand and took the weapon. Król walked back to the fireplace. Peter rose and, gun in hand, moved after him. Immediately, Kate rose too and grabbed hold of Peter's arm. 'Don't,' she instructed. 'Don't.'

Peter ignored her. 'What's to stop me putting a fucking bullet in your head?' he spat at Król, arm and gun shaking violently. 'Where is my daughter? How do we know she is alive? How do we know there's a bomb? I want to know. Right now.'

'Calm, calm, Peter, please,' replied Król scornfully. 'First, there is nothing to stop you from putting a bullet in my head, but it will not help or speed Amy's release. In fact, if you do so, you will be sending her to the grave. How do you know she is alive? You must trust me. There is a bomb. That much you need to believe. Amy, you will get her back when we are done here. I will not expect you to make any of your jury deliberations under excessive duress or undue influence,' Król continued as if he had rehearsed these lines a thousand times, 'and finally, I promise to abide by our collective verdicts, once we follow the rules as I have set out. I believe that this is all very fair. Do you agree?' No replies came. 'Again, I'll take that as a yes. Finally, you can hold onto the weapon. But please, do not shoot yourself with it, not yet. Now sit, please.'

Peter dithered, unsure of what to do, and eventually, all he could do was retake his seat. Kate followed suit.

'Now, can I get a vote of approval for these proceedings and the actions of this court?' Król spoke aloud.

'Approved,' proclaimed Kate without hesitation. Peter looked at Kate, and again, she nodded to him.

'Approved,' said Peter.

'This court is now in session,' declared Król.

XI

It was random chance that I met her. Not destiny, not a fate predetermined, just chance. I watched her through the window as she came scurrying along the footpath, head ducked beneath her satchel, the rain dancing high on the concrete pavement. Her flimsy yellow summer dress glued wet to her body as she descended the steps to my uncle's tavern on Jablonowskich Street. She slipped as she entered, and the satchel fell from her raised hand and landed on the floor, sending books and papers spilling across the room. I moved instinctively to help her. Piling a few books on top of each other, I handed them to her, and she thanked me coyly. Her drenched hair clung steadfastly to her head as droplets fell down her cheeks. I'll never forget that first image of her or the feelings, the rush that coursed through my body. Never. For some reason, I was immediately drawn, no… captivated, by this girl. I couldn't tell you why, but I knew there and then that something special was occurring.

I watched her as she removed her saturated cardigan, hung it over a vacant stool and then sat down on the seat next to it. Thankfully, the bar was mostly empty. I think this gave me the courage to speak to her. I pointed to the book atop the pile, Meditations on First Philosophy, *with the face of Descartes gazing up from the cover. 'The father of philosophy,' I said to her. She looked at me curiously. She stayed silent. 'It is only by stripping away all perceived knowledge that we can attain, without any doubt, that which is certain knowledge,' I quoted to her.*

'Cogito, ergo sum – I think therefore I am,' she replied, and then she smiled. I can see that smile now. I will always see that smile. We exchanged some small talk until the downpour turned to sunshine. A fresh multicoloured rainbow now crowned the late afternoon sky.

'What's your name?' I asked as she made to leave. She blushed ever so slightly. That look on her face, that worried searching in her eyes – I see those eyes now like she was still before me. I see that face like I still hold it delicately between my hands.

'Jude.'

Jude.

For some crazy reason, I started to sing to her as she walked to the door.

She stopped. 'Can you make sad songs better?' she asked.

'If you come again, I'll try,' I replied.

She seemed to consider this for a moment and laughed and smiled that smile, and then she was gone. I watched until she boarded her tram, and it snaked up the road and left my sight. I was sure I would never see her again.

Król reached into the black holdall and pulled out a bundle of papers of varying shapes and sizes. There were files and documents bound by elastic and others by clips. Taking great care, he duly arranged them in orderly piles on the coffee table before him. Next to them, he placed one of the candles that Kate had lit when the lights had failed.

'Crimes have been committed. Our task is to seek justice for these acts. To examine the evidence before us' – he waved his hand at the display of papers that were now spread across the table – 'and to find guilt where guilt lies.'

'Crimes have been committed; is that not a statement of fact?' enquired Kate. 'If this is a court, does it not believe in innocent till proven guilty?'

Król nodded. 'Yes, that is a fair comment. I am corrected; thank you, Kate. I restate, crimes have been alleged.'

Peter shook his head back and forth in an exaggerated show of dissent while Kate stared silently at the items that had been spread across the table.

'Our first case seems open and shut. I, Nicholas Król am the defendant. I am accused of, and I confess fully to, the following crimes: the premeditated abduction of a child and the premeditated killing of a child.'

Peter and Kate gasped simultaneously. 'Wait a minute, wait a minute,' exclaimed Kate aloud. 'You swore that Amy was okay! Is Amy alive? Tell us now!' she continued.

As she spoke, Peter lunged furiously across the coffee table, barrelling into Król's chest and sending both of the men sprawling towards the fireplace. They landed hard on the wooden floor. The gun that Peter had been holding spilt loose. He grasped desperately along the floorboards to retrieve it. Behind him, Król was clambering to his feet. Peter grabbed the gun, swung around and thumped the side of the weapon into Król's face, the velocity of the impact sending both of them tumbling back to the floor. Somehow, despite the blow, Król rose first and flung himself onto Peter's back, straddling him. Król grabbed the hand in which Peter held the gun and banged it forcibly downwards, the impact against the floor releasing his grip on the revolver. With both hands, Król grasped Peter by the hair, wrenched his head upwards and proceeded to thump it down hard onto the wood. Kate screamed and leapt to her husband's defence. She flailed at Król with her fists over and over until, at last, he relinquished his hold and turned his attention to her.

Wrapping one strong arm around her waist, he half pulled, half lifted her towards her armchair, where he duly dumped her. He walked back to Peter, and, using his hair and his shirt collar for grips, he dragged him across the floor on his knees and, hauling him upwards, he shoved him back into his chair. For a long moment, they all gasped for breath.

Król grabbed the revolver and placed it on the coffee table. Blood was congealing in his mouth, and he spat it into the fire. He turned and stood between them, his eyes bulging in fury. 'This is not a game. This is my court. These are my rules. Final warning!'

He then picked up the monkey wrench from the table, walked towards Peter, lifted the wrench high and smashed it down onto Peter's hand, which had been resting on the arm of the chair. Metal, hand, wood: one had to give. Peter screamed in agony. Kate rushed again to his side. Król returned the wrench to the coffee table. He walked to the fire, threw on some logs, righted his seat and sat down.

He had allowed violence to take control, and it had felt good. This could all end very quickly if he chose. He clenched his fists tightly, knuckles cracking under the pressure. He would have revelled in smashing Peter's face to a pulp. Instead, he poured another whiskey. He gulped it back and set the glass down hard on the table. There was still work to be done.

Turning again to face the couple, he repeated aloud, 'There will be no more contempt of this court. Understood?'

Peter whimpered quietly in his chair, his limp hand resting awkwardly in his lap. Kate surveyed the scene of wreckage before her. 'We understand,' she said.

Midnight

Explosive waves of pain reverberated inside Dan's skull. He grimaced in agony and struggled to open his eyes. He lay sprawled on the floor somewhere. He glanced around, but the room was just dark, gloomy shadows. What objects he could detect were blurred and fuzzy. His eyes weighed leaden, and he longed to close them, but he didn't, not till he could tell what was going on, where he was. The pain kept coming in horrible, relentless waves.

Had he been drugged? His head was too cloudy and sore to work it out. Something stirred near him. 'Who's there?' he mumbled with difficulty. Silence. Only his own heavy breathing answered him. Still, he could sense that he was not alone. He tried to lift himself, but he couldn't coordinate the effort, and he fell back to the floor. He shivered in the extreme cold. He remembered the snowstorm that had come to town. What else?

Another movement. Dan swung his arm and caught hold of something, somebody. He held on. 'Who's that?' he asked. He could discern a trouser leg as it pulled away, but his eyes were closing, succumbing to the fog. He fell again into the dim, murky blackness.

12:01a.m.

Kate stared coldly at Król, who was lifting papers that had fallen from the table during the scuffle. Who was he, this self-declared judge? Who was he to judge them? Yet here he sat in complete control. Whatever it was he wanted, he could have it in return for Amy's safety. Kate tried to collate at warp speed what she knew and what she thought she knew. He had seemed polite and quiet when they met for the first time when he called out to her on the beach. His voice was gentle – apologetic even – knowing then, as he did, that the very utterance of her name would open this portal to hell. On the sand, he whispered to her so that Amy would not hear. He carried letters written by Peter to his wife. Letters filled with sex and lust and obvious contempt for both Król and her. Letters written as if neither of them existed or mattered, as if all the tender and quiet moments they had each shared with their adulterous partners had been naive and silly and counted for nothing alongside their crude carnality. Kate's secrets had been shared, too, traded as intimacies. Traded *for* intimacies.

After she'd read them, she agreed to meet him in his hotel. She'd been wary to do so, but he had seemed as lost as she was. Solace was to be found in the fellow afflicted. Nothing then could have led her to believe that any of this might unfold. He'd been respectful, dignified even. Yet here he was, this menacing avenger. Król looked up from the documents. His cheek was bruised, and he had a small cut under his right eye. The flames of the fire flickered behind him. *There was more to all of this,* thought Kate. *What though?* Abduction. Killing a child. He had admitted to these terrible crimes. She dared not think the thought, but she couldn't stop it. Was that child Amy? He said she was alive and that she could be saved. Had he lied?

Król rose from his chair and stood before them. 'I speak now as the accused and confessor of these terrible crimes. All that remains is for this court and jury to convict me and agree to my sentence.'

Kate shook her head. Was he admitting that he killed Amy? Was that it? After all the posturing? It still didn't make sense to her. He'd killed a child. There were two children on the sleepover. What about Niamh? Why would he kill Niamh? Which child was still alive?

XII

I waited every day to see if she would return, and then, after nearly a week, the rain brought her to me once more. I went behind the bar, poured a brandy and put it down before her. 'For medicinal purposes,' I said. Then I poured one for myself. 'On the count of three?' She looked cautiously at the drink, still wary of her new Descartes-quoting friend. 'One... two... three!' We both lifted the glasses and sent the fire down our throats. She coughed and then laughed aloud as if startled by her own behaviour.

She was a student at the university, studying politics and philosophy. 'A dangerous mix,' I joked. She'd come to Kraków from Chrzanów, a small rural town some fifty kilometres west of the city. Her parents farmed the land there. She was in her final year, and after that, she wasn't sure what would come next. Friends had talked of moving to Warsaw, others Germany, but to her, both seemed a long way from her parents. For now, she was enjoying Kraków, and after that, she would see where opportunity took her. I told her that my grandfather had taught at her university before moving to Oxford at the outbreak of the war with my father in tow. That my father had been an eminent professor in England. That both were now gone. That my mother had died giving birth to me. That my uncle owned the bar where we sat and that I lived in the attic overhead. I couldn't stop talking, my life story spilling out word after word. For some reason, I'd yearned, no needed, to bare my soul, to impart everything to her. I'd never been a big talker. In Oxford, my father was usually immersed in his research and studies. Presence was comfort enough, our silences too. Yet with Jude, I couldn't stop the flood of gushing consciousness. She graciously listened, a dutiful reservoir to well my life's torrent.

Finally, the old clock behind the bar struck 6:00p.m., reminding her that there was somewhere she needed to be. Again, she rose, thanked me for the drinks and then hesitated in the moment between what we had shared and what we might be. After what seemed like an eternity, she bent low, smiled that smile, and sealed our love with a kiss on my cheek. I knew there and then that we would gravitate towards each other forever: she, my sun, I in orbit, fuelled and given life by her radiant warmth and love. I know that sounds crazy, something a teenager might profess, but honestly, that's what I felt, what I knew. I still do.

12:05a.m.

Peter resembled a down-on-his-luck boxer, his body a dishevelled canvas of cuts, blood and bruises. His hand was swollen to an absurdly unnatural size and shape. He looked punch-drunk, his head down and lolling, eyes fixed on the floor. In the shadows of the candlelight, his face reflected a ghoulishly unhealthy pallor. He must have sensed Kate's gaze, for he met her stare long enough to share a moment of misery.

Steeling herself, Kate stood. She would fight this with all she had and win this twisted game. She addressed Król. 'Every defendant has the right to defend himself or to be defended, is that so?'

Król nodded, 'Yes.'

'As you have already confessed, you are not in a position to defend yourself. It is only right, therefore, that I assume the role of conducting a defence for you.'

Peter stirred and blurted aloud, 'Kate, are you crazy? This man has abducted and killed our...' and there he faltered and stopped, unable to finish the sentence. 'He's a child-killer for Christ's sake. The only solution is a bullet to the fucking head.'

'That is hard to argue, Kate, is it not?' agreed Król.

Kate ignored them both. 'Let us do this by the book. That was your instruction.'

'OK,' replied the smiling Król. 'As you wish.'

Kate wasn't sure where she was going with this idea, but something was leading her forward: the tenuous thread of a plan. Something told her that this was critical to Amy's well-being. She tried frantically to cajole a haze of flickering thoughts into one beam of clarity. Start again, think this through. This man is English and of Polish descent. He has come to Blackcliff to satisfy this crazy vendetta. He delivered love letters to her, proof of both their spouses' infidelities. He has Grace's phone. Nobody has seen Grace or the kids since the school closed. He arrives at the lighthouse, uncaring that he may end up stranded by the weather. He is holding their daughter Amy hostage somewhere. Grace and Niamh, too. Only he knows where. There is a bomb primed to detonate at 2:00a.m. He has a gun, and he seeks revenge on Peter. Yet, there had to be more. Why take Amy, Grace and Niamh? Why convene this *court* of his and then put himself on trial? Something didn't add up, but she couldn't figure out what. Maybe he was just a madman. Yet somehow, he always seemed to be in control, steeled at every step by an inherent determination. What could she do? Keep asking questions.

'You said that your crimes were premeditated. What did you mean by that?' Kate asked. Król smiled.

'You are a trooper, Kate. To be admired! What I meant was that they were pre-planned. They were not a reaction. In any man's book, that would be defined as premeditated.'

'Were *all* of your actions premeditated?' Kate asked, surprised by his answer. It didn't make sense. His coming here to seek out Peter had seemed hot-headed and impulsive. The children and Grace? That made no sense either. But she had struck a chord, something important, a shadow of knowledge. A change appeared in his face, nearly imperceptible but altered, nonetheless.

'Yes, they were all premeditated,' he continued.

An icy shiver ran through Kate. It was only then that she fully realised how calculating this man was, how planned his behaviour had been. These were not just the hot-blooded actions of a wronged husband. Instead, he had been plotting against them, watching them, preying upon them. All the while coolly biding his time, waiting for his moment to pounce. For an instant, she couldn't breathe. Whatever this was, it was everything to him. He had nothing else. Nor did they.

It seemed that Peter had come to the same realisation: this man was not for stopping. Peter got up, staggering a little as he did, and once more attempted to rush Król. Król quickly lifted the gun from the table, aimed and shot. A deafening blast thundered through the house, rose through the chimney and was sucked away by the gale outside.

12:10a.m.

The impact of the gunshot sent Peter buckling to the floor. Kate rushed to where he lay writhing and wailing in pain. Blood gushed steadily from below his knee. Kate grabbed a cushion from the chair and told Peter to hold it to the wound. 'Call an ambulance,' Kate yelled at Król.

He shook his head nonchalantly. 'We can't do that, Kate, come on, you know that. They couldn't get here anyhow.'

'Fuck you!' shouted Peter angrily at Król between groans of pain. Kate rushed to the bathroom. She grabbed a towel and soaked it with hot water under the tap. She yanked open a drawer and fished around until she found some scissors. In the medicine press, she dug out an elastic cotton bandage. Quickly, she returned with her makeshift medical kit to where Peter lay squirming on the floor. Kneeling beside him, Kate cut the blood-soaked trouser from his lower leg to reveal a grisly red hole. She wiped away some of the blood and tissue with the wet towel. She grabbed the whiskey bottle from the coffee table and splashed some of the golden liquid over the wound. Peter shrieked aloud.

'What a waste,' remarked Król dryly. Kate wrapped the strapping tightly around Peter's leg until the wound was bound and sealed tight.

Peter snatched the bottle of whiskey from Kate with his good hand and swigged back a desperate mouthful. Kate rushed again to the bathroom and returned with some painkillers. She handed Peter three times the dose, which he washed down with another gulp of whiskey. 'Please end this now,' Kate pleaded to Król. 'He needs urgent medical assistance.'

'I cannot do that, Kate. I am sorry. We must finish what we have started. It is only a leg wound. Let us conclude our business, and then you can get help.'

'What, are you a bloody doctor now, too?' she asked incredulously. Król just stared back at her, stony-faced. 'Help me lift him,' Kate instructed. With Król's assistance, she bundled Peter back into his chair. She propped the damaged leg on a small side table, placing a cushion under it as she did. All the while, Peter moaned in agony.

'I told you both. I was very clear,' sighed Król. 'No more contempt.' He stared at Kate as he spoke but kept the gun pointed in the direction of Peter. 'Now, where were we? Yes, I had confirmed that these crimes were both planned and premeditated. I've freely confessed to them. Two verdicts are permissible: Guilty or not guilty. What shall it be?'

'Guilty, you fuck,' said Peter.

'Have you killed our child?' demanded Kate. 'Tell me the truth.'

Król paused for a moment.

'I have killed a child. I have abducted children. I have confessed to this. Do you really need any more?'

Kate couldn't think straight. She was losing track of what was happening. What else could she do? A flood of defeat drowned her sinking soul. She could feel the trapdoor closing above her, but she had no idea how to stop it. One thing was clear: if he harmed her daughter, she would kill him stone-dead.

'Guilty,' she said.

'And so we have it, unanimous verdict,' said Król. 'To sentencing. We are to be bound by *Lex Talionis*, the first written code of law – an eye for an eye. In the case before us, we face multiple crimes, killing being the most heinous. Therefore, this crime shall be punished by an act of equal measure: execution. I, the guilty party, offer to exact the punishment myself. So, are we all agreed on the sentence?'

His gaze shifted from Peter to Kate and then back to Peter.

'Agreed,' said Peter. 'And I am happy to pull the trigger, you fucking psycho.'

Kate felt light-headed. Why the big performance? Why come here in the middle of a storm just to kill himself? Why say to her that he would act honestly and that Amy would be returned if they played his game, knowing all along that he was going to end his life? She had acted fairly but for nothing. There was still one thing she needed, though, and it was non-negotiable.

'Before you do this,' she said slowly, trying not to let

the emotion of the words engulf her, 'I need to know where my daughter is, dead or alive so that I can bring her home. Without that, I cannot approve your sentence.'

'Trust me, Kate. You will know, that I promise, regardless of how you vote. You may abstain if you wish.'

'I abstain,' Kate said.

'As judge and casting vote, I vote with Peter, the death penalty.'

12:15a.m.

Dan woke to a force ten earthquake sending seismic tremors of pain through his skull. He had no idea how long he'd been out. He tried to lift himself from the floor, but it was impossible.

'Fuck's sake,' came a voice. A man's voice. A voice he knew. Dan squinted to get a view, and it was then he recognised the unmistakable face looking down upon him, Tommy Molloy. Suddenly, Tommy was pulling him upwards, lifting him from under his armpits. Dan's feet attempted to find a grip as he struggled to stand. He couldn't, and he toppled backwards onto something soft. His falling weight dragged Tommy down on top of him. Tommy pushed his palms into Dan's chest to lever himself upright. Dan was lying on a bed, and now Tommy was standing over him, saying something that he couldn't make out. All the while, the pain continued to screech through his skull.

A memory came drifting through the mist. He was driving to Grace's house. He couldn't remember why.

'What's going on, Tommy? Why? Why are you here?'

he asked groggily. Tommy looked uneasy as he stared down at him, an odd expression on his face.

'Where's Grace?' Dan asked.

'I don't know,' said Tommy defensively. 'There was no one here when I arrived. The back door was wide open. The side window was broken. You were on the ground. You were out of it.'

Dan tried to gel the pieces together to make sense of what Tommy was saying, but he couldn't. Another memory flashed brightly through the haze: Amy, Kate's girl.

'Is Amy here?' he asked.

'No. I told you already the house is fucking empty. Will you wake up? Something is fucked up around here. Somebody broke in, man.'

'You?' asked Dan.

'No,' Tommy replied angrily. 'Listen, I don't think you are thinking clearly. You must have fallen and banged your head.'

What Dan was clear on was his immense dislike for the man standing over him. He didn't believe him and knew he hadn't ever fallen anywhere, at any time that he could remember. His mind went foggy again, and he lost track of his meandering thoughts. Peter Kavanagh was driving past him in the snow. Dan was waving after him, shouting for him to stop. And now, somehow, he was here, back home? Was he waiting for Grace? No, there was something else. Kate was talking to him. They were lying on the heath down by Warren's Cove. She was leaving for New York. He was going to Garda College in Templemore. He moved to kiss her. Violent tremors of pain vibrated through his head. Kate was gone, and Tommy was back.

Dan tried to rise but couldn't. His teeth chattered uncontrollably in the cold. He felt terrible, the worst he'd ever felt. 'Tommy, please ring the station. Get some help.'

'I've no phone,' replied Tommy after a long moment.

'Go to my car outside, use the radio. Just press the button on the side of the voice box after you lift it.'

Tommy looked down at him, assessing the potential outcomes. It wasn't in his make-up to help anybody. He walked to the door and flicked the light switch. The bulb above Dan's head seared his eyes like a desert sun. Shrill, sharp bolts of pain electrified frazzled synapses. He held his hand up to block the lacerating glare. Tommy had walked to the bedside and was staring down at him. Where before he wore an arrogant, bitter visage, now Dan detected something else. Fear.

12:15a.m.

Król appraised the couple before him. Peter was broken. Head down, hand bust, leg shot. Kate was twitchy, uneasy. A cornered animal, but still ready to spring and fight. She caught his gaze and returned it, unwavering. He could see that she wouldn't give up, not until the last breath had left her body. He could feel it so close now. His own last breath. A great relief settled upon him.

'You do not disappoint me, Kate. You are what I hoped you'd be. Resolute. Determined. You even tried to defend my case. You don't deserve any of this. Then again, neither do I.' Król rummaged in his bag and pulled out two white envelopes. 'These are for you. One is from my wife, the other from me. Please read them when I am gone. I hope they bring some sense to all of this. None of it was my design – I was as much a pawn as you.' He propped the letters against the silver candelabra on the small table next to one of the armchairs.

'More bloody letters!' exclaimed Kate, shaking her head disconsolately.

'I came here to be a voice for those who cannot speak. If I do not tell their story, if I do not seek justice, it would be as if they never mattered. I can't have that,' said Król.

'Justice for whom, for what?' exclaimed Kate. 'What about Amy's justice?'

That hurt him. Kate was right; the children were innocents caught in the chaos.

'All will become clear soon, Kate. Bear with me just a little longer.'

He lifted a file from the table.

'This brings us to our second case. The trial of Peter Kavanagh. Mr Kavanagh is accused of adultery and unlawful killing.'

'Killing?' sputtered Kate.

Peter lifted his head and scoffed in derision. 'You are pathetic, truly pathetic. Why do we have to endure this any longer? You actually enjoy this sick bullshit. Go ahead, please, just shoot yourself as we agreed, and be done with it. Or have you not got the nerve? Are you only tough enough to attack women and children?'

Król raised his eyebrows, pursed his lips outwards a little, nodded seriously, and gave all the outward expressions of having carefully considered Peter's outburst.

'We shall see, Peter. When the time is upon us, we shall see,' he replied, lifting the gun again as if judging the weight of the lives held within it. 'However, we must continue, for now, we come to your hour of judgement.'

Król looked to Kate. 'I know your thoughts are elsewhere, Kate, but focus, please, for here is your chance to save your daughter's life. I said it would be you who decided when the time came: who lives, who dies.'

'You said Amy was dead?' roared Peter.

Kate looked into Król's eyes, searching for proof of life, for salvation.

'I said I had killed a child,' replied Król, 'but I did not say it was Amy. Amy is very much alive. In this storm and with the night upon us, you will need to reach her soon, but we have important matters to conclude first. And quickly.'

XIII

Most days, I would walk the fifty yards to the end of the street and cross over to the Planty Gardens that circled the outer perimeter of the Old Town. There, on the park bench next to the university, directly opposite the statue of Copernicus, I would sit and wait for Jude to come from her lectures. Jude's arm wrapped lazily around my waist, mine about hers; we would walk the gardens until we arrived back to find Copernicus awaiting our return. This might sound silly, but I remember on those strolls noticing for the first time how intricate and beautiful the spring flowers were. It was as if Jude's presence had turned my world from grey to colour. We talked about everything new couples do. Her studies. My days in Oxford. Where we had travelled to (nowhere really for me), where we'd like to go, and what music we liked. Our favourite foods. The books we loved. We retold the histories that had conspired to place us in that bar on that day when the rain came – two unique paths, now one. I didn't truly believe that it had been foretold, but oddly, it had started to feel that way. I could hear my father's voice in my ear... *what will be, will be.*

When I kissed her, I kissed her whole face, her eyes, her cheeks, her nose, her forehead and finally, her lips. They were kisses dreamed of in desire but earthed in overwhelming affection. I wanted somehow to relay to her in these small touches that I would adore this face, this woman, for all time. I couldn't explain it, but as I said before, I just knew.

'Will you show me where you live?' she asked with a shyness that melted my heart. I'd been reluctant to take her to my flat, to take anybody for that matter. Later that night, I cleaned and cleaned. Two black sacks accounted for the empty bottles and the decayed and rotten contents of the fridge. Bedclothes were dumped, and the bathtub took an eternity to scrub. My uncle advised on newly cut flowers, oven-baked bread and freshly brewed coffee. If nothing else, their scent would help mask the mustiness.

The next day, she came. There was no lift in the old building, so together, we climbed the ten flights of stairs to the loft apartment. I paused at the door and held her hand in mine. 'Are you sure you wish to enter?' I asked her. 'I may never let you go.'

'Who says I'll want to leave?' she replied, and I've never forgotten that look in her eyes as she said it. Excited, happy, serious, scared, crazy.

We drank wine and talked for hours. When night fell, we made love for what seemed an eternity. It was our first time, and I couldn't get enough of her. I wanted to consume her. We woke in the dark hours before dawn and wrapped *in blankets, we went out to the balcony. There, we gazed over the rooftops of the old town. Thousands of years of our ancestors' endeavours lay before us. The old university buildings, the parapets and spires of cathedrals and churches, the Grand Square. Away to our right on an elevated bank of the Vistula, the fortified walls of Wawel Castle, the resting place of our kings, poets and martyrs.*

'I have never seen Kraków from such a height!' she exclaimed. 'How beautiful it is. You are so lucky to have this.'

'What is mine is yours,' I replied, and I meant every word. I pointed to the stars above and told her how my father had taught me to read the night sky. I showed her how to find the North Star Polaris, then the constellation of Orion, the mythical Greek hunter. I showed her the red supergiant Betelgeuse, resting on Orion's shoulder. I explained how it was slowly dying and that what we saw was a photograph of the past, a picture of a vanishing light.

We stargazed until the sun rose, and then we went back to bed and made love again. I remember feeling that if we stayed in that bed, we would be safe forever. That the universe and everything within it could not touch us.

12:20a.m.

Dan shielded his eyes from the light as best he could. 'For God's sake, turn it off,' he pleaded. Tommy stared at him, not moving. Dan saw the look on Molloy's face, and a surge of panic flushed through him. 'What is it, Tommy?' he asked.

Tommy just kept gaping. 'I didn't do that to you,' he said.

'Do what, Tommy?' Dan asked nervously. He wiped his dripping nose with his cuff. Blood.

'They'll say I hit you or some shit like that. I didn't,' Tommy stammered. 'You fell.'

'It's okay. It doesn't matter. Just call in for help, will you, quickly, for God's sake?'

'Call in and explain this mess? Fuck that, no way,' Tommy moaned. 'I know how it works. That Sully fucking hates me. He'll stitch me up, same as my dad. I need to get out of here. I thought you were the person that broke in. I was looking for Niamh. I need to find her, Dan. None of this is my fault, okay?'

Dan was sifting through the soupy fog, trying to remember what had made him so worried earlier. What was it? He'd been here with Grace that morning, hadn't he? Where was she now? Where was his mother? Was she okay? Was she coming, he wondered? He could remember falling in a ditch as a child, and she came to him. He thought she would help, but instead, she hit him hard. 'Be more careful!' she'd roared. He'd cried and cried. Was she here now?

He was back in the room with Tommy. There was a mirror resting on the locker by the other side of the bed. He was too queasy to rise himself. He couldn't even feel his legs with the cold. 'Tommy, bring me that mirror,' he said, pointing to it.

Tommy fetched the mirror reluctantly and then held it up for Dan to see. Dan caught his breath. Around each of his eyes, the skin had discoloured. It was like he had two black eyes, but worse. Blood dripped from one of his nostrils. A bump protruded over his right ear. He turned his face and saw dark bruising. He knew these symptoms from his training – the nausea, the light sensitivity, the excruciating pain. It all made horrible sense. He was bleeding internally. Blunt force trauma to the skull. He needed urgent medical help.

'Turn that off,' he barked, pointing to the light above him. Tommy did as he was told. 'Now go out… call this in now.'

'Tell me you'll back my story, Dan? I can't go inside again,' replied Tommy.

'If it's the truth, I will Tommy. It is true, isn't it? You didn't do this to me, did you?'

'No, no way,' came the reply, but as Dan looked into the nervous shifting eyes before him, he knew that Tommy was lying. 'Okay, Tommy, call it in.'

12:20a.m.

Król peered at the bedraggled mess before him. 'Peter Kavanagh, politician, husband, father and respected pillar of the community, you are accused of adultery and unlawful killing. How do you plead?' he asked as he leafed through the file in his hands.

'I don't recognise this thing you call a court,' Peter replied.

Kate rose to her feet and spoke with as much calm as she could muster. 'Judge, Nicholas,' she said, deliberately now using his first name. 'I understand that it was horrible to learn that your wife was having an affair. I, more than anyone, know the pain these actions have caused. It was my husband having that affair also, remember? Is all of this needed? I beg you, it's past midnight, time is running out, there are two children out there who need our help.'

Król turned to look at Kate, a pained expression on his face. 'Kate, I am so sorry. I have another confession to make. I was not entirely truthful when we first met. In fact, I lied to you. Believe me, it was never malicious. I had to get your attention, and I am truly sorry. The letters, Peter's letters to his lover, that was not my wife.'

Kate shot Peter a shocked glance, but he looked as confused as she was. 'What do you mean?' she shouted angrily. 'Who the hell is she? Why...'

'It is all here in lurid detail,' Król interjected, his hands gesturing to the papers on the table. 'A report from Max Trzoslo, a private investigator,' he said, lifting a thick brown A4 folder aloft in his hand. 'He hacked Peter's email account and found details of his affair with a woman named Margaret Nowak from Warsaw.' Trzoslo tracked Margaret down, and she was more than happy to hand over the love letters once Trzoslo didn't mention the liaison to her husband. They are the letters I gave to you. 'Remember Margaret?' said Król to Peter. 'It seemed in the end that you really loved her, how romantic. You kept sending her letters even though she asked you to stop.'

Peter cowered silently, his head in his hands. 'Margaret was a senior official with the Polish Investment Authority.' Król continued, 'Peter met her on a business trip. The big shot from Brussels with promises of grants and funding. Easy pickings, I'd say.'

'I don't... I don't understand,' stammered Kate, her mind whirring. 'I thought you wanted to teach Peter a lesson because of your wife.'

'I'm sorry, but I had to get your trust,' he replied.

Kate felt dirty. She thought of how she had let this man take her. She had felt sorry for him, for herself. Then, after, she, lost in her own guilt. And why, for what? The sins of Peter? This man took her daughter, and she repaid him. How? She shuddered at the thought. Was any of what he said true? What about Amy?

'We must proceed without further interruption,' said Król.

Kate snapped back to the present. There was no time to feel sorry for herself. She turned to her husband. 'Peter, please, listen to me. Tell him what he wants. Amy is the only thing that matters now. We must finish this.'

'Okay, okay,' Peter groaned. 'I am innocent. I haven't killed anybody. Is that too much for you to grasp?' said Peter angrily, as somehow he managed to aim a spit at Król's feet from out of his bruised and bloodied mouth.

'The court notes your plea and your contempt,' said Król, fixing him a withering glare.

Kate fought hard to focus amid the noise and mayhem. Her daughter had been abducted. Her husband was on trial for adultery and killing, and all the while, time was running out. Yet, so many things didn't make sense. At first, she thought this man was just another jealous husband. Another angry, bitter man looking for revenge. But that wasn't it. So, why the stalking, the trial? Then, a shadow crept into the light. This was a hanging court. They were slowly, but quite assuredly, being led to the gallows. Kate scolded herself for not spotting the trap sooner. Król had spoken of precedent, and now it had been determined. His own punishment was set at death. An eye for an eye. He was happy to burn in the fires of hell once Peter burned with him. Suffering loves a companion. What had gone before was just the preamble. Here was the main event. He was loading the gun, and they were going to fire it.

XIV

Time passed. Blissful time. We were completely consumed by each other. One day, a few years later, as we walked through the Planty Gardens, Jude turned to me, a broad, mischievous smile lighting her beautiful face and told me the best news that I had ever heard. I was to be a father, and our two would become three. We talked excitedly about the future, about how different everything would be. The longer we talked, though, I could feel her withdrawing a little, becoming silent, sad even. I asked her what was wrong, but she said it was nothing. I wouldn't go a step further. I pestered her until she told me. 'I'm worried that you won't love me as much when the baby arrives,' she blurted and then burst into tears. Like a fool, I laughed, and she slapped my arm hard. Gradually, I set her mind at ease, and I assured her that I would love her even more. She pulled me close to her side, and we strolled towards the castle.

That night, when we lay side by side in our bed, Jude seemed agitated, lost in thought. She nestled her head onto my chest, and then, in a gentle whisper, she asked me to make a promise. I went to reply, to swear that I would offer her whatever she wished, but she stopped me, put a finger to my lips and told me to listen. 'Never let anything come between us,' she said quietly. I smiled broadly and kissed her nose. How could I? I thought. It was impossible. Yet, she saw what I couldn't, that her request was layered in complexity. Like an astrophysicist's quantum maths theory, I should have guessed there were a million permutations.

12:25a.m.

Kate sprung to her feet. 'Wait, wait,' she implored.

'I am listening. State your objection?' said Król, lifting his eyes from his papers.

'How can a man be expected to enter a plea when the nature and details of his alleged crime have not been disclosed?' she asked.

'They are the rules of this court,' said Król calmly, 'any reasonable person should know the extent of their actions and what consequences have ensued from those actions. How can a man not know he has committed adultery? That he has not killed? We do not talk of idle matters here. I have noted your objection, but it is overruled.'

Kate sat down. Peter wasn't grasping what was at play. Maybe he didn't care anymore. He looked horribly pale. He needed hospital attention and soon.

'Kate, did you believe your husband to be a loving and caring husband?' Król asked.

'Yes,' said Kate belligerently.

'Are you sure of that answer, Kate?'

'Yes, I am.'

'OK, we will proceed. Have you ever considered leaving your husband?'

Kate knew where Król was leading her, but what could she do? 'Yes,' she replied. Peter raised his eyes, sitting up again as best he could.

'Thank you for your honesty. It is noted by this court. Why did you consider leaving your husband?'

Kate didn't answer for a few moments. Her eyes met Peter's, and in that briefest of moments, she saw whatever they once had and all the time they had shared dissolve and drift away. A swell of sadness engulfed her. These were words she thought would never leave her lips. Yet, she had held her side of the bargain, for what? She could picture Peter's cold back turned towards her in their bed. Motionless, detached.

'Because he wasn't the husband I thought he'd be. Because if he loved me, he didn't show it enough, and he made it so hard for me to love him in return. But I did. I loved him. I always did. When I learned of his infidelity, when I read those letters, I guess that was the final straw.'

Peter hung his head.

'Again, the court must commend you, Kate, for your candour in providing us with this character assessment of your husband.'

'It's hardly a crime not to be the husband or father of the year,' Kate retorted, her voice rising with anger.

'True, true,' Król replied. 'For the record, the infidelity you refer to is the affair between Peter Kavanagh and

Margaret Nowak, and the letters mentioned are the letters in evidence on this table,' said Król.

'Did you ever suspect your husband of having other affairs?' he continued.

Kate could see Peter's eyes shift, alert again, panning furtively from her to Król and then back again. He sat rigid, a cornered rat.

'Kate, do you believe that your husband had affairs with other women besides Margaret?' asked Król once more.

Kate hesitated. Again, it struck her that life would be easier with only one gender. 'I suppose I considered it. He was away so much, even when it seemed unnecessary, but I'm not sure if I ever believed it. Then you brought me proof. I guess if there was one, there may be more. What does it matter to you? They weren't your wife. Our child's life is in danger,' Kate continued. Król ignored her question.

Kate wondered if she should just leave and walk out the door. Would he let her? Would she have any chance of finding Amy? Where might her precious baby be? This was all so bloody hopeless.

'We have established a profile of the accused and what he is capable of,' said Król. 'In summation, you are not of the view that Peter Kavanagh was an ideal husband or father.'

Kate had stopped listening. The clock on the opposite wall showed twelve-thirty. It would take twenty minutes downhill to reach Peter's car. Then, who knew how much longer it would take to find where Amy was? They were wasting valuable time. She walked to the window and drew back the curtains. The snow still came. Would the roads be driveable?

Peter was still arguing.

'Apart from this bloody assassination of my character,' he shouted, a tortured look on his face as he held the towel against his wounded leg, 'are we actually going anywhere here? Our daughter is missing.'

'Have we enough time?' said Kate.

Król paused for a moment, assessing the question. 'Peter's car is at the bottom of Cliff Road. After reaching that, you will need thirty minutes, maybe forty. We still have time. We need to finish this.' Kate nodded, ignoring an exasperated Peter to her right.

Król handed her a photograph. It was a young woman, maybe late twenties or early thirties, very shapely and attractive – a pretty face with long dark hair.

Król held out his hand, and Kate handed the photo back to him. He then showed it to Peter. Recognition shone clear in his eyes. 'Do you know the young lady in the photograph?' Król enquired.

'Yes,' he stammered softly.

'Sorry? I didn't hear that,' Król replied. 'Can you repeat your answer?'

'Yes. I do,' repeated Peter.

'What is her name?'

'Tanya.'

'Tanya who?'

'Tanya… Tanya Wagner.'

'Correct. She is Tanya Wagner. German, living in Brussels and the daughter of Commissioner Wagner, a work colleague of yours with whom you also socialise, is that correct?'

'How do you know this?' asked Peter, but he knew already. Tanya had not stayed quiet after all.

'We do not have time for that. Answer the question, please.'

'Yes, it is correct,' Peter said.

'Would you classify Mr Wagner as a good friend of yours, both as a business colleague and as a social acquaintance?' Król asked.

'Good enough. We work together,' replied Peter.

'Fine. Did you tell him that you were fucking his daughter?' asked Król.

Kate felt her pulse quicken.

'No, I did not, and I was not,' replied Peter.

'You deny that you were fucking his daughter?' asked Król.

'Yes,' Peter said.

'I warn you, Mr Kavanagh, this court will punish perjury. Your good wife has displayed exemplary honesty. I demand the same of you. Do you still deny it?'

'Yes.'

'Your continued contempt is noted,' said Król.

12:30a.m.

There comes a moment when crystal clarity cuts through all the fog and haze. There is a purity to it that cannot be altered. It slices its way through the clutter and the noise to beam a searing light on truth. Kate understood in that moment that she'd been hiding from the truth for a long time. She'd been living the life she thought she should be living: the happy wife, the successful family.

Aloof, yet involved. Respectable. If anybody spoke of their family, it could only be good things. They hadn't blotted their copybooks, not till now. But now she didn't care. Her marriage, her future, the scandal that would surely come, none of that mattered. She would rebuild their life, hers and Amy's. They would find a way to start again, to move forward if they were afforded that golden chance.

She knelt beside Peter. His head low, he seemed to be teetering on the edge of collapse. She whispered into his ear. 'None of this matters, Peter. None of it is important. Confess. Our marriage is over. I've read the letters. I don't care anymore. It's okay, just let it go.' His embarrassed eyes looked away. 'We need to find Amy. That's all that matters. Tell the truth so I can go and get our baby.'

Tears fell from his eyes. He nodded. She lightly caressed his shoulder, rose from her knees and sat down again.

'Did you have an affair with Tanya Wagner?' asked Król.

'Yes,' Peter said in a defeated tone, no effort this time at denial.

'Were you, for a brief spell, seeing both this girl, Tanya, and the previous woman, Margaret, at the same time, unbeknownst to either and, of course, unbeknownst to your dearest wife?' asked Król.

'Yes,' Peter said in a low whisper, barely audible.

Kate rose and walked to the other side of the room. 'Sit down, please,' Król asked her, but she ignored him. Król stared after her for a moment but then returned his attention to Peter. 'My, my, Mr Kavanagh, quite the

Lothario. Verdi's Duke would be envious. It is difficult to see how you managed to do any work for us poor citizens. How reassuring to see that our elected officials are busy toiling earnestly on our behalf.'

Peter offered nothing in defence.

'He's admitted to having the affairs. Can we move on, please?' Kate cried in exasperation.

'Is it true that Tanya was also an employee of yours, that she accompanied you on business trips, and that you gave her a promotion?' asked Król.

'Yes.'

'Did you go on weekend trips with her when you told your wife that you were at political or business summits?'

'Yes,' Peter said, eyes glued to the floor below him.

'Can we please get on with this?' screamed Kate again. Król ignored her.

'Did you visit Poland on one of those trips?' asked Król. Peter stiffened a little.

'Yes. I did, but it was business.'

'Where did you stay in Poland?' asked Król.

'We were in Warsaw for a conference, some hotel there. I can't remember.'

'Did you visit Kraków the next day? Saturday, the 17th of July, driving from Warsaw with Miss Wagner in an Audi hire car, staying that night at the Imperial Hotel?' asked Król.

'Yes, I think so,' said Peter, staring down at his fidgeting hands. 'It was a long time ago, I can't remember every single trip I went on, every hotel I stayed in.'

'Yes or no,' said Król.

'All right, yes.'

'You went out to dinner, and when you got back to the hotel later that night, did you have champagne ordered to your room?'

'Yes.'

'Did you leave the hotel the next day in your hire car at roughly 1:00p.m. and drive towards Warsaw?'

'Maybe, yes, I think so. I can't remember the exact times,' Peter stammered, any remaining colour now fully drained from his face. 'Where did you get all of this information?'

Król ignored the question. 'A few miles outside of town, did your car leave your side of the road for reasons unknown and crash into the side of an oncoming vehicle?'

The room fell silent.

'I will repeat the question. Did your car leave its side of the road and crash into an oncoming vehicle?'

Peter closed his eyes and buried his head deep into his chest.

XV

Jude had secured a promising job in one of the large marketing companies. I was still sober and now managed the bar after my uncle Maciek had taken ill. Theia was a joy. We alternated our hours to look after her. She laughed and laughed. She was the happiest of little children. When she was five, we travelled to England to visit Oxford and the graves of my parents. Before we knew it, Theia had started school and was making new friends. We had all we could have wanted. You know that feeling you get when times are so good, you wish that you could just press freeze and replay, over and over. Yet, I always knew it wouldn't last. Happiness is light stolen from darkness; it always fades. We managed seven years in the sun.

It was the end of the summer. It was one of those days that went on forever into the golden glow. Jude had driven for about ten minutes along the narrow country roads that led away from her parents' farm. She reached the main artery that offered Katowice to the west and Kraków to the east. She drove east, returning to the city. She said that it happened as if in slow motion. They had been the only two cars. The other car gradually began edging towards her side of the road. No sudden movements, just a steady veer. She felt sure that the driver would correct their course at any moment. She hadn't registered the danger fully at first, for there shouldn't have been any. It was a sunny day, the road was wide and in good condition, and there was no traffic. Then, as danger loomed large, she froze in that briefest moment of shock and awareness. The shock that comes to those who are the victims of random chaotic events, events that none believe will ever befall them. The awareness that arrives with the knowledge that you possess no control over what happens and when it happens. Whatever is about to occur will occur, with or without your approval.

All of this in the blink of an eye. She frantically turned the wheel in a vain attempt to steer from harm's way, but it was too late. The bang struck like a thunderbolt, and her car careered out of control sidelong into the ditch. Jude was catapulted first sideways and then forward, her head smacking forcibly into the steering wheel. The protruding keys ripped sharply into her cheekbone. She must have blacked out for a minute or two, for when she came around, it took her a moment to realise where she was and what had happened. Then she remembered. She looked behind her, and in that instant, she knew nothing would ever be the same.

12:35a.m.

Peter had tried to forget, but the memory always lurked, resurfacing when he least expected it. How long ago was it now, three years? Sure, to look at him, you'd never know. On the surface, everything was smooth and calm, but below, snagging currents swirled. Guilt you submerge in the dark, but somehow, it rises from the deep to confront you.

They had laughed and joked as they left the hotel, both a little bit fuzzy from too much champagne the night before and not enough sleep. Leaving the city behind, they settled into the drive back to Warsaw. They were messing about. He was fondling Tanya's breasts – God, she was so young and perfect. Hangovers always left him needing more. She leaned over and started to undo his trouser zip. He'd been distracted, and within seconds, it had happened.

In that briefest moment, in that immeasurable time between one existence and another, everything changed forever. His car was drifting out of lane, but he hadn't noticed. Only a few metres, but enough to alter the trajectory of a multitude of lives. He lifted his eyes just in time to see that another car had entered the main road on the opposite side. He could see the driver clearly. A woman. She looked at him in a funny kind of way. Calmness, or was it shock? A recognition that this wasn't right but also an understanding or a hope that he knew what he was doing, that he was in control and that at any moment, he would change course. But he couldn't, and he didn't, and if anything, his flustered grab at the wheel turned them even closer towards the oncoming car. In that nanosecond, he saw the look on her face change to panic. He could hear the blast of her car's horn as it attempted to veer away from a collision, but it was too late. He braced for the crash.

The cars collided, and the force shoved Peter forward into the wheel and then backwards into the seat. Next to him, Tanya screamed as her head hit the dash. Their car rebounded back onto the correct side of the road and careered forward at a sideways angle to the driving lane. For a fleeting moment, frozen in shock, he did nothing. Then awareness returned, and he broke, regaining control of the wheel. He steered into the hard shoulder and stopped. The road was silent behind him.

They had travelled roughly fifty metres from the point of impact. He could still picture the stunned look on Tanya's face as she waited for him to say or do something. Her forehead was bruised and cut; otherwise, she seemed unharmed. His heart was beating a million beats per minute. He opened the door, stepped out and nearly fell over, his legs wobbling like jelly beneath him. He gazed nervously back down the road. Tanya stayed inside sobbing as she peered through the rear-view mirror.

Large black skid marks led his eye to where the other vehicle now lay on its side in the opposite ditch. The two near-sided wheels hovered precariously at an angle over the edge of the road. It had all happened so quickly. It could have been much worse, he told himself. It could have been a head-on collision. The other driver must be okay. She had to be. At worst, minor injuries, cuts and scrapes. Then he heard the scream, and he froze. He looked all around. There was nobody. It had been a split-second decision. If he were arrested, it would be a political matter:

police reports, media coverage, a diplomatic fallout, and possibly even a trial. There would be damages to pay, too. Tanya stared on silently, eyes wide with shock and fear. She waited for his next move. She was young; she didn't deserve this. Neither did Kate and Amy. Peter sat back in the car and drove away.

He called in ill for his Warsaw meetings and they left Poland later that day from Chopin Airport. He and Tanya ended their affair, neither desiring any lingering reminder of their near miss or what they had left behind. He had meant to search online for news of the accident or any hospital reports, but he never did. He just let it drift. It had been so difficult at first to sleep, to remove the events from his thoughts, but eventually, as time passed, it became easier to bury the memory. Now, the skeleton had clawed its way out of the swamp. Bad deeds exhumed.

'Peter,' Król roared, shaking him from his thoughts. 'I repeat the question. A few miles outside of Kraków, did your car leave its side of the road for reasons unknown and crash into the oncoming vehicle?'

Kate had walked slowly back across the floor and stood by her seat, watching him, waiting for his answer.

'We did crash into an oncoming car, but it was only a slight bang. I don't think we crossed the central line. I don't think it was my fault.'

'I have warned you before about perjury. Do you want to reconsider your reply?' asked Król.

'I can't remember exactly what happened, but that's what I think happened. That's what I remember.'

Król glared at him for a moment and then resumed his questioning. 'Did you leave the scene of the crash without checking on the other vehicle?'

Kate gasped audibly, holding a hand to her mouth. Again, Peter paused to try and gather his thoughts. 'I stopped and looked back. It was a slight bump, that's all. Everything seemed fine.'

'Did you see the other driver exit her car?'

'No. But that doesn't mean she wasn't okay.'

'So, you left the scene of a crash without checking on the other vehicle and its passengers. A hit and run?'

'It was not a hit and run,' Peter wailed.

'Then what?' asked Król. 'What is it you would have us call it?'

Peter didn't reply. What could he say now that would make any difference?

12:40a.m.

'I called it in, Dan. I guess they'll come as soon as they can. I left a message on a machine,' said Tommy without much conviction as he sat in a chair next to the bed.

'Good,' mumbled Dan, but he wasn't sure what Tommy was talking about. The room spun around him. He tried to say something, but he couldn't find the idea, let alone the words. Why was Tommy Molloy here? Where was Grace? Dan closed his eyes and drifted.

A voice spoke. 'Dan.' A faint sound, then louder. 'DAN!' A man's voice. Somebody was shaking his arm. It was Tommy. Dan tried to get up, but none of him moved. He couldn't see Molloy's face, but he could feel his hands holding his. Their warmth, their life. That was all he had now; there was nothing else. Tommy was saying something over and over, but Dan wasn't sure what it was. Was he dreaming, or was this real? There it was. 'Forgive me. Dan, please forgive me.'

Dan couldn't figure it out. What did Tommy want to be forgiven for? Dan struggled to get the words out anyway. 'I forgive you.' He could feel his hands being squeezed tighter, and he wasn't sure, but he thought he heard someone sobbing.

Dan couldn't keep his eyes open. Sleep beckoned softly. He knew he had to do something, find something, but he couldn't now. He had to sleep. He was so cold and tired, unable to do anything else, only sleep. That soft shroud would cover him. He closed his eyes, welcoming the honey warmth that flowed through him. On that gentle wave, he drifted away.

12:40a.m.

Król lifted a file from the table, and holding it under the candlelight, he rifled through the papers inside. 'It's all in here, Peter. Interviews with hotel staff, phone records, receipts, times, and a sworn statement from the only witness to the accident. Trzoslo was very thorough.'

Peter lifted his head. 'A witness, what witness?' he asked.

'A local farmer, Jacek Bilowski. He was on his tractor in a nearby field. You had driven past, and by the time you came to a stop, your view of him would have been obstructed by a small crop of trees. He said his attention was averted to the road because it sounded like a car was driving too fast. That was your car,' said Król, pointing an index finger at Peter. 'He saw the other car, heard it slam on the brakes in an attempt to avoid yours, and then came the crash. He gave a sworn testimony that the collision occurred on the opposite side of the road to yours. He was adamant that it was your car at fault.' Król paused for a moment, allowing his words to sink in.

'The location of the brake marks bore this out, as did the location of the crash debris.' Król carefully placed photographs from the scene of the crash on the table. 'Mr Bilowski identified the colour of your car and had a rough opinion as to the shape and model. That was enough for Trzoslo to check with Warsaw Hire companies, and guess what? He discovered a navy saloon fitting the description, rented to one Peter Kavanagh the day before. The hire company informed Trzoslo that the car was returned with damage. However, the driver was happy to accept fault and pay up there and then. He didn't want to contest liability or make any insurance claim. They thought that was odd, but they didn't complain. It's all here,' said Król as he dropped the folder on the table with a thud.

'Did you see the other driver, Peter?' asked Król.

Peter didn't respond.

'She saw you. She described you in detail. Now that I've met you in person, you are a perfect match. The other driver, that was my wife.'

Kate drew a deep breath.

Król rose from his seat and circled Peter's armchair, speaking as he strode.

'Did you hear her scream, Peter?'

Peter's eyes moved furtively as he shook his head to say no.

'I repeat, did you hear my wife Jude scream?'

'No,' replied Peter, 'I don't think so.'

Król paused, fixing his gaze on Peter, who seemed to have shrunk further into the armchair.

'You don't think so? That's odd because Bilowski did. He heard her, and he was further away. He ran to his farmhouse and called the emergency services. That took him over twenty minutes. Nearly half an hour was wasted – precious time for the injured. And now here you are again, time-wasting once more. Amy's precious time.'

Król lifted a piece of paper between his fingertips. 'A signed affidavit from Tanya Wagner detailing and attesting to the same version of events already outlined and confirming that she did hear a scream.' Peter was whispering something to himself over and over, inaudible to anybody but himself. Then, he lifted his head and admitted that which he'd managed to convince himself wasn't true.

'I heard her scream,' he whispered.

Król walked to Peter's side.

'Repeat that.'

'I heard your wife scream,' said Peter again.

Król towered over Peter like a wild animal ready to rip its prey to shreds. Instead, he stepped away.

'Say it again so that there can be no doubt.'

'I heard your wife scream,' said Peter slowly and clearly.

XVI

Jude lay motionless on the hospital bed. I didn't recognise her straight away. I had to look twice, three times. Her soft blonde hair had been replaced by an assortment of probes attached to her shaven scalp. Both eyes were black and swollen. Her nose had been broken, and most of her face was concealed by bandages. Her right eye socket had been smashed. She had been lucky her eye was saved. For some reason, the airbag hadn't deployed. They speculated that a side-on collision and the car's age were factors. An array of machines and monitors read her vital signs. We think we control our bodies, but they survive without instruction. Our lungs rise and fall, our hearts pump blood, our livers filter toxins, all this without our conscious intervention. Body without soul. Through it all, she slept.

She'd suffered a traumatic blow to the skull. They'd induced a coma to quell any further swelling. They said she wasn't really aware of what was happening around her, but crucially, her brain was still active. However, leaving her asleep for too long risked infection setting in.

On the fifth night, I was startled awake from my half-sleep in the visitor's chair. Jude had bolted upright in the bed, eyes bulging, pupils dilating wildly. One arm on the handrail kept her semi-erect. The other cupped her stomach as her face contorted in pain. 'Theia, Theia, where is Theia?' she sobbed aloud. I tried to comfort her, but she grabbed my face in her hands and turned it to hers. I couldn't look her in the eye. I couldn't let her see. 'Theia?' she whispered in a scream, her name ripping through both of us like a shockwave. Our lives and our entire existence becoming that one name and question, a question that Jude could barely muster the courage to ask. A name she could barely emit from her mouth, as if by doing so, by bringing her daughter's name into that room, the truth too would enter, and it, and she, would be extinguished and would disperse and drift away on the air, lost forever. One name asked for everything or nothing. 'Theia?'

12:45a.m.

'Your wife Jude... did she survive?' Kate asked hesitantly. Król began to speak, but the words seemed to catch in his throat. He coughed and started again. 'Yes and no,' he said, his voice wavering, tears forming in his eyes. 'She was never the same. I lost her in that crash. We lost each other.'

'I am so sorry,' said Kate, not fully understanding but wary to ask further. She lifted Król's file from the table along with the torch she'd left there earlier. Shining the light onto the file with one hand, Kate began leafing through the contents with her other. As she turned the pages, names, times, places, and faces downloaded into her mind at warp speed. The damaged lives of others were reduced to data. Then, a name she hadn't seen before. A surgeon's report. Test results, medical notes. Coma. More brain injuries.

'Who is Theia?' she asked slowly, softly.

Król rose from his seat and, turning his back to them, he stood before the fire. He lifted some dry logs and tossed them in.

Kate kept scanning the report as quickly as she could.

'Your daughter?' she asked, her voice faltering as she did.

Król turned to face her, his eyes filled with tears. His face bore such a tortured expression that Kate had to glance away.

'She'd called me earlier that day. She told me of her fun time on the farm. She'd chased the chickens, milked a cow, and played games with her grandparents. Then she told me that she loved me most like she always did and that she'd see me later. She asked if she could sleep with her mammy and me that night in our bed. I said yes. But she didn't sleep with us. She never came home.'

Peter put his two hands to his head, palms over his ears and began to rock back and forth, emitting a slow, soft whimpering sound as he did. Kate's chest tightened. She could hardly breathe. Król reached into his holdall and lifted out a photograph. He held it out in front of a head-down Peter.

'Look.'

Peter kept rocking, eyes on the floor. 'Look!' shouted Król angrily. Peter snapped his head upwards and eyed the photograph. Król walked to Kate and showed her the picture. Kate hardly recognised Król, but it was him. A younger, happier, more animated man. A contented man, a broad grin lighting his face. A glint in his eye as he looked adoringly at the smiling woman next to him. Between them nestled a laughing young child, her arms wrapped about the woman's waist. 'My wife Jude and my daughter Theia,' he said. Król walked to the small table and carefully placed the photograph resting beside the two white envelopes.

XVII

The ground in the cemetery had frozen hard. In that unforgiving dirt lay the remains of our daughter Theia. I tried to visualise her face, but it wasn't right. I listened for her voice, her laugh, yet nothing came. An old woman passed and patted my shoulder gently. 'She's in a better place now,' she said. I struggled to restrain myself, to not shout obscenities at her. Eventually, I stopped visiting. I thought somehow there'd be solace in that graveyard, yet all I could think of was how meaningless everything was.

Most parents would sacrifice themselves to protect their children. I wish I had been afforded that chance. She'd been in a coma since the accident, though hers wasn't induced. We couldn't stir her. Months passed. Jude had recovered, but Theia still lay asleep, the only signs of life, the electrical impulses on the monitors. At first, Jude wouldn't leave her bedside, day or night. We would sit talking to her, playing her favourite songs over and over, hoping they might spark something. Jude prayed to all the saints and all the gods who might care to listen, but none did. After a while, I suggested we alternate stays, with one of us getting some proper rest at home, but Jude would have none of it. She slept in a chair or on the floor in a sleeping bag. Slowly, as time drifted by and nothing improved, the guilt obverwhelmed her. I told her it wasn't her fault, but she wouldn't listen. She fell so low. That broke my heart more than anything. My Jude, I couldn't help her. I couldn't do anything. They gave her medication, but it changed her. She became a zombie, hardly aware of her surroundings. In the end, she stopped visiting. She stopped doing anything.

All the while, our little baby slept silently, and if she could hear me, she showed no sign. She never did wake. The doctors reported no cranial nerve reflexes. Irreversible brain-stem dysfunction was the diagnosis. They suggested, delicately at first, more forcibly later, that there could be no positive outcome from delaying the inevitable. They wanted to pull the plug. It was the humane thing to do. I said no. Never. The hospital sought a court order. At home, Jude seemed to be mirroring her child. She was rarely conscious, unable to deal with what was happening. I held them at bay as long as I could with injunctions and protests. The court visits and candlelit prayer groups became a welcome distraction from the empty reality of my bedside vigil. I did my best. I swear I did. Not a day goes by that I don't regret that decision. How did I let them convince me? How I flicked the switch.

A year or so later, I read a newspaper story about a boy from Leicester who'd been declared brain dead. He, too, *had been in a car crash, and all his doctors insisted that he couldn't recover. His father demanded an independent opinion, and a new neurosurgeon agreed to see the boy. Incredibly, this physician said he could detect brain activity. Together, they convinced the hospital to slowly take the boy out of his coma to see if he improved. He did. Later, the boy said that he could hear the voices talking all around him as he lay motionless in his hospital bed. He heard them declare that all was lost. And then he heard his father say no.*

I have never stopped wondering if my little Theia had been able to hear us all along. Did she think her father would save her? Did my baby girl know I was there? Did she know that my world had ended? Did she hear me say yes?

12:50a.m.

Kate closed her eyes and prayed. For forgiveness. For mercy. This nightmare was infinitely worse than she could have ever imagined. Misery defiling misery. She had to find a path through this deluge of suffering. She could never change what had happened; she could never make it right for this man's daughter, but he could return hers. She had to keep going. There was no way out now but to see it through to whatever the end might be. Nothing could prepare you for this, a hanging court in her own home presided over by a righteous and vengeful judge. Her husband's life teetering in the balance. Blood on his hands. The fate of her daughter dangling by a thread. Every minute, a minute closer to... Should she continue to argue? What defence did Peter have or deserve? The question entered her mind and lingered longer than she was comfortable with. How can it feel to be

243

the parent of a dead child? Could anything be more cruel or unnatural? Kate thought of Amy, and again came the tears. Time was not their friend, and if anybody needed her help, it was her daughter. Yet she couldn't – she couldn't just leave Peter to the mercy of Król. She had to do the right thing.

She scanned Król's file as she paced about the room. The police report, the investigator's notes, the hospital files; all appeared damning. Yet, an idea had formed, a possible way forward. She began.

'Firstly, I want to say how dreadfully sorry I am for your loss. What you have endured is harrowing. It should not be the fate of any parent.' Kate looked straight at Król as she spoke, and he nodded, accepting her heartfelt wishes, saying nothing. 'And I am also sorry for these things I am about to say. Please understand that I only say them because we are in this court, your court, and I must play my role. I must respect this process that you have started.' Again, Król nodded his understanding.

'So, your case is as follows. We have an adulterous husband. That much is clearly proven, but adultery, no matter how dishonourable, is not a crime in any part of the civilised world. Indeed, you yourself have slept with another man's wife.'

Peter lifted his head. 'How do you know that?' he asked her. Now, he could speak.

Kate, to her shame, felt no shame. 'Because that woman was me,' she said, and for a very brief moment, the words gave her a vengeful pleasure. She chided herself. She needed to be better than that, better than these two men before her. Peter glanced from Kate to Król and back. 'Bitch,' he spat, anger burning in his eyes.

'Are you serious?' asked Kate incredulously. 'You have some nerve. The only reason this man is here is because of you. You brought all of this to our door. How dare you, you self-obsessed prick. You have no idea, do you hear me, absolutely no idea how many times I've been hit on all these years? By men like you, men who don't care about the damage they'll do. But I never, I never. I would never. Not until I read your filth and I saw your contempt for everything we built.' Kate lifted the pile of letters and angrily flung them at Peter. The ribbon opened, and they scattered across the floor.

'I trusted you. I trusted us. It was me here all the time, minding our baby, making our home,' Kate shouted angrily. 'It was me encouraging you when you wallowed in your self-doubts. I sacrificed my career so you could play the hero, the small-town man making it big. While all the time, all along, you, you were out screwing whatever you could. Well, shame on you, Peter, shame on fucking you! Let all of this be on your head. Our baby is in danger because of you! This man has lost his child because of you. So no more of your self-pitying bullshit. Amy doesn't have the time for it.'

Peter opened his mouth to retort and then thought better of it and shut it again.

12:55a.m.

The clock on the wall showed 12:55a.m. Kate had one hour to save her daughter. She pushed the awful negative thoughts away. If she considered the implications of failure, of running out of time, she'd wither and collapse.

Holding on to every ounce of composure she could, she resumed her argument. 'As I said, adultery is not a crime. Next, we have the car crash that so tragically resulted in serious injury to your daughter. Here, I see problems. The first major issue is that we have a police force that closed this case, according to these notes. They never prosecuted my husband, nor did they contact him in any way. We only have your prejudicial investigator's file. We have not been afforded sufficient time to assess the truth of his evidence. Secondly, per his report and from your own words, your daughter was alive when she reached the hospital. How are we to know what standard of medical care she received while there? Were there delays? Was valuable time lost by the medical staff? None of this is clear. The evidence presented is one-sided. It is sparse, and, in many cases, it is uncorroborated. We have had no chance to counter these claims.' Kate kept walking, circling the room.

'Finally, and most importantly, the accident response unit verified that your daughter was not wearing her seat belt. That seems to me to be the biggest contributor towards her injuries. My husband cannot be culpable for that. Please forgive me for asking this, but was that not your wife's responsibility?'

Kate paused and waited nervously for Król's reaction. Her words left her feeling horrible. They unsettled her. She had no heart, no wish to say these things, things that she would never dream of saying, not in any normal world. Yet, in this world that consisted of the three of them in this lighthouse, on this clifftop, where every move could mean the difference between winning and losing, life and death, then she had to, she had to fight for Peter's life, for the life of her child, by any means necessary. To challenge a grieving father, to question the mother of a dead child, these were awful things, but she'd been left no choice. It was he who had chosen to open the wounds.

Król's fiery eyes narrowed. 'No, Kate, adultery is not a crime, on that we are agreed, no matter how it hurts the innocent. However, in many civilisations, it is deemed so, and it is punishable by all manner of vicious acts. Leaving that aside, what Peter's adulteries illuminate for us is the very essence and character of the man. Unfortunately, it seems your husband is best viewed in the shadows. He has a lengthy affair with a married woman. Then he would rather be fucking a young and impressionable work colleague than be at home with his wife and daughter. How many more were there? Was there no satisfaction at home, Kate?'

Kate didn't rise to the bait. The jab stung, but the whys and why-nots were irrelevant now, as were the acts. Peter was away again, finding his wallowing pit on the floor. He was proving as useless in time of need as he had been in the good times.

'You are correct, Kate; valuable time was lost. The bang to Theia's head caused internal bleeding, and by the time she reached the hospital, she had lapsed into a coma. If the emergency services had arrived maybe ten or fifteen minutes earlier, had she made it to the hospital quicker, they might have stabilised her, stopped the bleeding and prevented the damage.' Król wiped his eyes and cleared his throat. 'My wife's phone was found fifty feet away in a field. If the farmer had brought his phone with him, he could have used it. If your husband had reported the incident, then who knows? All these ifs. All these little things make the things that happen, happen the way they happen. Both Peter and Tanya had their phones. An emergency call from either could have changed everything. So yes, valuable time was lost, but not by the hospital. It was lost because of your husband!'

Król walked to Kate and took the file from her hand. He searched through some of the pages and then held one out for her to see. 'Here,' he said aloud, his finger pointing to a line on the hospital report. 'The response time of the emergency services.' He moved his finger. 'Here, the arrival time into the emergency ward.' Again, he jabbed. 'Here, the time of surgery and the time Theia was attached to the life-support machine.' Then he stabbed his finger forcibly into the page. 'Here! The date and time that I allowed them to turn off the machine. So, as to my wife's culpability, no, I never thought that she was responsible for what happened, but she did. She had fastened the belt, but Theia opened it to retrieve a fallen toy. A child hardly deserves to lose her life for that, does she?'

A thought came to Kate. Had he slipped up? Yes, she felt sure that he had. Had she worked it out?

'It wasn't Amy you were on trial for, nor Niamh, it was Theia. She was the child you referred to, the one that you killed. Wasn't she? You killed her when you gave permission for her life-support to be turned off. If you, Nicholas Król, have already been tried and convicted for the killing of your own daughter, then how can my husband be responsible for the same crime? If that is true, then this is not an eye for an eye; it is two eyes for one, and it doesn't add up.' For the first time, Kate felt like she could win this battle. Even Peter seemed bolstered, his head lifting from his knees. They waited on Król.

'Well done, Kate, you are right. I ended my daughter's life and...' Król struggled as the words caught again in his throat, 'every day since has been a living hell. However, my little Theia wasn't the only innocent victim,' he continued. 'Jude was seven months pregnant with our son.'

1:00a.m.

Peter tried to gather himself. How much more suffering could be unleashed? He felt ill. He'd caused it all. He couldn't deny it.

'We were to name our son Konrad after my father. He arrived stillborn. Jude and I never recovered from that,' said Król. 'So, count them up, Kate. How many dead eyes do you need?'

Kate remained silent, for what could she say that would dam this torrent of woe? Peter buried his head in his hands again. He could never have imagined so much horror, so much sorrow.

After a few moments that seemed like an age, Król spoke into the void. 'My daughter died due to the actions and inactions of your husband. My unborn baby son, too. I demand that this court gives me justice. I ask the jury to find Peter Kavanagh guilty of killing through misdemeanour and omission. I decree that in line with the precedent agreed tonight, should the court find the defendant guilty, then the appropriate punishment is a life for a life.'

Peter couldn't argue anymore. He'd lost the will to fight. It wasn't just that it happened; it was how it happened. He'd left the scene of an accident. An accident caused by him and his mistress. They'd left a car teetering upside down in a ditch on a country road. A pregnant mother and her young daughter fighting for their lives. He'd heard a scream but fled like a coward. As time passed, he'd convinced himself he hadn't heard it, that he'd imagined it. Tanya had never spoken of it either, not till now. He'd never wanted to know the reason for that scream, but now he did. He couldn't bear to meet Król's eyes, to see the sorrow and hatred they held. He thought of his own parents. They had raised him to be a good person. Where had he gone wrong? He hadn't meant for any of this to happen, but it had, and it was he who was responsible. And Kate. The disgust in her eyes. The hatred. He could issue a million apologies now, but they would all ring hollow and useless. He felt light-headed, as if he might pass out.

He sat up as best he could. It was time to do the right thing, to try and save his daughter. Peter's words came unsteadily, his waivering voice not sounding like his own.

'Nicholas. Can I call you Nicholas? I'm not sure I deserve to.'

Król listened silently.

'I understand why you are here. I am so sorry, believe me. If I could go back, I would change it all. I can't. I know I am to blame for this, but please believe that I never intended harm.' Neither Kate nor Król spoke as he paused, searching, it seemed, for words that could never truly express his remorse or in any way make better his actions.

'Please know, for what it's worth, that I have suffered these years too. Of course, not like you, but I have. What happened never left me. It haunted me. It clung to me. All of this,' Peter said, waving his hand at the files of evidence on the table, 'Kate and Amy are innocent. This is not their doing. Tell me what you want from me. Tell me what I need to do to get Amy back.'

For the first time, Peter felt that he saw something in Król's eyes that hadn't been there before – a glimmer of humanity.

'Thank you for your words, Peter,' replied the sombre judge. 'First, we must ask the jury to cast its vote in your trial. So, Peter Kavanagh, are you guilty of these crimes?'

'Yes,' came the immediate reply from Peter.

Just from stating that simple word, from accepting responsibility for all that had happened, Peter could feel the cross lifting from his back. It had only been a few short years, but it had felt like an eternity.

1:02a.m.

And with that, it was gone. The raging anger, the hatred that had consumed him. Król could see that Peter was just another man who had fucked up. Not very different to the countless others who had gone before him. He didn't see the devil he had hoped to see. Still, he had to finish this, to end it once and for all. For Theia. For Konrad. For his beloved Jude.

Kate stood by him at the fireplace. She spoke softly to him so that only the two of them could hear. 'This is wrong, Nicholas. I think you know that. It is time to stop. Please don't let your grief submerge you. Don't let hate win.' Her eyes looked into his, imploring whatever good remained within him to rise. She took his hands in hers, holding them together as if in joint prayer. 'You have broken Peter, his body, his spirit. Our marriage is over. Enough is enough. All these wrongs don't make a right. None of this will bring your children back. Please return Amy to us. I promise we'll never talk about this night to anyone, ever. You have my word on Amy's life. We all walk away. That will be justice of a kind. Please, Nicholas, please.'

Król closed his eyes for a moment. He considered how far he had come. Could he leave it all now, just walk away?

'I'm no priest, Kate. There is no forgiveness to be found here. For you, for Amy, I am truly sorry. But now you must decide. Peter or Amy. Whom do you choose? Do you find Peter Kavanagh guilty or not guilty?'

1:03a.m.

Król crossed the room and handed Peter the gun. The long, narrow barrel, the satin metal boxy finish, the warm wooden grip. Even in these circumstances, with it to be the instrument of his demise, Peter couldn't deny the elegant beauty of the thing. Tears fell from Kate's eyes. Oddly, this comforted him. She still cared. He thought of his daughter. How he loved her so. How he would miss her, and she would him. Daughters saw no ill in their fathers.

'Kate, do you find your husband guilty?' asked Król again. Kate knelt low by Peter's armchair. She put her face to his and kissed him. He put the gun down and wiped the tears from her cheeks with his good hand.

'It's okay, Kate. It really is. Do what must be done. I forgive you anything that you might feel needs forgiving.

This is all my fault. I'm ordering you to do it for Amy. Please.'

'Are you sure?' Kate asked.

'I don't think I've ever been more sure of anything,' he replied.

Kate kissed Peter on the forehead and turned to Król. She had no choice. She had to save her daughter.

'Guilty,' she said.

Król spoke. 'Peter, you and I have been charged with terrible crimes. We have both been found guilty, and our sentences have been agreed. Our lives in return for the lives we have taken. It is time. Utter your last goodbyes, and say your final prayers. Then do not think further – just act. When you have acted, I will tell Kate where to find Amy and how to deactivate the bomb. Then I will follow you, and all of this will end. Our time here will be over, and we will be at peace.'

Peter rose awkwardly to his feet, his injured leg stretched out straight to one side. He met Król's eyes. Dark still pools filled deep with sadness. He could feel himself drawn towards them, into them, his soul buckling under their irresistible weight. Król nodded to him. Here in this hell, they had found a communion of sorts.

'You are a man of your word?' Peter asked him.

'Yes,' Król replied. 'If I am nothing else, I am still that.'

'Promise me that Amy is alive.'

'She is alive.'

'Promise me, please.'

'I promise you, Peter, on the memory of my children.'

Kate emitted a sobbing wail of emotion. She believed him.

Peter beheld the story of Król's face. Pained, resolute, truthful. He believed him. A euphoric rush flushed through him. His baby would survive this – he would deliver her to safety.

'You will tell Kate where to find her?'

'Yes, Peter, you have my word.'

'There is still time to get there, to turn off the bomb?'

Król looked at the clock on the wall. 'Yes, but we need to act now, quickly.'

Król went to his holdall and retrieved Kate's phone. He handed it to her. 'You cannot be here for this. Make your way down Cliff Road to Peter's car. In ten minutes, I will call you, and I will tell you where to find Amy.' Kate stared at Król and then at Peter, her cheeks wet with tears. Kate returned to Peter's side, took his face in her hands and kissed his lips. They hugged, each holding on for one last time to the life they once shared.

'I'm so sorry,' mumbled Kate. 'There's nothing else I can do.'

'It's okay,' he told her. 'I never thought things could get so messed up. I didn't mean to hurt anybody. I thought I could do whatever I wanted. You can't. Nobody can. Don't forget, tell Amy I love her. Tell her I will always love her. Don't tell her the bad things, please. I am sorry, Kate, so sorry. I do love you. I always loved you. Please remember that. I just couldn't get out of my own way.'

'Shhh… shhh, don't…,' she said as she brushed the matted hair from his bruised face. He rested his head on her shoulder. Felt her skin, her hair, her warmth. Her familiar scent comforted him. She had loved him once; nothing could change that.

Peter dug his car keys out of his pocket.

'Here, go quick. Find her.'

Kate stared at him one last time, and then she turned, left the room and was gone.

XVIII

Jude had been hearing Theia's voice. She was convinced that her child's spirit lived on. It was as if the two of them had merged into one. Jude was so frazzled, deluged by dose after dose of stupefying medication. She mumbled things over and over, and I could hardly make out her words. This wasn't my Jude, not the girl who rescued me, who took me into the light. Maybe the cocktail of antidepressants and other chemicals had wired her to a higher frequency, one I couldn't tune into or didn't want to. For if Theia spoke to me, what would she say? 'Daddy, why did you let me go?'

As I failed Theia, I failed Jude, too. When she needed me most, I couldn't help her. There was nothing I could say or do to make any of it better. And wasn't I part of the problem? It had become unbearable to look into each other's eyes… to see our dead children looking back at us. That was a hell worse than death.

Slowly, the months came and went. Time was a tortuous blur for both of us. Days suffered one into the next. Jude didn't leave the apartment. She hadn't been to work since before the accident. She would spend endless hours in Theia's bedroom, lying on her bed, touching her clothes, smelling her hairbrush. We hardly spoke. What was there to say? In the silence, we barely hung on. I was drinking again, as much as I could stomach and then more. Still, the emptiness wouldn't fill. Maciek tried to help, but what could he do? What could anybody do? One morning, I woke up hungover and tried to rise, but the pain and sickness pinned me to the sheets. I felt Jude near to me. She caressed my head softly, back and forth, back and forth. 'Go back to sleep, my love,' she whispered delicately, over and over. I told her that I loved her and that I was sorry, sorry for everything.

'I love you too,' she replied, 'always.'

I must have dozed off. I could hear the voices of children laughing and playing. We were at the playground in the park. Theia was running and climbing. Every few minutes, she would look back to where Jude and I lay on the picnic blanket, and she would wave and laugh, reassured by our presence. Jude held my hand, and we looked into each other's eyes, and I knew that there in that playground were all the things we ever needed.

I woke with a startle. I was alone. My head pounded. I could hear the plip, plop of dripping water. Not loud, but repetitive, drip, drip, dripping a hole in my brain. It was coming from the bathroom. I struggled from the bed and stumbled my way to the door. The trickling water hailed me louder and louder. 'Come quickly,' it pleaded.

I found her in the bathtub. At first, I could only see her hair as it bobbed on the water's surface like a lily pad in a pond. As I crept closer, I saw her submerged body. Empty medicine vials lay discarded in the mess. I attempted to pull her from the bath, but I lost grip and fell forward with her, both of us half-in, half-out of the tub. Eventually, I managed to haul her limp body up and over the rim, and my darling Jude fell backwards into my sodden arms. I embraced her tightly as together we slumped to the wet, tiled floor. I pushed her chest frantically and gave her mouth-to-mouth, but there was nothing – our final kiss. I coiled myself about her and whispered over and over that I loved her and that I always would till the end of time.

1:07 a.m.

Kate stumbled down the steep descent as fast as the drifts would allow, the tumbling snow propelling her forward as she went. She checked the time. Fifty-three minutes. On she pressed. She felt her pocket again for the car keys. She knew they were there, but she still had to check. She had to do something. She passed two sets of tracks that were going in the opposite direction, upwards. For stretches, the tracks became singular. Kate guessed Peter had walked in Król's footprints. It struck her that she'd left her husband to die. What else could she have done? That was the choice she'd been offered, Peter or Amy. Król could have killed her and Peter if he had wished. It was the only way. On she pushed, one eye on the path downwards, one eye on the phone in her hand, waiting for that precious call.

She passed the ruins of the old school on her left, its vertical walls, the last structure visible not covered in white. She removed her gloves and immediately felt the icy air bite at her fingers. She scrolled until Dan Brady's details appeared. She pressed the call button. Dan needed to know about Grace and Niamh. Kate trusted him not to intervene at the lighthouse until she had received the vital location information from Król. Dan would help her to end this. There was no answer. Her heart sank. Kate pulled back on her gloves and stumbled on as fast as she could go.

The storm was gusting again, and thick swarms of snow swirled about her. The cold air filled her lungs as her chest heaved from the exertion. Her numb cheeks tingled in the biting chill. All the while, in her right gloved hand, she clutched her phone. Still no call. It had been over fifteen minutes since she'd left the lighthouse. She dared not consider what the call signified when it did come. What had preceded it? Her decision. Peter's sacrifice. She shivered hard in the unrelenting cold. None of this would leave her, not until she, too, was dead in the ground. Time was ebbing away, slipping through her fingers. How long had it been? Eighteen minutes. Why hadn't Król called? Would he keep his word? Without that call, she was lost. She could do nothing out here on her own.

It was hard to lift her aching legs, but somehow Kate kept going. It seemed to take an age, but at last, she reached the last major turn in the road. Far to her left, she could see the lights of Blackcliff. On the edge of town, the church and its cemetery. There, her parents lay. If they could see her now, what would they say or do? It seemed preposterous amidst the silent white expanse that this nightmare was really happening. A few hundred metres ahead at the foot of the road, she spotted the outline of Peter's snow-covered car. She was nearly there, but still no call.

When she reached the vehicle, Kate cupped her hands over her face and blew hot breath to warm her frost-bitten skin. She fished the car keys from her pocket and pressed the alarm fob. Welcome lights flashed in response. She heaved open the snow-covered door. In the passenger seat sat Amy's teddy Buster. Kate struggled to retain control. Half sitting in the driver's seat, she put her foot to the clutch and pressed the start button. The Range Rover purred into life. She fetched a jumper of Peter's from the back seat and backed out of the vehicle. Bundling the jumper, she used it to wipe clear the snow from the windows and mirrors. Next, she grabbed the ice scraper from the glove compartment and scratched away at the frosty layers that clung to the windscreens. All done, she climbed back into the driver's seat and shut the door behind her.

The heat from the engine was working, and soon, the coatings of ice and fog had dispersed sufficiently to allow her to see clearly. She slowly reversed the car in a ninety-degree arc, taking great care not to slide into the roadside ditch. Any mistakes now would prove fatal. She was ready. Kate stared at her phone, urging it to ring. Nothing. She leaned forward, resting her head on the steering wheel, and began to cry. Tears came in heaving sobs that rose through her exhausted body. Suddenly, blue lights began dancing across the dashboard. Kate sat upright with a jolt and stared anxiously out the window.

The night sky had turned indigo as flashing emergency lights approached. Her heart leapt – Dan at last. The Garda car stopped ten feet from Peter's. The door opened, and out stepped Sergeant O'Sullivan.

1:21a.m.

Peter didn't want to die. Now that Kate and the life he once loved had gone, the thought of dying without his loved ones overwhelmed him. Raw terror coursed through his veins. It was true what they said: a projection of your life reeled before your eyes. A million recollections flared like the bulb flashes of an old camera: flashing thoughts and memories downloading into some essence that survived this realm.

He locked in a vision of Amy. A memory of a time when everything in his world was good. A moment that encapsulated more meaning and joy than a whole existence. He could see it clearly. Feel it. The smell of the sea filled the air. Seagulls squawked loudly, and the sun's rays warmed their skin. He touched her delicate hair, her soft face. Together, they walked, hand in hand, wandering barefoot across the sandy beach. It was one of those long, lazy afternoons in Blackcliff that seemed to go on forever. They collected shells and skipped in and out of the foamy wash. The breeze blew through her wavy red hair, and her freckled face glowed in the hazy golden sunlight. She looked back at him, her mischievous smile beaming. Her purity always astounded him. Her absolute perfection, untarnished, unspoilt. He prayed that she too might retain this memory, lock it away for when she thought of him.

And if she thought of him, that somehow he would return in those moments and whisper again in her ear that he loved her more than any father ever loved his daughter.

Peter looked to Król. He'd damaged this man, damaged his family. And now all of that damage had been returned. All the turns that led in any good direction had long been passed. There was no escaping, no hiding, and the journey ended here. It was always going to end here.

Król spoke, and it was as if he had read Peter's mind. 'We both had everything, didn't we? Loving wives and children who adored us. A place to call home. There's not much more than that, really. Family. Love.'

'It's a shame that you have to be standing on the ledge to see it,' Peter replied. 'You don't know what you've got till it's gone and all that.'

'And here we are, on the ledge,' said Król.

'Can I have a cigarette?' Peter asked as he suddenly felt an irresistible longing, a stronger craving than he'd felt in years.

Król rummaged around in Peter's coat for a moment and then returned with the pack and a lighter. He dug out a cigarette and handed it to Peter. Peter placed it between his lips and, Król lit it.

'Want one?'

'No, thanks,' said Król, 'they'll kill you.'

Peter smiled and blew a circle of blue smoke into the air. The nicotine rushed sweetly through his bloodstream.

'I'm sorry... for what it's worth, I'm so sorry,' he whispered.

A moment of forlorn silence sat between them.

'I am too,' said Król.

Peter shrugged.

'Are you ready?' asked Król as he watched the smoke rise to the ceiling.

'No,' said Peter, shaking his head. 'Are you?'

Peter could see tears of emotion forming in Król's eyes.

'I thought I was, but if I go and they are not waiting for me, then what? Was this whole existence for nothing?' He paused, and it looked as though the thought pained him as it formed.

'I hope not,' he finished.

Król walked to the coffee table and lifted his pocket watch. He closed over the cover. He seemed lost for a moment as he rubbed the back of the piece with his fingertips. He then placed it on the small side table next to the letters and the photograph he had already left for Kate. He returned to where Peter stood. He lifted his phone, ready to dial Kate's number.

'It's time, Peter.'

Peter closed his eyes. He lifted the pistol and brought the barrel level with the side of his head. He began to yell as loudly as he could. Nothing coherent, just noise. A guttural death roar. One final act of defiance. One final act of living. A roar that would drown out his whimpering tears and wash away his sadness and fear. In all the noise, it would be over before he lost his nerve. He pulled the trigger.

1:25a.m.

Instinctively, Kate pressed the lock-doors button. She needed that call from Król, and she needed this vehicle.

They were her passage to Amy. Nothing, and no one would stop that. She lowered the driver's window halfway, took a deep breath, and faced the sergeant.

'Hi, Kate, I was expecting to see Peter.'

'Hi, Sergeant,' said Kate.

As she was about to say more, her phone buzzed loudly on the passenger seat. Kate grabbed it and put it to her left ear, the ear furthest from the sergeant.

'Kate. It is over,' said Król without emotion. 'Amy, Niamh and Grace are in an old shed at Grace's farm. The shed in the backfield, out of view of the house. It is nearly hidden by overgrowth. The number eight will turn the bomb off. Just press the number eight, nothing else.' Kate knew the shed. She'd grown up playing in and around it. His voice paused for a moment and then continued nearly inaudibly, 'I'm sorry, Kate, goodbye,' and with that, he was gone.

Kate could feel Sully's eyes burning holes in her head. She didn't trust him, never had. She quickly processed whether to tell him everything or not. Her child's precious time was ticking away. It would take at least twenty minutes to get to the farm at regular speed. In the snow, she had no idea. The car clock read 1:27a.m. If she told Sully her story, would he believe her, or would he dither and delay? When he learned of a bomb, would he stop her from searching? She couldn't risk telling him. She had to move fast.

'Everything okay, Kate?' he asked.

'Yes, Sergeant. Everything's fine,' Kate said, trying hard to stifle her internal panic, but even to her, the words sounded unconvincing.

'You seem upset.'

'No, I'm fine, really,' she replied.

'Who was that on the phone?' asked the sergeant.

'Peter, why?'

'Peter?' The sergeant's tone suggested he didn't believe her. 'Where is he?'

'At home.'

'I see,' said the sergeant, eyeing her suspiciously.

'I was just heading up to your place, Kate,' said the sergeant. 'I'm looking for Dan.'

'Dan? Why would he be there?' said Kate.

'He was worried about an email you sent to him. Something about a stranger? He said he was coming out this way. Now, we can't get through to him. I'd finished, gone home for the night, and now I'm back out working again. What's going on, Kate?'

A fresh wave of despair flooded through Kate. She had hoped that Dan might be at the farm, that somehow he might have already found the girls. She scrambled as best she could for a reply.

'A stranger…? Oh, he left hours ago. He was searching for somebody he thought lived close by. A foreign guy, he didn't know the area. Peter wasn't home, so I got a little worried.'

'He was looking for them in a snowstorm?'

Kate said nothing.

The sergeant continued to gaze disbelievingly. She returned his confused stare with one laced with exasperation. He was wasting her time, and this was the wrong time to be wasting her time.

'Kate,' the sergeant spoke slowly and sternly as he stared straight into her eyes, 'if there is something you want to share, or if you are in some kind of danger, it's best you talk to me now.' Kate returned his gaze unblinking. The sergeant knew she was lying. She'd never been a good liar. 'No. There's nothing, Sergeant. I just want to be with my daughter tonight, that's all. I've really got to go now, okay?'

'There's a red smear on your cheek.'

Kate looked in the mirror. Fuck. It was blood. She wiped at her face with her sleeve. 'It's just make-up,' she replied, her voice steely and resolute.

'You sure?'

'I'm sure.'

The police officer continued to eye her with suspicion. He looked behind her to the rear seats and then to the passenger seat – nothing to see, only Buster the bear peering back.

'These roads are very dangerous. Maybe it's best if we go up to the lighthouse together.'

'No,' Kate said.

'Why not? Where are you going?'

'To the farm, Amy is there.'

'She's not there, Kate,' said the sergeant and now his face spoke of confusion.

'How do you know?' asked Kate, trying to stop her body from shaking.

'Dan was there earlier. He said the house was empty,' said Sully.

For a moment, Kate just looked at the Garda. His story only confirmed what she already knew. She wasn't going back to the lighthouse, not for Sully, not for anybody. She had to move and fast; she'd wasted too much time.

'Follow me,' she said, and at that same moment, she stepped on the accelerator. The Range Rover leapt out of its bed of snow and spun forward along the slippery surface. Kate fought for control and, at last, felt a grip. She turned the vehicle away from its path towards the opposite ditch and steered it for town. In the rear-view, she saw O'Sullivan standing in the middle of the road, staring after her, blue lights flashing behind him.

1:25a.m.

Eyes closed, body trembling, Peter had pulled the trigger and waited for the boom. But all that came was a mechanical click. His legs had buckled beneath him, and he'd fallen to his knees. His trousers felt warm and moist. He'd soiled himself. Tears flooded that he couldn't control.

'Up,' Król demanded.

'I can't,' cried Peter, 'my leg.'

'An empty chamber. Try again,' said Król.

'What?' Peter cried. 'Fuck you! This is sick. It's inhumane.'

'I'm sorry, Peter, that was a mistake. It won't happen again. Remember Amy and Kate,' said Król as he waved the phone in his hand.

Peter closed his eyes. His body shuddered in nervous convulsions. Maybe his heart would explode before the bullet ripped through his brain. He stayed kneeling and pointed the barrel to his head again. He could do this. *Don't think, just do it.* He gritted his teeth, roared aloud and pulled the trigger.

Again, nothing, only the click and the empty chamber.

Peter began to weep aloud. He cried and cried because he had nothing else. He felt a firm hand on his shoulder, a silent reminder of where he was and what he had to do. 'Fuck you,' he shouted at Król, shaking his head from side to side, 'I can't, not again, I won't.'

'Fuck you too, Peter,' replied Król. 'In time, you will thank me. It's over.'

'What?' blubbered Peter through the tears. Was this another twisted move in this awful game? Król said nothing more and walked away. He had his phone to his ear, waiting. Then he began speaking to Kate. He told her matter-of-factly about the kids and the shed at the farm. He told her the number, eight. He said he was sorry and said goodbye. Peter remained silent, hardly daring to breathe. Were they truly done?

Król lifted the picture of himself, Jude and Theia. He'd done this for them. Would they have wanted it? He had felt certain that they had led him here, driven by their need to find justice. But now, he wasn't so sure. All this ugliness, it wasn't him, and it wasn't them. He couldn't finish this in their name. It would be wrong – no more. Kate was right. There had been enough grief. He had believed that these events were inevitable, just the unavoidable fall of destiny's dominoes. Not now. He was stepping out of that stream.

He turned to Peter. 'You're like a cat, Peter – too many lives. I'm allowing you one more. Make this one work. Remember what happened on that road in Poland. Remember what happened here.'

'Thank you,' whispered Peter weakly. Król nodded his head slowly in response. 'Call for help when I have gone. Your leg needs urgent care.'

'Where are you going?' asked Peter.

'Time stands still when there is nobody left to share it with. I can't endure that emptiness anymore. I don't want to live forever in that suffering. Not here, not without them.' He shook his head with finality. 'No more. I am ready now.'

Peter listened silently.

'Come and help me, Peter. Are you able?' asked Król as he stood over him, offering an arm of support. Using Król for leverage, Peter clambered up. Excruciating pain ripped through his leg and hand. He could barely stand. One arm wrapped around Król's shoulder, Król's arm about his waist, together they slowly shuffled along the corridor that led to the old lighthouse. On they stumbled through the connecting door and into the tower base. Peter leaned backwards, using the curved wall for support. Król crossed to the key lockbox by the door. 'What's the code?' he asked.

'4747,' replied Peter. Król lined up the dials, and the box swung open. He lifted the large key. First, he slid the two bolts backwards, then he inserted the key into the lock and turned it anti-clockwise.

For a moment, they just stared at each other.

'I'm so sorry,' Peter said. 'I never intended…'

'I know,' said Król, and with that, he started to pull the door towards him. It was stiff from lack of use, and its dead weight refused to budge. Król hauled again with all his strength, and this time, it jarred. Another tug and he had it open an inch. A gust of icy wind gushed into the tower and whistled up and around the spiral stairwell.

Król wedged his hand into the gap and pulled the door again until it had opened enough for him to squeeze through. Peter peered through the parting just in time to glimpse a silhouette descending the granite steps that led down to the sea. Peter heaved with all his might against the metal frame, and eventually, the door closed. The metal bolts clunked loudly as he shunted them across. He turned the key and slumped back against the wall.

XIX

I lie in the belly of the beast. It came like I knew it would. Time has stalled. Singularity. Space and time indistinguishable. Nothing here to love, to live for. Nothing can escape, not even light. Nothing to do but think and think and think and think. Gravity, pulling me apart. All around, the ghosts are whispering. They, too, stranded in this hell between life and death.

1:35a.m.

Kate wanted to put her foot to the floor, but she dared not lose control. She drove as fast down Main Street as possible, praying nobody stepped out from the shadows onto the road before her. The town was silent and peaceful, oblivious to her torment. As a child, she'd run and skipped along these streets on her way to buy sticks of candy rock or ninety-nine ice creams. This town had been the backdrop to her life, the stage upon which she played out her dreams. Now, none of it seemed familiar. It cared not for her and would still stand the next day and the next day, regardless of what happened to her or her daughter. They were not safe here. This was no longer home. Kate could hardly see ten feet ahead as flakes of snow hurtled in elongated darts at the windscreen. Again, she prayed. Here was her hour of need, God.

Kate sped by the police station at the top of Main Street. The building was dark, and the car park was empty. Suddenly, the lights of a patrol car were flashing in her rear-view mirror. Sully had listened. The police car pursued her out of town and into the darkness of the countryside. A few miles further, Kate turned onto the minor road that led to the farm. So many times, she had driven this stretch with her father. Then, the comfort of home awaited. Now, she dared not imagine what lay ahead. A few miles more, and she was nearly there. Behind her, the blue flashing lights were catching up. She broke and swerved sharply into the narrow lane that led towards Grace's house. The Range Rover slipped and slid as her heart pounded a million beats a minute. Eventually, the farmhouse came into view, and Kate made the final skidding turn into the courtyard.

Two police cars were parked, both with blue emergency lights flashing above. Kate's heart leapt in her chest. The back door to the farmhouse was open. Had Dan turned up? The young Garda Edwards appeared in the doorway, alerted by the sound of her arrival. Kate jammed on the brakes and jumped from the car. 'Did you find the children?' she shouted at Edwards as she ran towards the house.

'No, I've only just arrived,' replied Edwards. Kate brushed past him into the farmhouse. 'Wait, stop, you can't go in there,' exclaimed Edwards. 'It's a crime scene, Kate. Stop!' he called after her.

Kate's heart nearly leapt out of her throat. *A crime scene!* She gulped down her fear and ran towards the front of the house. 'Amy?' she called aloud. There was no response. 'Amy, Amy, are you here? Princess, it's Mammy.' She entered the master bedroom and stopped abruptly in her tracks. This was the room where her father and mother had slept. Where she had been conceived. The bedroom she would run into in the early morning for preschool hugs, hoping her dad had not already gone out to the fields. Now, on the bed, lay a body.

Kate moved closer. A pale, lifeless face stared upward. It was Dan Brady, her oldest and truest friend. She felt her stomach start to heave. Kate turned to Edwards behind her. 'You must help me find the children. We have no time to waste.'

XX

One day, a frustrated detective named Kowalski visits. He knows who the hit-and-run driver was that destroyed your family. He speaks of a political cover-up. A fire ignites within, fuelled by anger and hate, ever-renewable energies that run black and poisonous through your veins. Metamorphosis. A lost soul slouches slowly from the abyss in search of justice. In my hands, a bundle of letters. I see the woman and child on the beach. I call her name.

1:40a.m.

Peter dragged his battered body back along the corridor that led to the main house. He felt the prickly tingle on his face first. Waves of heat intensified the sensation the further he inched down the hallway. He could see the flickers of orange and yellow through the gap of the dining room door. He pushed it open further. The heat struck him like a hammer blow.

One of the candelabras lay fallen on the carpet. All around, papers and letters burned. Some flittered smoking in the air. On the opposite side of the room, flames were curling up the wooden legs of the piano. The curtains behind it ignited and were devoured in seconds. The bookshelves were next to go up. Peter froze, transfixed by the brutal ferocity being unleashed before him. There was nothing he could do. At best, he might save himself. He hunkered down onto the flat of his stomach as the smoke clouded upwards and began edging his way forward as best he could, his good arm dragging the rest of his body trailing behind it. Horrendous pain shot through his wounded leg. The raw heat began to sear the exposed skin of his face and hands. To his right, the two armchairs were now ablaze. Król's pocket watch, photograph and letters lay inches from the flames. Peter reached out to save them. He shoved the watch and letters down the front of his buttoned shirt, but he couldn't reach the picture. Slowly, it browned and curled backwards upon itself in the heat. First Jude, then Theia and finally Król, all fading to black.

Peter shuffled forward, but the fire was gaining with every painstaking heave. The harsh air burned at his throat, and it felt like his aching lungs might explode. All of the oxygen was being sucked from the room. He pressed on through the open kitchen doors, sliding painfully across the tiled floor. Choking black smoke curled in a thick cloud above him. One last thrust forward, and he reached the patio doors. Somehow, he hauled himself into a semi-kneeling position and reaching up, he turned the door handle. He cried aloud in pain as the scalding knob cut hot red into his palm. It didn't matter, the door was open. Never before had his heart greeted an icy draught of air with such elation. Something crashed behind him, and startled, he glanced back. Flames spewed through the doorway from the living room to the kitchen and stretched out towards him, trying with all their might to claw him back into the blaze. Peter bundled himself over the threshold, and at last, beneath him, he felt the cold welcome of the snowy earth. Within seconds, the kitchen was lost to the ravenous fire. Peter crawled away, leaving the inferno behind him. Only when the smothering heat became tolerable did he stop, turn and survey the damage.

A crimson trail of blood from his injured leg snaked back through the snow to the open door. A loud moaning noise rose ominously. Peter gazed spellbound as the long rear window of glass exploded outwards, spraying shards of crystal across the lawn and sending vomiting rolls of flame upwards into the dark sky. He slumped backwards onto the cold snow. He patted his pocket for his phone. It was still inside. By now, it was surely molten glass and metal. All he could do was wait. For Kate. For news of Amy. For help to come. Wait as their home burned to the ground before him.

1:47a.m.

Kate darted out the back door into the snowswept yard, Edwards following right behind her. The Garda stopped as the flashing blue lights of Sully's police car turned sharply into the yard. Kate kept running. Edwards quickly briefed Sully and then rushed after her. Suddenly Kate froze in her tracks. Even through the swirling haze of snow, she could see it. Out on the island, high on the clifftop, a flickering glow lit the dark sky. Not the steady warning beam of a lighthouse beacon, but instead a blazing inferno reaching to the heavens.

'Jesus, is that the lighthouse?' asked Edwards, catching up behind her.

'I think so,' said Kate.

On she went, there was no time for anything else.

Kate reached the gated entrance to the field and screamed aloud for Amy. Then Grace and Niamh. She closed her eyes and strained to hear. No sounds of life came. No child's cry for saviour.

Kate cleared some of the large, wet snowflakes from her frozen face as she pushed through the gate. If she never saw or felt snow again, it would be too soon. 'Amy! Grace! Niamh!' she called over and over as she ran. The field was badly overgrown, and the covering of white made it nearly impossible to find an unobstructed path. Kate couldn't even see the old barn through the blizzard. She advanced in the direction of where it should be, pushing through the snow and thick scrub. Edwards' torch shone over her shoulder, lighting a way through the dark.

Then a noise. A familiar sound. 'Did you hear that?' Kate shouted. A dog's bark. It came again. Then, some whining and more barking. 'Rocky!' A bolt of hope rushed through her. 'Good boy, Rocky. Good boy!' Kate yelled, moving as quickly as she could through the thick vegetation in the direction of the yelping dog. Kate's footing slipped and she landed in a scraggly bush, grazing her arm on the sharp thorns. Edwards grabbed her forearm and tugged her back to her feet. On they pressed, closing on the sound of the dog. The barking came louder and louder. Edwards was now leading, Kate at his heels. At last, ahead, the dark outline of the shed rose from the overgrowth, on its roof a strange yet familiar sight. She saw the eyes first. Amber lights in the night. The snowy owl. Sitting. Watching. Then she heard it, and her heart nearly exploded from her chest: a barely audible cry. A human cry. 'Amy!' she screamed.

'Wait, Kate,' called Edwards, but she ignored him. She darted to the shed and began frantically clearing the gorse that blocked the door. 'We don't know what's in there,' he cautioned. Kate looked at her phone, it was 1:58a.m. She was nearly out of time. She tugged on the door handle, and the door opened outwards. She turned back to Edwards and, lifting her two hands to his chest, she shoved hard, sending him falling backwards onto his rear in the snow.

'Take cover!' she roared at him. 'There's a bomb.' Before the startled Garda could reply, she'd squeezed through the gap in the door and was inside. Immediately, the dog was on her, paws on her chest, tail wagging ferociously. She pushed Rocky off as a muffled human gasp came from the rear of the shed. Kate could make out three figures huddled together on the ground. To the right, along the side wall on a shelf, she saw the lit electronic face of the device, exactly where Nicholas had said it would be. She rushed to it, ignoring the bodies. It was a smartphone, the screen displaying a countdown. Forty seconds remained. Thirty-nine, thirty-eight, thirty-seven. Kate held her breath and then pressed the number she'd been told. *Eight.* Her heart sank deep into her stomach. He'd lied. The countdown continued. Twenty-nine, twenty-eight.

The phone shook in her quivering hands. She wiped the screen clean with her cuff, steadied her hand and pressed the digit eight again. The countdown stopped. Kate swallowed hard and began to breathe again. Behind her, she heard Edwards struggle his way through the door. His torchlight shone firstly on her and then to her left, where Grace's eyes squinted in its glare. Next to Grace, the light illuminated two smaller bundles. All three were wrapped in what looked like sleeping bags. Another head lifted to catch the beam. There, looking back at them, blinking in the brightness, was Niamh.

Kate rushed to the huddled figures. Grace was shaking her head vigorously, mouthing something through the taped gag that had been wrapped about her face. Quickly, Edwards was beside her, kneeling, freeing her mouth. Behind him, Rocky began to whine aloud. 'Kate, no! Don't, don't!' Grace gasped.

'Don't? What do you mean? Stop it, Grace, don't you dare!' screamed Kate, her voice catching amid the welling tears. 'Amy, Amy, baby, Mammy's here.'

Niamh stared at Kate. In her eyes, Kate saw the bleakest despair, a look that would never leave her. It communicated to her the last message she would ever want to receive. It spoke of unparalleled and unending desolation. A crying Niamh buried her head into her mother's chest.

But they were wrong. They had to be wrong. Kate pulled at the third bag. Her daughter's red hair fell to one side. There was no movement. No sound. No breathing.

'We couldn't wake her, Kate,' cried Grace.

Kate ignored her and pulled the limp body up towards her as she knelt over it. Amy's cold, motionless face now protruded from the sleeping bag. She was gagged at the mouth, but her nose was clear. Kate pulled the gag down and held her tightly in her arms, kissing her face and her forehead. Still, no movement came from the lifeless form. Kate tugged at the zip and frantically pulled the cover away.

She lay Amy flat on her back on the stony shed floor. Placing one palm over the other in the middle of Amy's ribcage, Kate began pushing wildly. Over and over, she pumped. Kate tilted Amy's face backwards, opened a gap between her cold lips and with every breath she had, she began exhaling warmth into her daughter's frozen airwaves. Amy stared back at her, lifeless.

Behind her, yet sounding like far in the distance, Kate could hear Grace and Niamh sobbing, but she wasn't ready to cry yet. This wasn't over. On she pushed and pushed until it felt like her daughter's ribs would crack beneath her palms. Push. Breathe. Push. Breathe. Push. Breathe.

2:00a.m.

Here was a world devoid of arrogance and stupidity. Dark stony cliff face. Scarred granite hewn over billions of years, shorn by glaciers and ocean, only in these last moments of time exposed to frail humanity. Howling wind and crashing sea silenced all amid nature's fury. To these wondrous forces, mankind mattered not, and maybe there lay the answer to a question he'd no longer any need for. Waves smashed into the rocks, showering him with freezing spray. Down the granite steps he descended.

It was done now, and nothing on earth or in the heavens could change that, nor how it would end. He roared until his throat ached and his lungs emptied, but his scream was muffled away by the mocking squall. High above all the fury lay ungodly silence amongst the celestial orbs. Amid all the rage in the lighthouse, he had heard her soothing voice. Jude imploring him to be true to himself. He was not this vengeful man. He was her love, her husband, the father of her children. He could feel her close. Whether the fault lay with him or the stars mattered little now.

A vision of his mother came. Precious grainy photos of a time before his existence. She who had sacrificed all for him. A woman he'd never met but whose blood coursed within him, every beat of his heart propelling her essence through his veins. He thought of his father gazing to the skies, making the undecipherable cipherable. Sitting at his desk, head in his books, half-rimmed glasses on his nose. He remembered how people looked at him on campus and respected him, and he remembered the pride he had felt to be his son. He could hear his voice comforting him, telling him that we were all made from billions of tiny particles bound together, some so small that humanity couldn't yet observe them. These particles never cease to exist. All eventually disentangled and returned to their place in the universe.

Time is but a measure of change, his father told him. It wasn't linear. It didn't move from minute to minute, hour to hour, day to day. These were man's measurements. The past, present and future all exist simultaneously. Interlinked. Enfolded. Entwined. Twisting and distorting with the push and pull of the cosmos. They would all be together again. He could feel it, his atoms and cells counting down until they were released to the earth and the stars. Tick, tick, tick. Time ebbing invisibly through his fingers. Tick, tick, tick. Closer and closer. His time to die.

Król paused, his sodden, icy clothing clinging to his body. The snow bit into his frozen cheeks, cutting jagged at his eyes. Velvet flakes draped over him. A white shroud to die in. The ferocious swirl tried to raise him on its pallbearer blanket, but his frame held, weighed heavy to the stone by gravity and the earth's spin. He closed his eyes to the storm, to the snow, to the stone, to the sea. He stood in his own deafening silence, holding fast his final mortal thoughts, cradling them as if they and they alone were the keys to the universe and all its secrets.

He could feel nothing now. The icy snow no longer stung his flesh. He felt weightless, giddy even, as if he might float into space and ascend to the planets and the stars above. Beautiful Jude came like a shining light towards him. She was a vision of all he had ever wanted, all he could ever want. Oh, how he loved her. They were together again on his rooftop balcony, wrapped in the sheets of their lovemaking. All the universe was unfolding before them. Every instant of theirs mapped above. Moments to step into and out of. A universe so large they couldn't see it, so small that they were a part of all of it and it of them. Shared elements. Shared destiny. Shared time.

Jude wrapped her arm around his waist the way she always did. Theia came too from the light and held his hand. 'It's all right, Daddy. Everything is okay,' she said.

Down the last stone steps. Love flushing euphorically through his veins. He was at peace. The peace to let go. To step into that universal river of atoms. To begin again.

XXI

I will leave you these letters, my scattered thoughts. Jude's note, too.

You will understand why I did what I did.

I am sorry for the harm. I hope the scars heal in time.

These are all that remain.

Proof that we were here. That we lived. We loved. We existed.

***

To my love, Nicholas.

I am sorry that you had to find me that way. Maybe I should have gone somewhere, but I needed you near to me. To feel your presence as I left.

In truth, I had already left ever since that day. I couldn't leave her alone anymore, you knew that. Theia calls to me, and when I sleep, I am with her again. Now I will be with her always, to mind and love her. Konrad too. I am their mother, Nicholas. I am their mother. They need me.

This destroyed us. I saw us changing. It made me so sad, but I was full of grief, I couldn't stop it. I couldn't help myself. I couldn't help you.

I am their mother, Nicholas. I have no choice. I have to…

Please, please understand.

I am yours eternally. Never, never forget this. I will be waiting for you, I promise. Let that knowledge give you solace. The kids and I will be together, and someday you will join us. Don't languish in guilt. Be careful and choose the right path. Know that none of this was your fault. Not I, not Theia, not Konrad, not any of it.

I must tell you the truth now, as I am tortured by pain. Every time I look in the mirror and see the scar on my face, it haunts me. It is my brand of guilt. That day, as we turned onto the main road, Theia dropped her toy in the back of the car. She asked me if she could take her belt off to get it. She was such a good little girl. She would never take off her belt without asking me first. So dutiful and respectful, so innocent and beautiful. She asked me, Nicholas, she asked me.

I said yes. Her mother said yes. I allowed it, and that decision changed everything forever. I should have told you before, but I couldn't. How could I? To see her lifeless in the hospital, knowing what I knew. I feel so much better now that I've told you. For all of this, I am sorry. I am so filled with sorrow that it suffocates me. I cannot breathe.

I ask this of you, my love. Do not think of me as you found me. Remember me as I found you. That day I fell in love with you. Do not judge me; forgive me. Please never forget me. I am taking with me our best memories, our best times when we blazed together in the sky.

In love, time has no measure.

Eternally yours.

Jude.

Five Years Later

Snowflakes began to swirl above the narrow streets of Kraków, a light breeze lifting crystals high in the air only to fall slowly in wispy white blossoms onto the cobbled paths below – each an intricate, unique fingerprint.

Kate looked at the weathered blue plate on the wall that read Jablonowskich Street. 'Nearly there,' she announced in encouragement, pointing onwards. Arms linked, they trooped warily along the icy path until they reached the tavern. *Maciek's Café* read the sign. They picked their way carefully down the steps and entered the basement bar below. A travel guide might have described the interior as rustic. Neglected was the word running through Kate's mind. Choosing a table underneath the window, they watched the people pass up and down on the pavement outside. The rear of a tram snaked along the tracks and out of sight. Kate ordered coffee. Amy had lemonade and sweet fried *paczkis*.

After an hour or so, when they were warm again and fuelled for the afternoon ahead, Kate paid the bill, and they gathered their things to leave. As Kate began to ascend the stairs to the exit, she froze – an eeriness tingled under her skin. The vision of a sodden girl ghosted past her. A yellow summer dress glued wet to her body, a satchel of books cradled in her arms. Suddenly, the bag slipped from her hold, and textbooks spilt wide across the tiled floor. At the bar, a young man rose from his stool. Kate's heart thundered in her chest. She closed her eyes. When she opened them, both the girl and man were gone, yet somehow, she could still feel their presence, tangible, nearly touchable.

Outside, on the path, Amy turned to her, a concerned look on her face. 'Is everything okay, Mum?' she asked.

'Of course, love,' replied Kate, gazing assuredly into her daughter's eyes. Amy was a fledgling teenager now. All her life before her. They'd talked many times about that day when the storm blew into Blackcliff. Kate never wanted her to carry fear or worries in silence. Amy had shown the remarkable resilience of a child. She'd adapted and got on with things. While Kate saw everywhere the fragility of existence, Amy, like steel strengthened in the furnace, seemed possessed of a belief that she could survive anything. She'd already proven that. She carried this power with a lightness that made Kate's heart sing.

Kate brushed snow affectionately from her daughter's hair. 'It's nothing, baby, just a memory that came to me, something from the past. Come on, let's go,' she said. They strolled hand in hand back up the street towards the Planty Gardens. The grass lawns were covered in white. Cautiously, they negotiated the slippery path until they reached the statue of Copernicus standing proudly at the entrance to the university. A thought flickered and left Kate's mind. A realisation of how little she really knew of anything. Of what made the universe hurtle through space, of what made the planets orbit their suns, of the powers that conspired for her to be standing in this spot on this day. Of the miracle of new life and of how, on one frozen night, her daughter began to breathe again.

'Who was he, Mum?' asked Amy. 'A great man named Copernicus,' Kate replied. After a moment or two, they walked to the kerbside, and Kate held her hand aloft to hail a passing taxi. Cab after cab was occupied, but eventually, one stopped. The car drove south of the old city, then east and finally north around the ring road until fifteen minutes later, large wrought iron gates and sentried stone pillars announced their arrival at Cmentarz Rakowicki. Kate paid the driver, and they clambered out and entered through the open gates.

They strolled along the tree-lined avenues, marvelling at the endless array of ornate tombstones and decorative sculptures. Stone angels stood guard at every turn. A thin layer of snow covered all. Kate cleared some of the recent fall from the face of a gravestone and read the inscription. All about were memorials to poets, artists and actors. To soldiers of all nationalities. To young and old. Quills, brushes and guns now set down; all silently gathered side by side in eternal rest beneath the cold ground.

They passed an old lady as she tended to a loved one's plot. The stone declared that a husband and daughter had left her behind. Kate caught the woman's eye and nodded to her, their faces sharing an understanding, a knowledge that this grief would come to all. Further on, Kate noticed the gravestone of a young girl, only six when she died. Concrete angelic wings spread wide above, sheltering her from any further harm. Kate glanced at Amy, and for a moment, she felt dizzy. She was back in the shed, fumbling at the bomb, holding her breath as she pressed the number eight. Later, the police would confirm the device had been a fake. Nearby, the lifeless face of her daughter stared up from the shed floor. She remembered somehow knowing that Amy was still there, still alive, that she hadn't left her. How? That, she would never understand. A mother's intuition? A spiritual connection? She'd kept pushing Amy's chest and breathing her mother's air deep into her daughter's lungs. Edwards had taken her shoulders in his hands and tried to tell her it was over. And then, it came. A splutter. A breath. A reason to keep living.

Five years had passed since the snowstorm blew into Blackcliff. They now lived in London. No more clifftop walks or strolls along sandy beaches. No lighthouse. She'd sold the ruin to a retired German couple who dreamed of a life by the sea. The tower had somehow escaped undamaged, but their home had been gutted by the fire and eventually razed to the ground. The Germans rebuilt and opened a guesthouse. Kate sold her father's farmhouse, too. New hands had injected new life. Grace and Niamh moved to Ennis, with Grace taking a teaching job in one of the primary schools. They hadn't spoken in a long time. The sorrow that each of them felt with Dan's passing seemed to linger between them. He'd received a posthumous badge of honour for saving Bobby Kirwan's life. The funeral was the largest ever seen in Blackcliff. It seemed half of the country's blue force had turned out. They could never pin his death on Tommy Molloy, but it didn't matter. Tommy was found dead six months later from an overdose. Had guilt caught up with him? Stupidity? Regardless, he, too, was gone. Kate wondered if it was worse to be a survivor. Niamh with no father. Grace without Dan. Iris still somehow above ground even when she no longer had the will to be.

From the sales and insurance proceeds, Kate bought a three-bedroom flat in Camberwell. An '*up-and-coming*' location, '*her investment certain to grow once the area fully gentrified,*' she had been assured. It was a new start where nobody knew them. Their apartment was as safe as it could be, as safe as anywhere else. She set the alarm and bolted the windows and doors, whether they were in or out. They had a dog, too, a German Shepherd named Rex. Her neighbours remarked that he might be too large a breed to be happy living in a flat. She smiled and ignored them. Come too close, and he'll bite your face off. The local school seemed fine. It was only so-so on the rankings. Kate could help at home with the lessons if she had to.

Peter passed the items from Nicholas to the Gardaí. They'd given her a copy of the letters he had written. His reasons. His apologies. His life. She'd read them over and over to try and make sense of everything. Jude's words would never leave her till the day she died. Kate put the letters away under lock and key, and she wasn't sure if they would ever come out again. Only time would tell. A few months later, a parcel arrived in the post. It was Nicholas's pocket watch. Sergeant O'Sullivan said he didn't know what else to do with it.

Kate spoke to Peter regularly. They were friendly and helpful to each other, but they would never be together.

She didn't know his feelings on the matter and had, at times, sensed that he wanted more, but she had been clear, that part of her life was over. He'd been airlifted to Ennis Hospital that night for emergency surgery to save his leg. Although the procedure was successful, he would forever carry a limp. After his recovery, he'd moved to Dublin but still seemed to always be in Brussels. He only saw Amy one weekend in four, yet Amy seemed content with that. Kate wondered if he was happy now. She wasn't sure what even defined happiness. An obscure notion for those yet to confront true suffering. A comforting belief for those still blinded by ignorance or faith, for those who had yet to fathom our nothingness in the vastness of it all. She no longer judged her life in terms of happiness. Yet, if she admitted to it, they were happy, but, above all else, they were alive and making the best of it. Kate thought now of survival. Always. To exist. She was hardwired to fight, to muster whatever anger and aggression was required to keep them going. Minute to minute. Hour to hour. Day to day. One after the next.

Król's body washed up six months after that night, somewhere along the Kerry coastline. Sully had called her out of courtesy to confirm it was him. He thought she'd be happy, but she wasn't. She'd known he was gone, never doubted it. She should have sensed it that night in the lighthouse, but she hadn't. He'd wanted desperately to leave, to be shorn of his agony.

And now, here she stood by his graveside. Why? She wasn't fully sure. Nicholas had once used the word *closure*. Her shrink would probably have agreed. An ending? A beginning? Probably all these things. There was no closure, though, of that she was sure. She'd seen this gravestone before. Now his name had joined the list of the dead etched on the cold stone, a family reunited.

Kate read the names and dates in silence as the waning snow drifted about them. As the unpitying finality swamped her, it felt as if she might never catch another breath. Here lay emptiness. Here lay desolation. An entire family erased. No more life in this field of bones. And who cared? Who cried for the lost? It should be Peter here paying respect, not her. It could be Peter under the ground, not Nicholas and his family. But it wasn't. And it wasn't. Kate reached into her coat and removed the pocket watch. She touched the engraved planets etched on the gold case. She twisted the crown. Then she bent down on one knee, and with her keys, she dug into the hard ground until she had unearthed a few inches of fresh dark soil from beneath the snow. In the small hole she had made, she placed the watch face upwards, and then she packed the loose soil on top. She covered the disturbed patch with snow until all lay white again. She stood up and brushed herself down.

The evening was drawing in, and darkness crept fast across the city. Kate looked to the sky above and saw Polaris, the ever-fixed North Star. Unmoving, unwavering. Eternal. She turned to her children and smiled. Just the three of them now. Amy's survival had been the first of two miracles. The test had confirmed the second. Against all odds, amongst the death, the heartbreak and the horror, a new fingerprint had found life – Król's fingerprint. From the brutal cold of that storm, new life had seeded. Kate hadn't thought twice about her options. It had been the right thing to do, the only thing.

To move forward, not looking back. The only path time knew. There could only be room for love, nothing else. And she had so much love to give. She'd asked Peter to make a sacrifice, and to her surprise, he had said yes. He'd been magnanimous even. 'It is my duty,' he had stated. 'He will be my son.' Peter's name was inscribed as *father* on the birth cert. They swore that nobody but they would ever know. Amy could never be asked to deal with the truth; how could she? Nor would they ever tell the boy of his biological father, or his lost sister Theia, or of his unborn brother Konrad. Nothing good could come of that. The ghosts should sleep. Król would understand.

Amy tugged on her sleeve. 'Mum, we're bored. Can we go?'

Kate smiled and nodded. Of course, they were bored, surrounded by the dead and things that meant nothing to them. They were children, indestructible, or so they thought. But one day, on a day determined, when it was their time, death would come knocking at their doors. When it did, Kate hoped that she was already long gone, for what worth is the parent of a dead child? Till that day, every day, as surely as the earth spun to greet the sun, she would be there by their side. With hope. With love. 'Come on, Amy, Nick, time to go,' she said. Amy took the hand of her little brother, and together, the three of them turned and made their way back through the snow.

***

The May sun warms our limbs, and once again, the flower beds are in full bloom. We sit on our wooden bench opposite Copernicus. It is my father's anniversary. As I look at the statue, I see both men, the great explorer and my father, as if they are one and the same. Both searching the stars for meaning beyond our realm or understanding. In my hands their book. As I read aloud the final page, they are here with us, beside us, around us.

***

He lies alone on his deathbed in the small town of Frombork, away from the masses and the chattering classes. Despite the layers, his frail bones shiver as the winter wind blows hard from the icy Baltic. He is an old man now – seventy years he has managed. His father died much younger, when he was but ten. Now, it is his time. Has he achieved what he'd hoped? Has he done his father proud? He is content with his efforts. The name Copernicus will be remembered. He discovered a secret that nobody knew. Knowledge so profound it would shake the world from its slumber. His destiny. He had solved the puzzle, but the solution was staggering, his findings confounding the very laws of science, of belief, of common sense. The ramifications would change everything forever. What would their reaction be? Would they ridicule him, denounce his discovery? Or worse? Charges of heresy were whispered. What of it, they couldn't hurt him, not now. The mathematics had confirmed it. There was infinite comfort in proof. All we ever wanted were answers.

He remembered standing by the shore watching the setting sun. He knew that what he was seeing was deception, a magician's trick, an illusion on a grand celestial scale. The enormous ball of fire in the distance wasn't sinking. It wasn't sliding low beneath the horizon in its perpetual orbit around the earth. Instead, it was he and the sand upon which he stood that were slowly spinning backwards, away from the light, away from the sun and into the darkness.